As this child of the northern darkness came to me from the evil places,
As this child is now grown and is a woman,
As this woman will be a warrior,
As this woman will be a sorceress by my skill,
As this sorceress shall not be in the power of men,
As this woman is of the Way of Truth,
So this woman shall go forth into the world,
So shall she learn the way of the world,
So shall she bring light to the darkness,
So shall the power of the south pass by this woman to the north,
So now I give to this woman, her true name, Cheon, bringer of dawn.

—*The chant of Meon the witch.*

Cheon

of
Weltanland

THE FOUR WISHES

Charlotte Stone

DAW BOOKS, INC.
DONALD A. WOLLHEIM, PUBLISHER

1633 Broadway, New York, NY 10019

FIRST PRINTING, NOVEMBER 1983

1 2 3 4 5 6 7 8 9

DAW TRADEMARK REGISTERED
U.S. PAT. OFF. MARCA
REGISTRADA, HECHO EN U.S.A.

PRINTED IN U.S.A.

INTRODUCTION

It is a great good fortune that Cheon's story has been rediscovered after so many centuries. Its translation and presentation represent the finest work of modern scholars of the period, and people of later days and other worlds can now read and delight in this true story of the oldest times. Only the barest commentary is included, because Cheon's quick intelligence gave such an illuminating account of her deeds and times that anything more would be superfluous.

In the main Cheon is a truthful writer, and whenever contemporary records are available they agree broadly with her accounts. There are some passages where the strict truth has not been adhered to, but they are seldom boastful claims, rather the omission of little incidents of which Cheon was ashamed. Her tales of sorcery and the great deeds among the mythical figures of the age may be taken in any way the reader chooses. It seems certain that Cheon believed them. Her combative prowess is not in the least exaggerated, and in the case of the slaying of the great ape, a reliable contemporary writer agrees absolutely with her story. Her beauty is something the present author will not judge. Cheon had a great many suitors in her life and let their judgment stand. "The *grandest* beauty of the age," one witty historian wrote, and in this he was certainly right.

I

If I am to tell my story properly, I must begin with the earliest memories, even though many be fragmented and perhaps mere imaginings. Let me then tell only what is certain.

I was born in Weltanland, and there I dwelt as a child, in the warmth of green grassy meadows and woods with the song of insects vibrating through the long summer days. It was protected by the empire, almost a part of it, so that the noise of battle had receded, and life seemed as secure as the return of the stars in its tranquil night sky. My parents were simple folk, barbarians softened by the permanence of the land. Of my mother I remember the strong arms and woolly thickness of hair which were my shelter in those early times. I spent my days playing with my cats which she gave me instead of dolls, while my father and brothers worked ever in the fields. Perhaps I was large for my age—I remember my father measuring me with merry laughter.

Then came days when my father and brothers looked solemn and often took their crossbows and flexed them. I was not allowed to wander in the fields as before, and my mother gazed anxiously at me as I made daisy chains for the cats to wear as crowns. One day my brother returned from the fields with blood on his shirt.

"They are dead!" he screamed. "The Bunnish are victorious, none now stand before them. Advanced raiding parties cannot be more than an hour away. Get you gone to the great forest! It is the only chance you have to escape with Mallikawna, else she will be taken for the whorehouses of Bunedi and you will be ravished and slain."

My mother bathed his wound as he faded from consciousness. Then we heard the shouts of strangers approaching. Great men with brown beards and rough skins, with large noses and cruel mouths broke down our door. They carried swords and

6

shields and wore tall plumed helmets. One took me by the neck and swung me around, ready to throw me through the window. Some were holding my mother while others took turns to lay on her. I knew not what they did, only that she screamed. When they had used her for their needs, one casually lopped her head from her shoulders. They pierced Robar with their swords a hundred times, then left to join their comrades who were moving past the house in a host.

I hung by a foot as my captor raised me to show what a prize he had. Other warriors made offers for me, holding up coins as they pointed at me, shouting in their hateful language. I remained conscious, even though the whole warm cocoon of life had been stripped from me. I cared not whether he sold me or kept me for himself. As it happened, he refused all offers, for there seemed to be something about me which gave me value. I expected to be made to work in some dirty Bunnish kitchen, knowing nothing of men's ways with women. But as we traveled on, I witnessed more pillaging and saw youths slain brutally—bravely defiant or begging for life it made no difference. Women and girls were dragged screaming from their hiding places and always their shifts torn from their cringing bodies. Some were used like my mother, some taken like me. And I began to struggle when I perceived what took place with those who were not thought worth the trouble of stealing for later pleasure. But a hard blow knocked the sense from me, and I did not return to consciousness until we were making camp for the night.

Here my captor ate and drank his fill, calling out in his loud voice, laughing with a cruel twist on his lips. He forced wine down my young throat, nearly choking me. And later I experienced the lowest degradation a woman may suffer. How many children have been thus used in this world which boasts so much of the Way of Truth? I shall not describe what happened. It is a thing not to be written of, and every man I ever slay pays the penalty of these deeds though he be innocent of them. Let it only be said that my captor having lost his money at gaming persuaded his bestial comrades to annul his debts by slaking their lust on my child's body. I know not of my exact age, but I guess that I was little more then ten though I probably seemed older by my size. I lay, fevered and sick through the night, my foot tied to a stake in the ground. And I saw other girls, some my age, most older, but a few even younger, all similarly restrained. Yet I did experience humanity among that truthless host. A youth barely bearded who had watched my violation, approached when the older men fell into their drunken slumbers. He spoke with halting phrases in my tongue.

"What done is wrong. I no can stop. If I say it bad I too die. I come fight to be man. Bunnish warrior I am. I think war good, I see many flags and warriors. Now I not like it. I let you free, Weltanland girl, free, so you not be again like this night."

I answered, still proud. "Kill me now! Then I will be free."

Tears came to his eyes. "What happened bad. But not good die. Run to forest. There none find. One day be woman strong, can kill Bunnish men." In his eagerness to see me escape, he tried to whet my appetite for life by arousing a vengeful motive. How he succeeded! He cut my bonds and led me silently among the sleeping throng. The arrogant army for so long victorious kept no guard. The youth pointed out a path at the edge of the heath where his comrades camped.

"Run swift. Soon be in great forest where Bunnish warriors fear to go. There thing befall you, good, bad, I not know. Yet it better than before. Here lantern, not use till forest, then walk far."

I said nothing but ran as he said along the path until I was out of sight of the camp, among the small trees that dotted the plain.

Trees and shrubs gradually increased in numbers and in density, until I was in a thin wood eerily patched with moonlight. I could still see my path and I kept running as fast as my young legs would carry me. At last after stopping several times to recover my breath I ran into a pitch darkness. I uncovered the lantern as the youth had said. The path went on through the boles of gigantic trees behind which lurked wild fearsome beasts of my imagination, laying in wait for just such a one as I. Yet I feared even more to be caught again by the Bunnish men, so I kept on walking, taking one fork after another, always the lesser of two paths so that my pursuers might choose the wrong way. The terror and hate that had spurred me on had drawn on stored reserves and when they were gone I was ready to collapse. I turned off the path and fell onto a soft pile under one of the giant trees. And paralyzed by tiredness I slept instantly.

I woke in the twilight which passed for daybreak in the

forest. As I opened my eyes, I saw a great beast that lay close to me, with dark gray fur and eyes large and pale brown. And its mouth was rowed with tiny sharp teeth. And that it was a giant nightstalker,* the most feared of the night hunters in the great forest I doubt not, for there are many smaller kinds as I have seen since, but I have never again beheld a giant one. As soon as I moved it sat up and looked at me, for it must have found my stillness confusing but now I had attracted its attention. It paced around me until it took my legs with its jaws, firmly yet without biting. Though I thought it proposed to eat me on the spot, it was soon dragging me to its lair.

I wore only the torn remnant of my dress for my breeches had been ripped off by the Bunnish men, and as I was bumped and banged over the ground, the dress was gradually torn up and it disintegrated. I did not struggle because any difficulty it had, caused the beast to fasten its jaws more tightly on my leg, which was painful. Indeed I helped it as best as I could, making the least resistance to its dragging. I did not wish to die now, although I could see no way to escape. I debated with myself how I might be eaten and whether the beast would bite my head off first, as I hoped. And even in such a peril and before such eyes I felt embarrassed at my nakedness for my mother had taught me that to go with my loins bare was shameless.

The beast made a deep purr which seemed eager anticipation as it neared its lair and a good feast, yet I began to sense that it was uneasy. It did not like the burgeoning dawn and made greater efforts to speed up though it was ever tiring. Why it did not stop and eat me while it still had the chance I could not comprehend, but then I knew not that each kind of beast has its own special way of conducting itself and will rarely depart from it, even when by the standards of men it acts foolishly. And perhaps it had young cubs awaiting a meal. Such was its weariness that it took the habit of releasing me, then seizing me again, as one might when carrying a heavy load. It began to require longer periods of rest. And as it had let go its grip on me once again, I got up and hobbled away, thinking to escape my fate, but the determined creature, unburdened as it was, had no trouble following me. I cast about for some rock to throw at it, all in vain, as they lie deep below the ancient forest floor. Only a piece of wood appeared

* See glossary

suitable for a cudgel. Though I might merely anger the beast, I laid hold of it, for I knew that was my only course, and I dealt the creature the heaviest blow that I could upon its snout.

I jumped back in shock as my cudgel, made from rotten wood as it was, burst into pieces. I ran off, pursued by the beast whose nose grew a comical looking bump. And as I felt its evil breath on my neck, seeming to draw my life to a close, I saw a bone—the thigh of some dead animal—with which I hit my hunter. Thus we ran through the forest—a child eluding the brute at her heels, and every so often facing back with a fearful swing of her bone to fight off its pressing snout—until it flagged and I gained confidence to deliver it a punishing beating. Grunting with distress it turned tail and slunk off into the undergrowth.

As I realized that I was free, I began to feel unbearable thirst and I made for the sound of water which came from ahead, behind a cluster of tall thick trees, where I found a great cascade bouncing down a rocky incline, the like of those I had passed in my wild flight from the beast. I leaned in and drank at the cold stream until my belly seemed but a pouch full of ice, and thus having satisfied my thirst I felt hungry, for I had not eaten since the time I had fled from the Bunnish camp. There were many fungi on the forest floor, and fruits that had fallen from above, half-decayed or pallid and evil-looking ones that grew on low shrubs. Among these I picked a pale yellow cluster of berries and though they tasted bad I stuffed them in my mouth, and more after those for I was in desperate need of food. Then a pain developed in my stomach which grew worse and worse. Although I retched I could not void its cause, but like hot needles, it stabbed through my gut and burned my insides. And I lay many hours, racked with convulsions and continuous diarrhea, and a fever came to me which made me shiver.

That night death passed close to me in the forest where I lay like a worm that dwells in the earth. Yet next morning I was alive, and though weak I was able to walk, and even my hunger returned after I bathed in the stream. Evil insects tried to land on the wound where the beast had seized my leg to suck my blood, so I tied a great leaf around it with a wiry string-creeper, and I used the same as a tight waistband to make a skirt. As I was gathering the biggest leaves I could find to hang from it, I noticed a tree whose fruit I knew, for my mother liked to show me the many different kinds that grow in the fields along the footpaths that we trod. And a great feast I made of sugary juices and flesh until I could feel my strength again.

Then I walked on through the wood with the naive intention of finding a village full of kind people like those I had known before the coming of the Bunnish.

II

From the green translucent canopy far above, the harsh and melodious cries of birds came echoing down, and now and again some multicolored sky-dweller would swoop down and up, screaming as it went. There was little undergrowth, but some parts of the forest were lighter than others, and the dark places I avoided. I saw many shy animals that ran away at my approach. More than once I boldly chased one, hoping to slay it with my bone, eat it and wear its skin as part of my skirt. But furiously though I ran, these forest dwellers knew how to escape.

I came to a rocky ridge where I sat to eat one of the fruits which I had tied to my belt. And as I ate I looked around at various shapes that lay half buried in the leafy peat. One I recognized although it was covered with lichen and moulds, for it was a great skull. And all around I saw that there were others, a whole army of dead warriors, their rusted shields sometimes still discernible. I picked among them with my bone, and since I could excavate the soft peat quite easily, I began digging up skulls, helmets and swords, some well preserved. And buried beneath so many bodies that he could not be plundered of his rich armor, I found the skull of a warrior greater than all the others, with a massive helmet of gold appearance and hanks of black hair that yet clung to the bones. Long-haired and wild, he had been struck from his horse, and at his side lay a dagger of rich workmanship covered with fine writing, with blade clean as could be and many precious stones set into its hilt. Then another stone of brilliant blue I saw shining in the hole, and this skystone and the dagger I took, but having wearied of my macabre game I made away with my loot in one hand and my bone in the other.

Thus I wandered for many days, and my wound healed with great speed and the damaged tissues resulting from the rapes similarly recovered. At night I went always to the side of a cliff which I had found, with empty and inconspicuous caves to sleep in, and though I walked along beside it every day I never found its end. Sometimes it rained and great torrents poured from the top of the trees, which I watched sitting in a hole in the escarpment with a heavy heart, reflecting on my endless wandering. And I cried out of loneliness, though had I seen a man I would have run away.

So it was that to break my boredom I decided one day to climb up one of those tree trunks that had many stumps of dead branches all the way to the top. Leaving my bone at the foot of such a one, like a naked monkey I shinned up higher and higher, resting here and there on a good solid branch. As I reached the first layer of leaves, I settled myself comfortably and looked down at the ground some seventy meters below. I felt no fear but with great excitement I spat to see what long journey my saliva might have. And not content with this I piddled and watched the golden stream break into droplets as they cascaded toward the floor. Then mounting the last branches I emerged into the green luminous city of the treetops.

Here the world presented a different face for it was a great aerial garden like those I have seen in later life that surround stately palaces. Thousands upon thousands of blooms adorned the canopy, whether they were the flowers of the trees themselves or of plants that twined among them I know not. They hung in festoons, in clusters, in racemes, in umbels and in great balls. And among them flew millions upon millions of brilliantly colored birds, butterflies, dragonflies and leapers. So thoroughly intertwined were the boughs of the trees that even creatures like me who could not fly were not restricted in our wanderings, though we made heavier work of it than the fliers.

There were many monkeys and similar creatures which looked anxiously at me, as if thinking me a poor specimen of their own kind whose furry coat had somehow moulted. I scarcely knew or cared what manner of creatures they were,

as I only took trouble to search for large and perhaps dangerous ones, such as the three or four apes which sat many trees
distant eating fruit together, bearing beautifully mottled coats
of black and gray. But although they saw me, they took no
notice and I breathed easily.

Then I began to feel my way among the trees and wander
carefully about their great gnarled limbs, lest a branch be
fragile or I disturb the local population. I saw snakes, but as
there was none near my home, I knew not of their poisonous
fangs and lacking fear I took pleasure in their simple forms
and patterned bodies. Once, I took the tail of a small one and
held it hanging from my hand, wondering how such a limb-
less creature might effect an escape from this impotent position.
It seemed quite peaceable and hung there with gentle undulating wriggles. Angered by its disappointing exhibition, I put
the tail in my mouth to see if a soft bite might encourage the
strange beast to greater efforts, but to no avail. I kindly
replaced it on the branch where I had found it and it slithered
away. If it was a poisonous snake it was a very tolerant one.

I climbed even higher into a fork which towered above the
green canopy, and toes curled around a lower branch, I
surveyed my territory. Under my dazzled eyes nothing but
trees stretched on all sides with, in just one direction, a patch
of misty cloud hanging over the forest. After so many weeks
of my twilight woodland world, I relished the warm sun on
my body, and having thrown off my leaf skirt I basked in it,
so that I felt no more the biting and burrowing insects which
had plagued me on the forest floor. But as it was getting low I
climbed down to where the mass of branches was thick and
intertwined and hurried in the fading light in search for a safe
dwelling, for I feared to still be at large when night fell. And
a hollow I found, like a great cup filled with soft moss, which
I quickly made sure was uninhabited before I jumped down.

Yet hardly had I dozed off than I was woken by a furry
body landing heavily beside me. I started up with a cry.
Either this was enough deterrent to the creature, whatever it
was, or it felt easily disposed that night and in no mood to
fight for its lair, for upon a snort it scrambled up and made
off, as put out as I.

For a long time I found no enemies in that happy domain,
and I came to love many of the creatures which showed no
fear of me, such as the small furred animals which I would

stroke and pet and take to my hollow. Thus I lived in peace amid a menagerie like to that which is painted in ancient tales of the beginning of the world, though those wild beasts did not always like one another as I liked them.

One morning as I searched among the branches for the most succulent and tasty fruits, I noticed a dearth of the usual hordes of small monkeys and lemurs which often pushed and jostled at the favorite sites. I continued to eat my fill, thinking to take advantage of the absence of competition, but my pleasure was suddenly turned to fear by the sight of an ape's face with a cast I had never seen before in my leafy paradise. For it was an evil and rapacious face with eyes dark and bloodshot, and its mouth was open showing great stained incisors and two rows of savage-looking daggers. And as I saw it stalking me with the sharp eyes of childhood, it realized it had been spotted and abandoned stealth for immediate assault. I watched its whole body appear.

Slightly smaller than a man it had no tail but long powerful arms with hands ending in cruel claws and short legs with grasping feet. And its whole coat was striped green and black in a strange mesmeric pattern. And it swung toward me and leapt suddenly and with tremendous force, crossing what I had thought an impossible gap in the branches. I sprang down and scampered, half running, half swinging toward the lower part of the canopy and after I had nimbly scrambled down fifty or so feet, I glanced over my shoulder to see the creature watching my flight. To my horror it was recovering itself and beginning pursuit.

Down and down I went into low regions I had not explored, and farther into dark shaded parts where the trunks of the trees were just visible. And all the time as I went I could hear the sound of that devil-like ape chasing me. Then I saw a tree swathed in creepers which I aimed to reach. With the skill I had gained in the treetops, I lowered myself at great speed into the darker and darker spheres below until I reached the tree and passed it. But I still heard the sounds of pursuit, so that I kept bouncing and cascading down the branches, taking little heed of the scratches and bruises which covered my body. And suddenly entering total darkness I found myself on the floor of the forest.

It was a terrifying moment—I could not see to run, yet I feared at any instant the eruption of the carnivorous ape. I struggled several steps, bumped into a tree, stumbled on, using my hands before me, and in panic in the space of a few minutes I lost myself. I cowered against a big smooth trunk, wishing it could open to hide me from all unseen and unwholesome eyes which might prey in this forest of eternal night, and I strained my ears to the numerous little sounds around me, although I could hear no more the great crashes of the hunting ape. Still I sat for ages, shaking and haunted by fears and dared not move lest the creature or any other beast of prey stood near. As those dark menacing vaults stayed hushed and dead, a feeling of claustrophobia overcame me, and I began to cry and despair, yearning for the airy domains of the treetops which now seemed unattainable. But even as I wept, nature called upon me to act, for I was hungry, thirsty and cold, having nothing with me but a string round my waist with my dagger and a pouch for my jewel. So at last I gathered my courage and got up.

Then it was that a warm and soft hand suddenly grasped my arm with a vise-like grip.

What happened to me in that evil darkness I shall not write—it is not to be known. But in those pitch dark, dank and foul-smelling shadows, dwell men* who see no light and who live like filthy worms from the soil. And I lived there a time which I cannot think of without nausea, among the subarboreal people, and my body and soul were soiled by it. One day I escaped and that is where I shall recommence my tale.

---

*The subarboreal people of whom Cheon speaks are somewhat of a puzzle. At that time the forests of night which exist in Mnoy in our own day still existed in Hyperborea and in Weltanland as known to Cheon. It has always been supposed that no human beings could live without light of any sort in those deep and humid places. But recently a skull has been found in Ravennay (then Uravuni), which may throw new light on the subject. Of a primitive type, certainly not Homo Sapiens, it has greatly modified orbital sockets, suggesting a huge aperture for the eye of a creature living in condition of near darkness. In spite of her reticence at this point of her tale, Cheon describes a subarboreal man in her later works ". . . with eyes as great as a copper palmer . . ." which agrees with this hypothesis. The copper palmer of the time was three inches in diameter. Only further study at the sites of the now defunct forests of night can confirm the theory. It should be added that romantic tales of Dwellers of Night in the forests of Mnoy in our own day can be discounted on all modern scientific evidence.

III

As I emerged into the sunshine I was blinded by the daylight, dim though it would have seemed to any ordinary man walking among those dense trees. But I had not seen the sun for the two years of my captivity where the only light I had known was the red flicker of the subarboreal people's fire. Great afterglows formed in my eyes and I had to sit down until I could see around me. There was no sound of pursuit—the subarboreals would never venture out into the light. With my sight cleared I began to walk, picking berries along my path, which after the wretched carrion and fungus of the dark world tasted like nectar and ambrosia to me. Hardened as I was now to the ways of the forest, I had no difficulty in finding food and shelter nor in making a fire at night to drive off inquisitive beasts. But as I reached increasingly spare regions of woodland, I took stock of my situation.

My only possessions consisted of the dagger and the jewel in the pouch hanging on the rope round my waist. As for my person, while I had grown in strength and cunning like an animal attuned to the art of survival in the wild, yet I retained the sickly look of a tormented child. For my skin was white and pallid though it already became reddened in the filtered sun, and my back was scarred by the forest floor on which I had been roughly used, and still painful with the accumulation of lashings. Then I vowed I should never eat meat again nor allow my body to be used by men for their pleasure and my pain. Never would I be like the subarboreal women, a bonded slave, to work until fatigue made her drop, then yield to the masters and tormentors. But I would learn to fight as they did, and kill as they did.

It was on the fifth day of my wandering that I came with great suddenness upon a woman who gathered wild herbs by a little stream in a flowery glade. And as she turned to me I stopped dead for I had not seen the like of her. She stood

black and tall, wearing a shimmering robe with three golden
tiers in her hair which made her look even taller than she was.
Thus is made the everyday costume of an imperial Asg, as I
now know, for lost in an island clearing of the forest of night,
a forgotten mote of empire still remained. Though she must
have been beyond her fortieth year, yet she retained her
beauty, as many of the imperial Asg do. I would have fled
but for some childish desire for maternal care, and I was
peering at her over the bush where I half hid when she spoke
suddenly with low clear voice, in a musical tongue which I
knew not. But once seeing that I could not understand she
tried others, and at last the Weltan language which I had not
heard since my abduction by the Bunnish men.

"Who are you, strange naked one from the forest?"

My lips stammered as the Weltan tongue returned. "I do
not have a name." I said.

She smiled. "Then I shall call you Npin-Npan, for it
means girlchild in the old tongue. Though you will not long
be a child. Approach now and let me see you."

I approached but drew my dagger to show that I was no
easy prey. She laughed, a pleasant laugh more loving than
mocking.

"Am I to die then?" she jested. "Spare my life for I am a
sorceress and able to grant your wishes."

I would not have harmed her whatever she had done, for
already I wanted her for my mother. I stood before her, and
she examined me; my wounds, my matted hair and the begin-
nings of my womanhood.

"Yours has been a cruel lot," she said, "in keeping with
these times. Tell me now how you came to wander alone in
these dangerous woods."

And I told her my story, and her great eyes gazed as I
spoke.

"And what will you do now?" she asked when I had
finished.

"I will stay here with you," I said naively. She laughed
again.

"What if I am an evil witch, slayer of men?"

"Then you can teach me too to be an evil witch and to
slay men," I said eagerly.

"Then let us return to my lair," she spoke, gathering her
basket of herbs. "But first," she took off her pale green silk

stole and fastened it about my waist. "It is not seemly for a girl of your age to go bareloined."

"Do you live alone?" I asked, pleased that she covered me. "Or with many other witches?"

"Not alone, not with witches. With my two servants."

"Are they women?"

"A man and his wife."

I stopped abruptly. "I will not go if a man is there."

"This man is a good man. And besides I have power over him. You shall be safe."

"Will you always be with me when the man is there?" I asked.

"So long as you wish it."

Then I followed her, and the land became more and more beautiful as we walked, like a great garden with many colored blossoms, still lakes and slender flowery trees. And at last we approached a large house made from wood but with small stone parts supporting the walls and around it was a courtyard overgrown with weeds and used for chopping wood and storage. My heart soared as I saw it, and I wanted to run to it, thinking that my mother and brothers would be inside. But in the yard sat an enormous blond man working on the wheel of a handcart, so I hung back and when he looked up I clung to the Asg woman's arm, expecting that he would instantly tear off my scarf. Yet he waved only and asked a question in a booming voice pointing at me. The woman replied quickly in his tongue, which I understood not, then he smiled and in Weltan he said:

"I Bonz. I good fellow. I not do shameful thing. I have wife. You poor girl. You safe with us. She boss woman. She keep you now."

At those words a woman came out into the yard; she bowed slightly to the Asg, then looked at me. She had long blond hair braided into thick plaits and her blue eyes were icy like the northern skies, but she too smiled kindly.

"A Weltan child?" Her accent was strange though she spoke as well as the Asg, and when the Asg had spoken to her as she had to Bonz, the blond looked back to me. "The men who rule now in Hyperborea have set a base standard for the treatment of children. What can we say now about the great speeches which roused the rabble to betray the empire? Our children must be born free, live free and die free! So it was said by Undish II. Now they are enslaved as babies, raped as children and slain before they are big enough to resist. What a great free land we fought for!''

''She understands nothing of that.'' said the Asg. ''Prepare a bath for her and tonight she shall eat well. Npin-Npan I call her—she does not know her true name.'' She turned to me. ''I am called Meon, and this woman is Leidi, my servant. Come now with me, Npin-Npan.''

She took me in the house where she made me lie on a low couch, and she sat by me, divining my uneasiness at the proximity of Bonz. And while I dozed with my head close to her knees, feeling the soft freshness of cloth again, she seemed to gaze at a strange shaped piece of wood, which I did not at the time recognize as a book. Then she woke me and led me to a large room with green glistening floor and white columns of steam through which her blonde servant smiled and beckoned us. Beside her a huge metal bath was being filled with warm water pouring straight from the wall, or so I thought with my simple mind, for it was in fact piped from a source in another room. When it was full, Leidi left and Meon, having taken the scarf from my waist, helped me in, and I lay down until only my head was above the water. And because of the sweet smelling oils and salts which Leidi had mixed, I suddenly remembered my baths at home and that very scent when my mother's hands rubbed my legs, and I craved her laugh when she would wrap me in her big cloth. Yet I said nothing of my thoughts for fear that I might cry but I only asked Meon about her household.

Thus she told me of Bonz who came from a far land to the west where he was a warrior in the service of the empire. And when the empire collapsed, he joined a band of free-people but left them as he saw how cruelly they treated those who fell into their power; and he took with him a girl from Shambi, Leidi, with whom he was in love though she had a lover, the chief of these free-people who pursued them. So they fled to the forest after Bonz was wounded in flight, and there he became very ill and he was near to death when Meon found them in her clearing, but she healed him by her powers, and they swore service to her for seven years.

''How long have they dwelt here?'' I asked.

''Three years.''

''After that then can I be your servant always?''

''No, Npin-Npan, you will go one day into the world again.''

I immediately became angry and beat the bath with my fists and kicked up and down, splashing the water all about.

"I do not wish it," I shouted. She spoke softly, yet there was no compliance in her voice, only a knowing affection.

"You will not go until you do wish it. But one day you will."

"I shall not," I insisted. Though after a little I added, "Not for a long time."

She smiled. "Put your hair under the water, girlchild, so I can wash out the dirt and insects in it."

She washed my hair with scented soap and oil which made me dizzy, so rich and full of memories was their perfume. Then she bade me stand and washed and rinsed my body with gentle hands on my wounds. Afterward she wrapped me in a large towel and sat combing out my long hair in the yard as the sun went down over the trees. And while I heard Bonz chopping wood and Leidi preparing the meal, I was happy as I had not been since the day of the Bunnish horde.

"You said you would grant me wishes." I spoke thinking that it was as well to get what I could while the situation lasted.

"Indeed I can," she answered. "I can grant you four wishes. What will they be?"

With great excitement I began to cast around for what I could have until in a few minutes I had named hundreds of wishes, some outrageous, some ridiculous, some perhaps pathetic.

"You must settle on just four, child, else you will have nothing." Meon said. "So think before you speak, yet speak before I sleep tonight, or my power to grant them will fade."

We ate that night at the great wooden table in the central hall of the house, and according to my vow in the forest I refused meat which reminded me of the subaboreal world. Then Meon took me to my bed which was a little cot-like couch in her bedroom. She said that Bonz would make me a bed more suitable for my age the next day, and that she was now going to her witchery, but she was near and no one would come. I lay in the bed near to sleep yet in deep thought, and several times when she looked in I pretended to be asleep, for she meant me to forget my four wishes and hoped to avoid keeping her promise, but tired though I was, I forced myself to concentrate. At last she entered the room with an oil lamp and undressed while I kept my eyes shut, for I had no curiosity of her nudity. I knew nothing then of the function of clothes to conceal mystery.

When I half opened one eye, I saw her in bed looking at an old parchment in the light of the lamp, which she seemed to do for an interminable time. Then she put it aside and lay silent with a strange expression in her eyes. They half closed and her lips pursed up only to stretch again over her teeth. And she breathed heavily and noisily, grunting like an animal in pain or angry until she cried out and finally sighed. Then her breathing became even and I feared that she might soon fall asleep.

"Meon!" I said in the darkness. She started up.

"What is it, child?" Her voice was deep and not kind.

"I have ready my four wishes."

She laughed. "You are a bold creature. Do you not fear my wrath when you trouble me at this time?"

"Yes." I answered. "But you promised and you bade me ask before you slept."

"I did indeed, girlchild. Come then, sit by me and tell me what your wishes are."

I jumped out of my cot wearing the beautiful scarlet night-gown she had given me and I sat on her bed, looking down at her eyes where the moonlight dazzled. Indeed I now understand her smile, for I must have presented a comic sight, my avaricious face glowing as I prepared to make my demands.

"What then do you wish, my proud preying mantis?"

"That no man shall again do to me as the Bunnish men and the men of the Dark Place did . . ." She would have spoken but I went on quickly, "That I may grow tall and strong and skilled in the use of weapons, that I may slay men as I please. That I may be as you are, a witch skilled in sorcery, yet beautiful like the dawn as you are beautiful as the dusk. That I may be a queen as my father promised me, the queen of the Northlands." I stopped, pleased with my speech which I had been planning since I went to bed. Meon sat up and took my hand.

"It is said that such wishes bring sadness, for the first is the source of much regret, and the second of shame, and the third shall cause you guilt, and the fourth fear. Yet they are good wishes, so they shall be granted, and like all wishes made to an Asg sorceress, so they are already half-granted. For if you gain your second wish, then is not the first guaranteed by your own will which you have sowed deep in your heart? And I see by your body which is still that of a child but for the lightest of fleece on your sex, that you are not older than twelve years, yet in height you are already greater than Leidi, and not so much less than I, who am greater than the generality of women. Thus you will be taller and stronger than any woman I ever saw and likely not inferior to Bonz in size. And I shall order that he teaches you his skills in battle until you will overcome him in friendly combat. As for slaying men as you please, it will then be your choice.

"And I shall teach you the art of sorcery, so that you shall be a sorceress greater than I, the first Hyperborean sorceress, the greatest white witch, to carry the guttering flame of Truth into the Boreal night and there kindle the fire which shall turn the darkness into glorious light, and sow the seeds of a Golden Age when once more Truth shall rule the world. And as for your beauty, already I see that you will win more power by its dawning than by the force of your arms or the power of sorcery. For your skin is white like the snows of the north, yet your hair is black, burned by the sun upon generations of northern heads in southern climes. And as the orange glow of the sun brings forth its reflection on your skin, so like the dawn your beauty will bring joy to all who behold it.

"And queen you will be. For you have found the great stone of Thanda in the forest, and like her you will rule a kingdom greater than any white kingdom that went before. But sleep now, Npin-Npan, tomorrow begins your schooling as queen, warrior, sorceress and bane of men."

She led me to my bed and laid down my nodding head. And I saw her lips smile over me and a hint of mockery mixed with the love in her eyes.

IV

True to her word she was. At first she taught me only the Way of Truth,* and for all my time with Meon it was her obsession above all else that I must follow the Way. I was a lively and curious child who liked well to be rude and boisterous, practicing the ways of the world, and my very size and strength made my cavorting a constant nuisance. For my many mischiefs and minor transgressions I was punished by beatings at her hands while Bonz held me. My buttocks were always the target for her birch, though they were never bared nor was she angry as she flogged me. But though I feared the beatings and could easily be brought to book by threats of them, yet it was by love that Meon brought me to the Way. For I loved her with all my childish heart and spent many hours on projects designed to surprise and please her. When I lied or stole and she became cold, my world was such dullness and misery that she soon brought forth my tears, a thing she could never do by her birch. I would make every effort to obtain forgiveness but she always took her own time. I would rush into the house to find the birch, and then pathetically hand it to her while bending down so that my bottom was within easy reach of my longed for chastisement. Sometimes that was enough, and I would feel the blows like a fiery manna from heaven expurgating my guilt. She taught me the way of modesty, to cover my loins and later my breasts at all times save with her alone. And I became curious about her body though I kept those thoughts to myself.

Each day I spent the morning with Bonz, the afternoon with Leidi and the evening with Meon. Bonz liked nothing better than teaching me the murderous ways of his warlike tribe. He would laugh uproariously in the first weeks as I rushed furiously on him with a wooden sword, my face

* See glossary

23

twisted with anger. He would parry my blows with ease, then rap me hard on the knee or knuckle to kindle ever further my anger. "Your arm not strong. Your spirit, she too strong." he would shout as I finally lay panting on the ground. Yet before the first year was gone, I surprised him. I was thrashing away with all my force and the determination born of many frustrating fights when I shattered the bronze shield and my wooden sword by one tremendous blow. We stopped momentarily as he looked unbelieving.

"Thirteen . . . yes, thirteen . . ." he said, shaking his head over the fragments of the shield. Only after that day did he begin to show me how I might penetrate guard, avoid return blows and how to strike from the ground.

He taught me too the longbow, the spear and unarmed combat. At all I excelled. And he made me progressively stronger and stronger bows, until running ahead of my tale, at last when I was sixteen I could draw his own great bow. By this time I was his height inch for inch, and his face broke into a smile of triumph as I flexed the bow and transfixed a tree a hundred meters distant. But this was nothing compared to the feast of my seventeenth birthday—reckoned by Meon. For the whole year Bonz had made me bend greater and greater iron rods, stretch springs and pull down small trees. By then I stood six centimeters above him and held back in our fights lest I injure him. On that day he set up his big iron shield in an elaborate frame before a dummy warrior in his armor. And before we sat down to the feast, he made a great play of fetching a present for me. He went into the shed in which he forged his weapons and metal, and reappeared carrying a string and something which I did not immediately see as a bow, so large and thick it was. He gave both to me.

"It is a back-bent bow. You must string it now."

Although I did not believe such a bow could be strung at all, yet boastful as I was, and wanting to keep the role of prodigy a little longer, I took it. Using all the strength of my thighs and lower legs I managed to string it, which indeed in itself was an achievement. Then I picked it up, looking proudly at Meon, Leidi and Bonz. I faced the target and lifted it. All the exerted muscles of my back and arms appeared from my soft-seeming flesh like magic as I felt the bow give under my ripening power. Then I drew it, and Bonz shouted to his Rainish gods in joy, and Meon's inscrutable face glowed with pride, while I stood with the back-bent bow

stretched out and held the tail of the heavy-headed arrow. As
I released I heard a rhythmic succession of clangs, but the
shield moved not, and I felt my cheeks flame with shame—I
had missed and humbled myself and Bonz, though strangely
he was laughing with pleasure. I ran to the shield, then to the
armor, and then to a tree twenty meters behind. And in
the heavy iron shield was a neat round hole. In the armor was
another. And in the tree we could just see the tail feathers of
the arrow. So my back-bent bow was baptized, "Whispering
Death" as I loudly proclaimed, though after that I felt a little
foolish, and I sat down and we began to feast. A light breeze
set up a strange keening sound in the holes in the armor and
shield—two notes in unholy harmony.

Thus I was at seventeen ready to become the greatest
woman warrior the world had ever known. Strong and tall,
yet not manly in appearance, rather like an ordinary woman
of my race, fair-skinned, dark-haired and voluptuous, if much
larger in size, under whose feminine cover of fat a keen eye
might detect the great muscles which distinguish me from my
sisters. Fleet of foot too I was and could run down a mottled-
bird in a meadow.

Taking my tale again to my early days at Fnaboi, (so was
Meon's name for the place where we lived), I spent each
afternoon working in and around the house with Leidi, cleaning,
washing, cooking and tidying. She was a pleasant woman
who thought of little but her immediate problem—the insecur-
ity of the world; she often claimed she heard evil beings
approaching the house, and she longed for the civilized days
of "bondage" in the empire which she could remember. She
complained of Bonz, his noisy ways, his drunkenness (though
he caused no trouble in his cups, merely becoming merrier
and seemingly lazier), and most of all his lack of civilization.
She compared him unfavorably with some man—of Węltan,
as it happened—who seemed to represent all that she desired
in a partner. Unfortunately, like my mother, he had met
his death at the hands of the Bunnish men. Yet she loved
Bonz too. She would show me wooden carvings he had
made and say proudly: "He has made this for me. He wor-
ships me, it is plain."

I liked to be with her, doing the same things, talking
endlessly of Bonz, Meon and the people she had known
before. We never talked of my past. I suppose she thought it

would give pain to me. But she asked me if I intended to be a wife one day.

"No, I do not wish to do the shameful thing." I replied. "The shameful thing" was what she and Bonz called copulation.

"Oh, you will. Girls always think that at your age. You will change." she said.

"I will not." And I held her wrist to emphasize my certainty, not intending to hurt her. But already my hands were like cruel vises and she cried out.

"Npin-Npan!"

I ceased immediately but she did not bring up the subject of the shameful thing again. As for Bonz he never showed any desire for me at all. I have often wondered since, knowing the proclivities of men of his type, how he felt when we rolled both nearly naked in unarmed combat, especially when I was older.

Best of all I loved the evenings with Meon in her lair. It is not permitted to write of the ways of sorcery—knowledge given only by one sorceress to another, so I may not give account of learning of the Deep Knowledge. But she taught me also to read and write and the number magic which may be written. As I was an apt though erratic scholar, I made good progress. She treated me always the same, save when I departed from the Way of Truth—kind and firm, concerned with my well-being, yet never too soft nor too familiar. Whether by design or accident this had the effect of making me her adoring slave. Long after I was too big to overpower she could have beaten me whenever she pleased though she never did.

"To beat you through your submission, though you are well able to render me impotent, would be against the Way," she said, and far from endangering my obedience, my immunity reinforced it. Only on a few occasions did she show me any affection.

Once in my younger days I ran off in disgrace after telling a lie and dared not return for fear of her anger. And I sat by the stream where we had met, tearful and angry with myself and with her. And the sun dropped and I still did not return. But after midnight as I became afraid, I ran back to the house to find her in the yard looking for me with no coldness in her face. She held me in her arms for a few minutes.

"*I* deserve punishment for *this* is against the Way," she

said, meaning, I think, that her concern and relief had made her neglect her duty.

"It is the Way of Truth," I replied and I was right. I never did such a thing again.

The other occasion was near the end of my time at Fnaboi, and to some extent it precipitated my departure, as will be seen.

As I grew older and as I have said, larger and stronger, I began to feel restless. I loved Meon and I liked Bonz and Leidi, but I felt an increasing urge to explore the world beyond the confines of the clearing. And as my power increased I itched to try it on my enemies. The subarboreals I despised as animals in dirty holes in the ground, unworthy of attention, but not so the Bunnish whom I intended to slay, all of them and I hated beyond all moderation. Meon was sad when I told her of this, though she did not council me for she knew that to wreak vengeance on a whole people for the crimes, however evil, of some of them, was against the Way, and yet seeing my determination she feared to bring this final urge of base nature into conflict with the Way in my young mind.

Many times I asked to see the maps of Old Mbora,* so that I could know where were the provinces of Bububa and Shuba-Snudi now lost to the Bunnish.

"The kingdom of Bunedi lies to the north of Wnai"* Meon said. "And it is this which lies where the old provinces of Bububa and Shuba-Snudi once flowered. There the northern Bunnish have settled, farming and building villages. It is the southern Bunnish who destroyed the old city of Shuba, who are yet restless and warlike. By the destructive and unjust impulses of their great duke Cax they invaded poor Wnai and destroyed the republic. The duke wishes to set up his own kindgom in Weltan so that he might emulate the deeds of Undish. Yet his men so wild and unschooled in the Way burn and pillage like the barbarians they are." She knew this by her sorcery, for she could see things that happened in distant places in her water.

"It is the Weltan Bunnish who I would first slay," I said eagerly. "May I know where the Weltan Bunnish may be found?"

"They may be found all over Weltanland, outside the great forests. But talk less of this vendetta; it irks me."

* See glossary

So I examined maps by myself and planned my return to the land of my birth. I walked more and more often in the clearing and behaved in a youthful and boyish fashion, breaking branches, hurling rocks at animals and firing arrows at numerous harmless creatures. Most girls do not behave in this way but I believe that is because they feel eclipsed by the stronger and more active boys.

When I was sixteen, a strange and intangible yearning grew in me. At first I knew not what it was, only that I felt in very low spirits at times and very elated at others, and occasionally a great tearing sensation came to me, so that I clenched my hand and clamped my jaw. Only after my seventeenth birthday the truth of my feeling dawned upon me. When Meon spoke to me, I was exulted. When she was in her lair, or silent as often, I was in the pit of despair. It happened perhaps because of my alienation from the other sex, and because my great strength and power gave me no longing for the secure comfort of a man. So my burgeoning emotions settled upon Meon, mysterious center of my universe, as their object.

As I grew larger I no longer slept in Meon's room, and as my interest in her body increased, so my opportunity for satisfying my curiosity disappeared. I began to imagine I might save Meon from some great evil, and in her gratitude she might take me to her bed. I had no idea of what real love was like between man and woman and did not associate that with a bed. The cruel violations of the Bunnish and Subarboreals had no connection with my new emotions. I only wanted to have her close to me, in the warmest and most private place I could imagine. And I wanted to caress her body, though I knew not why. These feelings would reach their peak when she passed across the courtyard, wrapped loosely in a shining blue silk cloth as she went to her daily bath. I knew she came along the corridor outside my room on her way down, and one evening I contrived to be in my room as she returned, sweet-smelling and warm. I came out blocking her path. She smiled.

"Why do you hide from the sun in your room?" she asked. "It is not the way to be a warrior queen." I did not speak, only looked at her, my heart beating. "Let me pass now, Npin-Npan, I shall be cold."

"Come into my room, I want to be close to you. I feel it so strong," I said, truthfully but awkwardly.

"You must not press your wishes on others, Npin-Npan. Let me pass," she said.

"I shall not," I said. She faced me. She could no more pass than she could have flown. But she caught my eye. My hair was partially over my face because I could not bear the shame of my action. One eye looked through my long black tresses. I reached out and held her shoulder, gently as I hoped.

"Leave me be, Npin-Npan. You act wrongly."

I put my hand to her shift and pulled gently. "Only be naked with me, in my bed, for a little time." I said.

"Let me go." she said. I pulled and she tried to hold her shift. My strength triumphed and she stood naked before me. I trembled. She spoke in a strange tongue which sent a shiver of fear down my body. My eyes swam and I could not make out what I saw. Then suddenly her hand was rough and cruel, mine thin and feeble—once more the Bunnish warrior held my wrist and laughed cruelly at my feeble struggles. And by her sorcery Meon overcame my strength, hurling me into my room where I lay weeping on the floor. I made a ridiculous figure, a great amazon planning deeds of conquest slobbering like a baby.

Later I sat up on my bed afraid to come out of my room, not for fear of the Bunnish warrior who I well knew was an illusion but for fear of the wrath of Meon. Night fell and I got into my bed, putting on a scarlet nightdress, the like of which I had worn that first night at Fnaboi. When the moon rose, I heard my door open and Meon stood before me, her face calm, her eyes glittering in the moonlight.

"Why have you departed from the Way of Truth, Npin-Npan?" she asked.

"I know not." I replied.

"What then, if your desire is too strong for your honesty, and your strength too great for my power to resist—am I to be your plaything? A doll to be undressed and subject to your fancy and curiosity at your every whim?"

"No, Meon. Never again."

Meon smiled. "So you think when the fever is not upon you. Yet I knew from the first where your wishes would lead. Now the time for your departure is upon us. Tomorrow at first light you must leave this place."

I would have cried again but I had no tear left. I only hung my head in sorrow and shame. "And shall I never return?" I asked.

"Not for many years. And then if you come, you may not find me here."

"And shall I never see you again?"

"Yes, Npin-Npan, you will see me again, and I you."

I smiled in the darkness, for I yearned for adventure, and my sadness was tempered with excitement, now that I knew the parting was not permanent.

"I am sorry that I departed from the Way," I said, a phrase that had not passed my lips for a long time—since my childish sins.

"Such things happen to all. Passion does not easily serve the Truth." She was silent for a while. Then she spoke again. "Since this is to be your last night, speak your wish and it shall come to pass. A great feasting perhaps?"

I spoke as ever I do, direct and bold. "It is my wish that you come now to my bed, naked as you were before." I expected nothing but a jest. But Meon slipped from her robe so quickly and easily, I doubted not it was her wish also.

"I did not guess wrong." she said, and slid in between the covers, so warm and alive.

I knew nothing of the ways of love and only thought to lie with our arms about each other. But Meon sought to rouse my young passions to their first tempest. She took off the red nightgown and caressed me, all my neck, shoulders and arms, then my breasts, belly and thighs till I sighed with the new pleasure she brought me.

"It is the habit of sorceresses to love their own kind." she said, stopping her movements, leaving me itching for her hands. "Some take men also to their beds, but ever as serfs or playthings, and often use them cruelly. Only with women are they truly kind though they may show small cruelties to them too, to add flavor to their satisfaction."

"Is it for the sake of such small cruelty that you now cease your caressing of my body?" I asked.

"Just such a case," she said softly but caressed again my belly until her hand tangled on each stroke with the thick hair of my sex. That part of me was taut as my back-bent bow, waiting in both fear and eagerness for what might follow. When her hand suddenly plunged down into the fleshy marsh below, my arrow was released upon the instant and I rocked in an earthquake of feeling, my great body a danger to my

surroundings as it bucked and convulsed out of all control.
Yet Meon watched, all fire in her eyes to see the eruption of
the volcano which she had created. At the end I lay exhausted
while she spoke tauntingly in my ear.

"Where now is the amazon? By such a simple means, I
have made you the animal you are at heart. It will be long
before you feel my hand again, great warrior."

Later I tried to do to her what she had done to me but she
would have none of me. "I could not abide your childish
gropings." she said. "Even though I would please you with
an act of pretense if I could, I cannot, nor would it be in the
Way."

I ceased, not really abashed since I understood nothing of
these matters. But in the night I woke and lay half dozing
while I felt her on me again astride my waist sitting straight
up, her arms raised. I felt the warm wet flesh on my belly
twitching and sucking as she spoke:

"As this child of the northern darkness came to me from
the evil places,

"As this child is now grown and is a woman,

"As this woman will be a warrior,

"As this woman will be a sorceress by my skill,

"As this sorceress shall not be in the power of men,

"As this woman is of the Way of Truth,

"So this woman shall go forth into the world,

"So shall she learn the way of the world,

"So shall she bring light to the darkness,

"So shall the power of the south pass by this woman to
the north,

"So now I give to this woman her true name, Cheon,
bringer of dawn."

As she said these words a great light rose up until it
dazzled me, and I saw her hair stand up in undulating waves
to float around her head while her loins pumped her power
over me so that it flowed from her body to my sex and into
my body in a living stream. Her eyes opened wide, and her
mouth, and a sound rose around us like a million tortured
voices. And my body began to rise and we floated upward
until we hovered in the room above the bed, our hair shivering in long streamers around our bodies like strands of shimmering life, our arms stretched wide. Then the light faded and
we sank again onto the bed and slept.

I woke to see her beside me. I remembered both the

love-making and the strange levitation. And I knew that it had not been a dream but it belonged to the category of magic and represented my christening as a sorceress, warrior and future queen.

When we rose from our bed of love, I was prepared for my journey. Meon had made my armor by her sorcery. Light it was yet stronger than the finest iron. It had a helmet in the fashion of the rising sun with rays which served to deflect blows, on top of a covering for the head which also protected my ears and neck. My chest and back were covered by a breast-plate attached by bands around my back, and shaped to accommodate my breasts which were large and high. My upper thighs, buttocks and lower stomach were covered by a skirt of mail, flexible and strong. My shins had fluted armor with great extensions protecting the front of my knees and lower thighs. All my armor was of sky blue with wing-like ornaments and intricate patterns of flowers, suns, moons and symbols of power. Under it, I wore in summer from breasts to thighs a soft silk shift which prevented it from chafing the tender parts of my body which are a woman's pride. And for winter I had a leather jacket and trousers. All of it could fold until it was easy to carry in my pack, where I also kept less warlike garb—gowns, shifts, a book of sorcery, a map of Mbora and of Wnai, valuable and irreplaceable things in those times. I carried money in a large purse around my waist where I also put my Dawn stone, my dagger and a lock of Meon's hair, black and curly. My great bow, Whispering Death, I hung on my shoulder, and I had a sword in my scabbard, one which Bonz had made. At last I held my shield which carried the emblem of Cheon, bringer of dawn, a rising sun.

As I took my leave, Leidi and Bonz wept and so did I, and each embraced me and I tolerated Bonz though I hated it, not for him but for those before. But Meon wept not when she embraced me and spoke:

"May the Truth go with you!" she said, and I turned and walked away, my feet crunching on the dry leaves and my breath making steam in the air.

V

I walked all day, leaving the clearing I knew, headed for the part of the forest where Meon said that light always penetrated. I ate from the supply provided by Leidi, drank spring water and made good progress. To carry so much—my pack, shield, bow on my back and my sword at my side—was an irksome business, but I knew that so a warrior traveled and the weight did not trouble me, only the irritating awkwardness. I made a fire at night and slept without fear, waking with the sunrise on my face. The world seemed joyful now that the sadness of departure had subsided and I watched the birds in their morning activity, chased animals that I saw and went my way with a tune on my lips.

I saw no one as I entered the woodlands keeping my direction by the magic pointer Meon had given me. But I walked ever alone under the trees until I saw a hut set beside a stream which I approached warily. It was empty and appeared to have been for some time. And behind it I found three skeletons, one headless, one with ribs caved in and one with no obvious injuries. I guessed they had been some family like mine slain by the Bunnish. But I felt no fear, only a sense of excitement which pressed my steps on the way to Elling, the nearest town to my old home. And still I made no encounter when I emerged from the wood and continued along deserted grassy lands in the late afternoon.

In those times people were afraid to walk abroad for fear of meeting the bands of duke Cax who roamed around perpetrating any outrage they pleased under the pretense that they were subduing a recalcitrant province. As I know now they were unruly and disorganized, fighting one another as often as not over some prize in the shape of a village or hoard of money. They seldom fought over women, there being a more than adequate supply of homeless, manless creatures ready to fall in with any plan for some atom of security. Such women I

33

saw at later times running from their homes making the most direct offer to buy their lives with their favors. Some ran naked pointing to their sex, others learned two words of Bunnish and would shout out: "Me screw! Me screw!" in the vulgar language of the soldiers. Yet even those less favored by nature were often slain as they debased themselves. Among them were women who only a handful of years before had been ladies, bestowing their favors only after great courtships and expensive marriages. The men of Weltan were few and spent their days hiding unless they were of some use as serfs to the conquerors. But the times were not settled enough for many to be needed, hence only the very old were tolerated by the Bunnish who respected age more than youth.

The sun was low over the western hills when I found my home, and though it had been a long time since I had last passed the gate, I could remember it, and the garden even overgrown as it now was, and the white poles, now peeled and rotten, and the window of my bedroom from which I could see the blond downy slopes of the cornfield shivering down to the distant forest. And I walked up the three stoned steps where I had practiced my first jumps, and I opened not the door for there was no more door nor need of it. Inside nobody waited but the skeletons of my mother and brother, still lying where they had fallen, and weeds and roots had crept through the floor and begun to weave a green shroud over them. And a wind wandered restlessly through the holes where there had been windows. That evening I buried their bodies and I visited each house where lay the dead, unburied and unmourned. And late in the night I looked over the land, once neatly divided into fields, now invaded by weeds and young trees. I wept no tears nor felt any dread of lying among so many dead when sleep at last overtook me.

In the morning I hastened into Elling, fearing to find it deserted but it was thinly populated with a mixture of old Weltanmen, Weltanwomen and children, and Bunnish men who seemed peaceful enough, wearing only light armor. Some vague semblance of town life seemed to exist—whether the last dregs of the old or the first glimmer of the new, I knew not though the latter was more likely. There were inns in the main street which were able to offer food and shelter for money, even though as I found out, they feared the sudden eruptions of new bands of Bunnish eager to take the village from the present holders who had softened after a couple of years of easy living. Those who run inns, shops and brothels are the same in all lands, as I have discovered. They are avaricious and selfish yet at the same time the most civilized of all people, loving peace and orderly ways. And their optimism is boundless as they start their trade in the most unstable of places.

I entered an inn which looked inviting to me. Like all those in the town the landlady looked at me with wide-eyed curiosity. My size, my fearless bearing and my civilized speech all contributed to make her treat me with respect. A Weltanwoman of engaging face, she appeared to run the place with a Bunnish man, older than is common for a warrior, who no doubt felt his fighting days were over. I was given a key to a room. No bath was available, indeed the general atmosphere of the town convinced me that such things were in abeyance at least for a time.

As I sat during the evening at a bench and listened to the conversation in the saloon, I had to admit to myself that I was in a dilemma. I had come expressly to slay Bunnish men. But I had expected them to be like the pillagers of my home in appearance and in manner. Those that I saw here were quietly behaved, their beards neatly trimmed and many of them carried not even a sword. This did not make me change my mind, only caused me to hold my peace temporarily. Looking back I can see that my problem came from politeness. It is difficult for one brought up to be civil, to suddenly break out of habit to the extremity of killing a perfect stranger in cold blood without explanation. So I sat hoping that more aggressive Bunnish might make their appearance. And by an agreeable stroke of fortune I was rewarded in this. Had I visited this town any time in the preceding year, I should have seen only the remnants of a band of marauders who wanted to set up a new life in favorable time for them. Yet on this one night the peace was broken and as is often the case, I seemed to call trouble from a clear sky.

I heard much mumbling and many lowered voices talking of a "new band" and realized that the people of the town, Weltan and Bunnish alike, feared a group of new invaders who were in the neighborhood. It was even as I became sleepy that a great commotion sounded in the street and all at the inn tensed with fright. None moved but only waited in silence. And soon a group of a dozen or more men heavily armed crashed into the room. They did not immediately lay

about them, for they were easy and confident. Elling, they
knew, no longer housed soldiers. It had a representative of
Cax, but he, no doubt did not consider it judicious to appear at
such time. They were like any band of noisy, arrogant men,
enjoying the pleasure of terrorizing people who were impotent
to defy them.

Several tables were upset, drinks spilt and men tossed from
their seats to make way for the newcomers. Behind them
some women, all naked and on a chain came in and stood
where they were left, trembling. One was a Kariasg, tall but
bent in shame, her fine eyes filled with unshed tears, her
mouth hanging limp. The others were Weltanwomen, their
faces drawn with fear and pain. They bore brands on their
buttocks, but even while they were exposed powerless, my
eyes were drawn away to the obvious leader of the band. A
great monster with scarred face, reddened eyes and bellowing
laugh, he sat heavily on a table and called to the landlady in
his language which I now understood for I had been taught
Bunnish by Meon.

"Bring me wine and food, the best you have. If I don't like
it, your place will burn." The woman hurriedly brought a
great pitcher of wine to him. "Take off your clothes
woman," he shouted. "Don't you know I am the lord of this
land now?"

She immediately stripped, and as she was at that time of
life when the mystery is better than the full revelation it was a
sad thing to witness. Perhaps forty-five, with breasts and
buttocks that sagged, she cut a pathetic figure. He roared with
laughter and spiked her bottom with a fork.

"What's this? An old crumpled wineskin?" His men made
loud sniggers. The Bunnish man who lived at the inn was
cowering in the room at the rear and showed no sign of aiding
her.

Of the men who surrounded their chieftain, many were
only youths and few were more than twenty or so years, save
two who seemed too old for their parts. Their armor was
crude, some of it rusty and adorned with symbols for warding
off sorcery. Bonz had told me what signs to search for in a
true warrior—scars, and quick, uneasy eyes that looked for
attackers at the edge of vision. The great man at the center
had all these, but of the others only one looked somewhat as a
warrior should.

The party continued, never violent yet always on the verge

of it, drinking and eating, some of the younger ones behaving more crudely than I believed was their true nature. The woman of the inn was obliged to serve all, naked as she was, and put up with vulgar abuse, rough but intimate handling and frequent discussion among the gang as to who would first satisfy his lust on her person, or by what fashion she might provide the greatest pleasure. Her man still froze in the rear room. Though the women were afraid, yet I could not help noticing that they were less uneasy than the men. They expected at most a beating and a rape, for they had learnt from experience that this was a night when they could provide something with their living bodies and would escape in the morning. The men knew that their lives hung in balance, and Bunnish and Weltan alike they shook in their boots, too scared to move, taunted as they were. Only one made to leave but he was told to remain and he did not dare to defy the command.

At last Arkan of Beldus, as the warrior frequently called himself, decided that it was time for entertainment. The women of Elling should dance, he said. All knew what he meant and stripped themselves stark naked. An old Weltan played a little flute, hoping to win favor by this means. I sat and made no move to join this groveling throng who began to wobble their hips and lower their quivering bottoms in lewd simulation of the delights they expected to offer later. But at this point Arkan noticed me and brought the proceedings to a halt with a roar of anger.

"Did I not ask for dancing? Who is this great sow that she does not obey my orders? Stand up, woman, and approach if you wish to see another dawn."

I rose and walked two paces. "Since you ask impolitely who I am, let me say that I am the very dawn of which you speak, Cheon of Weltanland."

His face was red with wrath. Defiance surprised and irritated him, eroding as it did, his air of omnipotence. Yet old warrior that he was, he was suspicious, seeing my armor and my great size, and thoughts of the myth of Thanda must have been in his mind.

"Well then, Cheon of Weltanland, who wears the remnants of some warrior stabbed no doubt after a night with you in a whore house, take off your stolen armor and give it to me, for I see it is of good quality. Then wave your ass like these other whores and be thankful you yet live."

"I must give you notice in accordance with the Way that I shall slay you, old windbag, if you lay hands on me, though I would prefer not to give you any warning since it is my wish to slay you. For you have departed from the Way and you have come to this land by the force of your arms." This speech evidently shocked him into action.

"Seize this drunken young whore, strip her, then bring her to me for chastisement," he shouted. Two of the youths stepped forward, but I seized hold of the nearer and raising him above my head, I threw him at his comrade. The two flew like sacks hurled from a cart and smashed into a table against the wall where they lay, one with broken back, the other stunned. The old warrior acted now, instinctively, knowing that it was no whore with whom he was dealing.

True to his experience and cunning he made to settle the argument with no further ado. He could brook no rival in his sight and I would not obey. I must be slain. My experience was so little and I was so moved by my hurling of the young raiders that I might then and there have died at his hands. All banter and appearance of drunkenness vanished as Arkan of Beldus leaped up, drawing his great broadsword in a flash of the eye, so fast I barely comprehended it. Only by the bravery and unlooked for aid of the woman of the inn was I saved. She kicked a chair over into his path so that he stumbled momentarily, giving me time to act. I had expected the beginning of a fight to be a more formal affair, little realizing that suddenness and surprise could give the victory to the lesser over the greater. Now I seized my shield and just lifted it in time to block the blow he dealt with every muscle and ounce of weight he had. I used my sword hand to help support it—even so, the blow shook my whole body and sent a searing pain up my shoulders. For Arkan the shock seemed ever greater. Like a man striking a rock with an iron rod, he felt a numbing recoil rebound up his sword which shattered into several pieces. His arm seemed limp and he backed off.

"My shield! My shield!" he cried and the other soldierly looking man threw his shield to him. As he held it up, I saw no fear in his eyes, for vile creature though he was, he was a warrior to the end. I had drawn my sword and seeing him cower under the shield I raised it, crying out: "Die now, man who scorns the Way!" I struck at him with every ounce of strength in my young body. My sword sheared through shield, iron and bone, and clove him in twain from his head to the middle of his chest. The two symmetrical parts of his head fell different ways until they hung by the bloody sinews of his neck, wobbling as he crashed to the ground. I looked too long—a warrior must not be too curious for the results of her deed, and I could have been slain by his men even as I stood aghast at the terrible result of my blow. But instead of an angry band of men out for revenge, I saw a pathetic group, all horror struck by the end of their leader's life, his blood spurting around, mixing with beer and wine and covering our clothes.

"So dies Arkan of Beldus!" I said, looking now at his leaderless band. The same man who had thrown Arkan his shield made a faint movement to his sword-arm. I looked at him. I was the master.

"You have slain my brother," he said in the voice of a lizard.

"And by the blood-bond you must slay me," I said. He spoke not but the woman of the inn nodded.

"It is the bond," she said. And those others in the inn nodded, even the Bunnish man of the inn who had reappeared. "You must avenge your brother."

The brother of Arkan grew pale as he saw all approve. "It is a wrong thing since all see that this woman—or demon, as it seems—may slay me with impunity. How then will the blood-bond be served?" he pleaded.

"So that you will the sooner be by your brother's side, in the palace of the Ice-King." I said, remembering what I knew of the Bunnish gods. "As he obliges the winged-women to strip and dance, no doubt." My irony brought smiles to the lips of the Weltan folk who believed not in the Ice palace, but not to the Bunnish.

"Can you not see that she is but a demon of the glaciers?" came the reply of the brother of Arkan.

"I can see that you are no demon of the north, nor a man either," said the woman of the inn.

Foolishly he was goaded and finally drew his sword which I allowed, as it is in the Way, and then lopped off his head which fell very heavily to the floor, making a sound like a falling anvil, much louder than I expected. His body slowly toppled, spraying us anew with blood. Then my blood lust abated and I sat down.

"Throw the bodies of these untrue men in the street." I said, and several Weltans and local Bunnish did my bidding.

The remaining warriors were a sorry crowd. They knew not what would now befall them. Two of the youths wept, a sight which puzzled me.

"What ails you, Bunnish reavers? Is it not well to be rid of this tyrant?"

"We have no king now. We shall not know where to go nor how to gain what we need. And we may be slain since we are but newly come to manhood. Arkan promised us land, food, wine and women, all the riches we could want. Yet now for this small thing you have slain him, who would have led us south to the city of gold."

I saw then that even a bullying untrue king is better than none, and that even though he gained their allegiance by outlandish tales of cities of gold, land and women, yet still he meant life or death to them. Petty chieftains like him, as I later discovered, roamed the whole of Weltanland, all of Wnai. Sometimes they fought and if the king was slain, it happened that the remaining warriors joined the victorious king. And by this process, larger tribes and kingdoms formed. Without a king as these petty creatures called themselves, the groups soon fell prey to hunger and rapacity. These young men, such strutting cockerels before, now feared that the villagers might kill them, even if I chose to spare them. The speech of the lad was partially his spoken fear, and partly as I soon found, an attempt to replace their king. For one of the others spoke to me, suddenly seeing that I listened with interest to the whines of his friend.

"You may be our queen now that we have no king. We will show you loyalty. You may have always the finest cut of meat, the largest jewels and the most comely . . . the most . . ." He had been about to say the most comely women but saw his mistake and was silent. Even had I wanted to lead this unhappy and ineffectual band I should have refused, since by accepting I would have fulfilled the prophecy of my wish to be a queen, and as I dreamed of a great kingdom I must need avoid such pathetic role as this.

"I have no need of your impotent service. It is prophesied that I become a great queen, not the leader of a bedraggled group of cowering popinjays." I said. They sat then quiet and fearful as the others of the inn returned to their drinking, eyeing the newcomers with the beginning of contempt.

"What will become of us then?" said the youth who had spoken first.

"I know not and care not," I said but his whining irked me and I added. "What do you fear? You have your lives."

"We cannot obtain food and the villagers will kill us by treachery if we stay."

"It is well," I said, then added. "Yet if you remain and work in the fields, aiding these people in their defense against men like Arkan, perhaps good may yet come of your foolish raid."

The Weltanwoman looked at me. "You speak wisely, Cheon of Weltanland. Yet why not remain yourself? None would dare challenge you and you might live well."

"I have much to do, woman, and may not dally where I please." My speech was imperious, so elated was I at my first success against the Bunnish.

"What of us?" one of the women in chains suddenly spoke. "We have no protector now nor any means of obtaining food."

"You have your asses which you can sell to any who might lack the charm or power to obtain them without payment," said the woman of the inn. Another one spoke, who had dressed again in her robe.

"Those are cruel words, Jzelli, and untrue. No one here has money to procure satisfaction for their lust. And the soldiers may take what they please from such women offering no payment."

"May they, with these men, not help to till the fields in this region, which as I have seen, are not tended and therefore cannot provide food?" I asked.

"We want none of these riff-raff," said a man of the town. I rose.

"I shall not listen further to this strife. Were I to wish for a more stable life, which I do not, I would settle differences so that the town might grow strong and resist the incursions of every band of raiders who choose to amuse and enrich themselves at your expense."

"For one so young, you speak words as wise as your arms are strong." said the inn-woman, Jzelli. "Be you demon or as you appear, a maiden of freakish strength, you have done well this night for us, and you shall pay no tariff for your food and shelter here."

"I thank you, woman, but as it is the Way, so shall I pay my due."

It may be seen that at this time I was, as is common in

young people, somewhat grandiose and pompous in my speech. My belief in the Way was now as strong as even Meon could have wished though she might have regretted my lack of humor and mellowness. Yet I am sure that though one may grow in ease of manner by experience alone, the Way must be taught vigorously as had been my case. As I made to leave the room, the Kariasg woman spoke, looking proudly into my eyes.

"Since your strength be so great and since we must now fend for ourselves, do us the kindness of striking off these shackles which have no key."

I turned and approached them. I saw that I could not hope to break the iron which held their ankles, yet I could sever the chains which linked them together and remove them so that the women were free to go their separate ways if they wished. Thus I drew my sword and freed them without effort.

"It is a great evil when women are chained and led naked in the streets." I said and I left the room and walked up the wooden stairs to my chamber. Then I removed my armor, having bolted the door, and wearing one of my silken white shifts I lay down to sleep. But before I could begin to feel drowsy, I heard a knock at the door. I picked up my sword and shield.

"Who is there?" I asked. A voice answered, soft and low, in the Old Tongue.

"It is I, the Kariasg whom you freed from her shackles."

I could not be sure that some treachery was not afoot, so I called out in the Old Tongue which I had learned from Meon.

"I am armed. Should any enter but you who you have said, I shall slay them. Should *you* bear any arms I shall slay you. Do you understand?"

"I understand indeed. Yet open the door and I will come."

I threw back the bolt and she entered wearing now a dirty white towel about her waist—a loan from Jzelli, no doubt. I closed the door and bade her be seated.

"What reason have you for disturbing my rest?" I asked.

"To offer you my service in exchange for your protection and enough food for a frugal living."

I hesitated. In truth I needed a servant—one who might bring me food and drink, sparing me much demeaning labor. Although active enough when I choose, there is a great laziness about me. And I liked this creature well by appearance since she reminded me of Meon. Yet might she not prove a hindrance in my war against Cax? She would not be able to keep up with me if I hurried, she might become sick and need nursing. Yet might I not also become sick? Then one such as she might be the only way to survive. Two, if acting as one, can be safer and more companionable in the wild. She was not large like Meon, rather of average height and I could carry her if haste were essential.

"How can I trust you? Might you not slay me in my sleep?" I asked.

"How often the word slay is on your lips! How can you trust me? I have no protector. I am not strong and able as you. My early life was spent in pampered idleness, so that now I must perish unless I have someone who looks to my welfare. If after three years of being whipped, raped, half-starved and near-frozen, I find one whom I may serve, by what paradox shall I then destroy her? As for slaying you in your sleep, if you pass but one night in my company and wake to life in the morning, then are you not doubly safe in your bed? Gladly will I sleep by the door, so that by its movement I shall waken and with my screams rouse you to save your life, even though I have been thrust through a hundred times like a pincushion."

I smiled at her jest. "And how can I know your service to be satisfactory? If as you say you spent your early life in idleness you must be unused to work even for yourself. And by age I suppose you to be nineteen or more, to my seventeen years. Will it not finally bring you to anger, serving me— your junior by two years or more?"

"For service I have learned by hard blows to be quick to my tasks. By my cleverness—Kariasgs are wont to be more intelligent than Hyperboreans—(she said this without malice), I shall anticipate your needs. And by my knowledge of the way my servants of old acted I shall be sure to provide you with a high standard. As for my age, I shall not resent your orders if they are just and in keeping with the Way, which I know you to follow. By serving you, I hope one day to return to the land of my people where the empire still lives, and I can once again live tranquil in a land of peace."

"What has become of your mother and father?"

"They were slain in the Bunnish attack on Weltanland."

"As were my own." I said, amazed by what seemed a coincidence though the same story must have been told a million times in that region at that time.

"And do you accept my service?" she said.

"We must agree to a contract, so that afterward neither may complain of hardship."

"Yes. I ask on my side only that you protect me from harm and allow me sufficient food for my needs, except where you are only able to find food enough for yourself. And that you will help me, if it falls in your power, to reach the empire once more. And on the other side I agree to do your bidding in all things, save against the Way."

"These terms are not just. In service you must receive some reward which may be saved, accumulated and one day used to free yourself. I shall grant you twenty palmers each month, and one tenth of what I may take in booty or wages while you serve me. I shall provide you with clothes and you may at all times share my shelter. On your side you must agree also to act always for my interest and to warn me of any news you may hear which may be of use to me."

"So be it. Do you wish me to write this contract so that we may not forget its terms?"

"Yes. In two copies and in the Old Tongue."

"Does my mistress wish that I do it now, before sleeping?"

"Tomorrow will do well enough. Tell me now your name, Kariasg woman."

"Wanin."

"Then let us sleep. Both have need of rest. But do not wear that dirty cloth about your loins, rather a silken shift which I shall give you, which you may wear when you have need of clothes. Take off therefore that garment."

She hesitated. "It is not seemly to be bare loined before another."

"You are my servant and must do my bidding. Do not begin badly."

She took off the dirty towel and was once more naked. I smiled.

"And besides, are we not both women? And have I not seen all parts of your body but half an hour before?"

She nodded. "But for the sake of dignity. . . ."

"Before me you are dignified as you are. Before others you will be clothed. Here, sleep now on this blanket by the door, as you said."

VI

Wanin came to be an attentive servant, gradually learning my desires until she could foresee my every wish before I spoke it. She was intelligent too, and could say things which made me laugh. She was afraid of all danger, as are many Kariasg and Asg women, so that she kept close to me where she felt safe, and bore well enough caresses which I sometimes gave her. For my part I needed then, and need now, women near me at certain times. I liked my woman to be naked and prostrate by my side as I ate my evening meal from her hands. I obtained clothes for her from a trader in the town who was revealed to me by Jzelli. No one openly sold anything, only waited for trustworthy customers to be sent from trustworthy sources. That trader had many dresses, some made from rags collected over years, some taken, I fear, from the dead bodies of women after the first sacking of Elling. She had attempted to wash bloodstains from them but had not been completely successful. Yet Wanin found acceptable shifts to wear when she walked with me.

We stayed only a few days at Elling, during which people avoided me. Once one spills blood, one becomes an object of fear. And if I was fair-spoken before, perhaps another day I might be in another mood, and it was foolish to take a chance. When we left it was to start a kind of life of which I am now ashamed.

My eagerness to kill Bunnish soldiers was undiminished, and I spent my days finding them either alone or in small groups, and by one means or another arranging that they struck a blow or attempted to, then killing them as the Way permits. Yet I felt a vague sense of dissatisfaction and so did Wanin. At first she spoke often and served me with smiles, but as the weeks passed she became taciturn and glum, and though I knew what she felt, I could not accept the reason for our depression. The slaughter of Bunnish warriors was good and it must go on.

One night as I lay abed in a ruined cottage where we stayed, I felt oppressed by Wanin's silence. She had curled up in a blanket by the door.

"Why do you not leave me, since you find the life you lead so irksome?" I said after a long time. She sat up.

"Do you not find it so?"

"What if I do? It is my destiny."

"What destiny? To slay a few ignorant barbarians? A stirring future!"

I was angry now that she spoke the truth. "You mock your mistress, servant? Take care lest I thrash your buttocks as you deserve." I said, remembering my childhood.

"If the truth does not please you, then thrash me if it comforts you."

I knew she was right and I was silent for a little. Then I spoke again.

"But I must conquer the darkness. I am to bring the dawn." My voice was small and childish, and tears were close. Wanin answered softly.

"Why say you this?"

"So it was foretold by a great sorceress, when I was but thirteen years, who also foretold my great prowess in combat."

"She foretold well in the matter of prowess, so you must truly be the bringer of light. Might not your present life though, be a mere practicing and gaining of experience? Your destiny must be to lead others, who will triumph altogether against the barbarians of the north."

"It must be so. Yet where can I meet others, strong in truth, whom I may join? For surely I must serve before I may lead."

"You speak wisely now, Cheon of Weltanland, like a child of Truth. Let us then leave this place and journey south until we reach the borders of the republic which still lives, though in much reduced size, if tales told are true. There you will be welcomed as a warrior who will be needed. Later, when your prowess and spirit are known you will surely be chosen their queen. And I may be then raised to a lady who will in turn have servants."

"And I may drive the Bunnish hordes north again and make all Mbora safe for the Truth. . . ."

Thus we dreamed. As we lay trying to sleep, I heard Wanin move often and fidget and turn.

"What ails you, Wanin?" I asked.

"It is a trouble women feel who know the embraces of men. The brother of Arkan whom you slew was my lover—though I loved him not. Yet now I would feel his spike in my loins."

"Such a feeling will never come to me, since that too is foretold. You must not think to lie with a man under the same roof as me, your mistress. But as I am just, so I say that if you must have such a service, do it with my blessing. And if you find a man whom you wish to take as a husband, you may be relieved from my service."

Wanin laughed. "I shall not leave your service until I can return to Mnoy, my ancestral land. Mbora is a place now of terror only; even were king Undish himself to take me as wife, I would not marry him nor any other of Mbora."

For a while again we were silent. But other thoughts now came to my mind.

"One woman may lay with another, and great pleasure may be had by it. If you come now to my bed I will show you how."

"I know of such things. But I could not take pleasure with a woman. It is not a real thing."

"It is real. And it is not against the Way, as my teacher told me."

"Yet I will not, even though you order it as mistress."

"That would be against the Way." I lay, sad but not angry, until sleep overcame me.

The next day we set out for the south and our spirits rose again, since we were hoping to become queen and lady. The route we took followed an old road of Wnai, built with flat stones, with many bridges and broken arches. Inns and hostelries lay in ruins and villages were deserted. No doubt the road was used by bands of Bunnish and was an unhealthy place for traveling. The weather was less warm as autumn began to fade, but our march was always toward warmer climates, so that we did not suffer too much. We passed gradually from the kind of trees that I knew from my childhood into the region where groves of subtropical trees and generally more lush vegetation spread. I enjoyed the days though I walked more slowly than I would have wished, since Wanin could in no manner keep pace with my usual speed. We ate differently, for Wanin liked meat and would clean and roast the small beasts I slew with my bow over an evening fire, while I ate only vegetables, nuts and fruit, as well as a quantity of dried beans and cheese which I had brought with me. Usually we found empty villas and mansions in which we slept—sometimes with unburied skeletons sharing the shelter with us. Wanin wept to see neglected houses and overgrown gardens which reminded her of her home.

"In such a room I was presented to the world." she would say, or, "In a garden, by a pool like this, once I used to play the flute and feed my birds of paradise." And at other times, "But then came the Hyperborean barbarians to kill and burn."

"I am a Hyperborean, remember, and I have given you protection," I would say, and she would add:

"The northern Hyperboreans I mean, of course."

In the evenings sometimes to give me diversion she would tell of those days which seemed so bright and colorful, so warm, carefree and exciting that I too would shed tears when she spoke of the terrible end of it all.

On the road we rarely met others. Sometimes we saw figures in the distance looking up, like startled sheep, before disappearing into the nearby woods. Then would I draw my bow, and leaving Wanin in the safety of the open meadows, walk into the tree-lined region to see if danger lurked. Only once did we see a great band whom we heard from long distance by their noise and clamor. They came up the road from the south and we hid in the woodlands to let them pass. Well schooled I was in concealment by Meon and Bonz, and I stood quite near yet invisible to that company. There were many—I counted more than five hundred, with prisoners and accompanying women. They marched untidily and they seemed disconsolate. Their armor, though mainly rusty brown, was of better cast than that I had seen in Arkan's group, and they looked soldier-like for the most part. They wore helmets with a single horn to the fore, with a cloth the color of terra-cotta covering their neck and shoulders. But among them I saw suddenly a group of five men of different type. Their armor was clean and bluish in color, and their helmets were made in the fashion of eagles' heads with small wings to the rear. And they were taller and more noble than the Bunnish. Their eyes were not fixed in brutality and rapacity as were their comrades'. Many prisoners walked with them—Mortons, the Hyperboreans who dwell in southern Wnai (Mortonland), and tall

Kariasg women, all naked. After they had passed safely I asked Wanin:

"Who were those whose armor was unstained and so blue?"

"They are men of the west, from beyond Anala, beyond Ynashawi, in Wdeni* which fell to the Hyperboreans near a hundred years ago—Odon it is called now by them. They are not like the Bunnish, for many follow the Way, and they have laws in their kingdom which protect the weak, as was the imperial way."

"Such men make a good impression compared to those with whom they travel."

"They are helping in the war with the republic. It is their military craft which enables the savage Bunnish to defeat the Kariasg in battle, by virtue of superior numbers."

"Is it by military craft or by superior numbers?" I said.

"By both." she replied.

"Why are so many Kariasg women taken and no men?"

"Because our men do not surrender. And if they do they are slain." Wanin's words, as always, were contradictory.

In twenty days we came near to the border with the Wnai republic. As we neared it so we were obliged to leave the road to avoid the many troops of warriors who used it. In the woodlands we could usually keep away from them, but all the land was filled with armed bands and once we nearly stumbled into a huge camp of Bunnish men whose drunkenness and unsoldierly carelessness enabled us to escape before being seen. How such men could win battles I could not understand. At the end we traveled at night, until we crossed the border near the great city of Bnoi, now in Bunnish hands, and entered at last a civilized land. With war so close we were not surprised that the country here too was deserted and it was several hours before we came to a garrison town where people still lived—Msapa which stood in a strategic place at the top of a ridge with earthworks to the front and side. We were immediately challenged by guards, Mortonland men who called to us.

"Take care for we are charged to kill all who do not answer our challenge. Who are you?"

"I am a warrior woman come to join the republic so that I may aid it and fight under the banner of the green palm tree.

* See glossary

For it stands for the Way of Truth which I am bound to serve.'' I said.

''Either that or you are a spy serving the Bunnish.'' said one guard. ''Keep in sight and have your hands well clear of your weapons, and empty, palms upward. Then approach.''

We did so. The guard was dressed in fine armor painted with the green palm, his helmet in the form of palm leaves spread out. He looked at me and spoke, using the Old Tongue which I had used.

''You are not like a Bunnish woman nor any other I have seen. Come with me and you shall see the chief of mercenaries.'' He bade his comrade keep the guard and led us through the great gate of the fortified wall which looked new.

The town still had civil population and civic life. I had never seen such splendor, though later Wanin told me that this was a small provincial town with nothing to excite interest to a civilized person such as herself. But to me the wonders were endless. Every building seemed like a fine work of art, with no bare brick or blank space to be seen anywhere. Beautiful carvings of nature, some entirely of beasts' heads, others of vegetation, all in burnished metal, copper or silver, or painted in fine, clear colors, covered the houses. The streets were laid out like a garden with fine tropical plants standing in great tableaux in squares and courtyards. I knew now what were the meanings of damaged brickwork, clumps of weeds and bare areas in Elling. The Bunnish had stolen all the carvings, torn from the buildings, burned the gardens which they thought harbored evil spirits left by the Kariasg, and grazed their animals on the ornamental vegetation. Walking among these gracious monuments and in the wide streets were the Morton and their masters, the Kariasg who were so beautiful that I stood in wonderment gazing upon them, but my guard urged me on.

''You gape at these people, little knowing that it marks you as a barbarian and thus causes the citizens unease,'' he said and I hurried on. Wanin too was embarrassed by my gaucheness and walked well away from me.

The barracks of mercenaries was a large building commandeered for the purpose of housing the paid troops from different parts of the world. It surrounded a courtyard set out with fine lawns and fountains, but which was now being used to drill men of a type I had not seen. Tall they were and brown-haired with the looks of young gods, fair-skinned and gray-eyed.

"Of what place are these men?" I asked.

"They are Namzens, from the Rainish lands far over the sea to the west. Brave men, and true, if all our mercenaries were as these, Wnai would be in better heart. Our own Mortons cannot claim such warlike skills as these."

A Kariasg was putting them through some maneuver, whether of battle or ceremony I knew not. It seemed more like to the latter, though if so it was a sore waste of energy at such a time.

"You will not be with these men but with a mixture of Shambi and Weltanmen, if you are accepted, though there are no women warriors here, and I doubt that general Mbopa will want one, for the trouble you may bring."

We entered the building and the guard spoke in Morton to another who sat at the entrance, so that we could not understand. Finally we were led up some stairs and into a sun-filled room where a Kariasg sat, his pale blue costume making pretty play with his brown skin. He was a lively looking man and not pompous or aloof.

"You may dismiss your servant," he said. "Kariasg though she be, she may not listen to what passes, since it could be of assistance to spies."

"Wait in the courtyard, Wanin," I said and she left with the guard. The Kariasg bade me sit on a chair.

"I am general of mercenaries for the eastern frontier. I welcome good warriors though they may be Weltan, Shambi, Namzen or any other. Yet I have no women warriors. To the south are some Morton women, held for a last stand, to the west a Namzen regiment which has women who fight alongside their men. Here we have unattached Namzen men only. I think the time too late to send you west. The Odon are on the move, giving heart to the myriad Bunnish. Here too we await imminent attack, and urgent news of the Sunedi from the south who have promised aid in return for money and territory. If you wish to go south to join with the Morton, you may. But I cannot risk quarrels among my men inflamed by desire for your favors, nor have I means of testing you for the truth of your statement to the guard. I must therefore let you depart, whether back to Weltan or south to the reserves who are waiting at Namna, I care not."

"Sir, I have slain more than a dozen Bunnish men in the

north. I ask no more than to join battle with them if they come here. I have money and food, I am no burden. As for your men, they will have none of my favors. I am a woman who, by sorcery, cannot ever be bedded by men nor do I wish it, since my taste is in any case for others of my own sex."

With a booming laugh in his rich baritone he said: "Indeed? I have often heard of such things in the imperial lands and in Wnai but thought them the product of degeneracy and mblobe. I little guessed that even among the barbarians such a confusion exists in these matters. The pillage and rape of a town may thus be a more complicated affair than one is wont to suppose. Be there *men* who likewise prefer the embrace of other *men* in the north?"

"As for that I cannot tell you."

"What is your skill as a warrior?"

"I am quicker than others with a sword and strike more frequently. My blows are heavier than those of the generality of men, indeed in my short experience as a warrior, I have not met any who seemed even a half-match for me."

"These are useful skills, no doubt, yet not easily tested without risking injury to some soldier who is sorely needed. What of your bow which you carry at your back? It seems a heavy weapon, a freak among bows."

I took it off and handed it to him. It was strung already.

"Bend it, sir general, if you can."

He smiled, a wide smile, his white teeth so bright, his skin so dark his pale green plumes shaking with his amusement. He lifted it and made to draw it, his muscles standing out like thick ropes of hide. Veins on his head bulged and sweat broke on his forehead. Yet great Kariasg warrior that he was, he could not bend *my* bow, Whispering Death.

"It is a marvelous bow certainly, though I should be slain long before I let loose one arrow." he said, his smile less bright yet persisting. He threw it to me. "Draw your bow then, woman of Weltanland."

I drew it, so easily, pointing it at him though without arrow.

"Thus might I slay many Bunnish before even they know from where come the harbingers of their doom."

"Thus indeed," he said. He walked to the window and leaned out. "Wnova, let one of the Namzen hurl his shield high in the air, that this woman may show if she channels her strength with matching aim."

The Kariasg who drilled the Namzen spoke in a strange tongue and one of his men turned, serious, to the window. With a polite motion he indicated that he was about to throw, before his round shield shot up glinting in the sun. I fired at it as if it had been a rainbird such as I hunted in Fnaboi. We saw the shield quiver, then a sharp clang came to our ears. The Namzen caught it, showing us clearly where the arrow had holed it, close to its center. He called something in his own tongue and all his comrades set up a roar which, as I know now, they name a cheer. Mbopa turned to me.

"Such a warrior as you cannot be sent away. You shall fight with the Weltan, that they might see how one of their own women may eclipse all the men of Wnai, Shambi and Namzen. By this means may they summon up their blood, for in a few days it will be needed. Take now these palmers in payment for a week's service and for lodgings which you may find yourself. It will be better if you do not cause a wonderment in these barracks which offer little privacy. Report to me each morning and you will drill with the Weltan and Shambi."

"I thank you. I shall fight loyally for the Great Palm banner."

Thus we remained until the great battle which I will presently describe. Before that, you may hear how I witnessed something which gave me a strange mixture of pain and pleasure, and how I became jealous and departed a little from the Way.

VII

We found lodgings at a hostel which was comfortable and indeed luxurious to my eyes. After eating a good meal we remained to drink and speak with the other soldiers. They came from their barracks to fill their bellies with wine, hoping to fill the women's bellies with other than wine. Kariasg and Namzen favored this tavern, brown gods and white gods they seemed. Many women came also, and as is common in time of war, were free with their charms. Wearing light costumes they lured the warriors, perhaps in some half-conscious desire to fertilize their wombs while their men's loins still pulsed with blood soon to be spilled forever. Several soldiers made tentative overtures to me but I informed them crudely that I found men repugnant as bedmates. However a young Namzen who spoke the imperial tongue stayed all the evening with Wanin.

Many merry steps were danced to the wailing-horns and keening-reeds in time with a Kariasg drum. The brown and white soft limbs of the women flashed in and out of sight, and under thin silk breasts great and small leaped high and low. Wanin's face went from brown to an orange-honey, and she became more and more mellow and entwined with the Namzen who would say only such things as: "You like wine? You like to dance?"

I left, irked by so much happiness which was barred to me. I lay abed and slept. Our room that night had two beds and was divided by a curtain. This curtain it was that must have emboldened Wanin to bring the Namzen upstairs to quench the thirst between her thighs. When I went to bed it was my habit to fall into a deep sleep almost at once, and this Wanin knew. She wasted only fifteen minutes before coming in with the man who tried to be quiet, though she had to hush him up. Strange feelings came over me as I listened to their suppressed giggles. I used my power as a sorceress to peer round the curtain, sure of their not observing me. Their preliminary love play hardly conformed to that subtle game of gentle advance and insincere retreat of which I have read so frequently in books. Simple creatures that they were, they could not wait to reach the main course of their intended pleasure. The Namzen divested himself of his armor and with comic pride indicated the size and readiness of his organ which to my eye seemed nothing out of the ordinary, but appeared to excite Wanin into stripping off her garments. She allowed him to grasp her sex and somewhat roughly, as it appeared to me, knead it for a few moments. Then without more ado he threw her back on her bed and aided by her spreading her thighs with unbecoming eagerness penetrated her to both their sighs and their grunts.

I cannot be pleased with the sight of males in their mating but I watched with interest to see how Wanin behaved. As it happened, she got less than she hoped. The half-drunk warrior started well enough, his muscular young body giving her several minutes continuous relief as he pleasured himself. But too soon for Wanin he spasmed in climax, then lay panting while she tried as best she might to bring her own pleasure. From underneath her movements were too restricted and she rolled him over so she might more easily supply the propulsion for her lust. He lay docile while she squatted down and more by her dexterity than his rigidity managed to mount him. Then she leaned forward and with commendable determination began the unpromising attempt to satisfy herself. Her brown buttocks reciprocated with less franticness than his had but with greater staying power. The most comical aspect was her continual battle not to lose her grip on him. Each time her excitement increased she forgot herself and raised her rear too high and slipped off. Her face betrayed greater and greater anger.

"Can you not wake?" she hissed. "I have not taken my pleasure."

He groaned drunkenly. I began to laugh, so that Wanin might hear me and turn. She looked round and I laughed more.

"Your steed shows less ardor than is desirable in that role."

She reddened and made to move. But I turned from irony to icy anger. "Stay. You will displease me greatly if you move. My anger will be painful for you and dangerous for him."

She stayed, feeling some fear now, yet conscious of her humiliation. I walked to the warrior and held my sword, point to his throat. He opened his eyes.

"Move slowly, Namzen, lest I end your life by an accidental movement born of nervousness. Leave this poor creature since you serve her ill."

He slid out slowly and got to his feet, no doubt thinking himself in a drunken dream. When he made to pick up his armor, I spoke.

"You shall have your armor tomorrow. Tonight, return to your companions and show them what little substance there is in your boasting of nights of untiring service to the goddess of lust."

He made to suddenly pick up his sword.

"Don't, Digivil!" Wanin screamed. "She is invincible. A demon of death."

"Fear not," I said. "I shall not slay him. But perhaps I shall release those fruits I see hanging, for they irritate me . . ." As I spoke, he made a thrust but I easily parried and with my skill unarmed him. I looked as if to measure a blow which would make him the last of his line and he backed off to the door.

"I little thought what I should find in your bedroom," he said. "May Thunderhead lead me to a woman with no murderous giantess hidden in the shadows of her chamber next time." He left the room, afraid even this mild reproof might bring my wrath upon him. How he explained his strange reappearance to the companions he left—with many a jest and knowing wink scarce fifteen minutes before—I never discovered. Doubtless he told the strange story of the evening of drinking, the warm wet Kariasg and the ghost of Great Thanda many a time in later life, if he survived the battle Shruvorga. I was alert for his sudden return with companions, but not surprised when it did not materialize. Few men complain of being bested in combat by a woman.

After he had gone I turned to Wanin. In truth I had been roused to lust by seeing her eager efforts to satisfy herself. And because of this I spoke dishonestly.

'I told you not to consummate your animal desires under my roof, did I not?"

She still knelt in her vulnerable position and as I spoke, my eyes went ever to her soft and rounded end. She looked at me over her shoulder.

"Yes."

"So you disobey your mistress and deserve a thrashing."

"Forgive me for I was in dire need and the wine dizzied my brain."

I softened my voice. "I will forgive you . . ." I approached and knelt beside her. "For I know your need is great." And thinking that as her body was roused by the Namzen, so might she settle for my caresses, I stroked her flank. But because she was angry for my having spoiled her fun, she was in no mood to oblige.

"My need is not so great as that." she said with hissing anger.

"Then you shall be flogged," I said, thus departing from

the Way. With my belt I beat her bottom since I could not caress it, until it was reddened and she wept with the pain. And even as I controlled her naked body in its struggles, I felt again such lust as longed for some relief.

VIII

We remained one week only in Msapa before rumors of Bunnish movements followed by definite news forced us to move out to meet the enemy. I spent the time in reading books of sorcery in the learned rooms of the town and practicing my weaponry with the Weltan. Brave men and eager for the fray, once they saw that I was indeed a mighty warrior they treated me with respect, though coolly. The Shambi did not drill and by their manner and behavior I thought them to be treacherous fighters, as like to join the enemy as fight them.

When walking with Wanin one morning we saw a shop selling many things including strange beak-like objects. She asked if she might purchase one.

"What is it, that you wish to have it?"

"It is a scenter, for the delight of the nose."

"Buy it if you like. Your money is yours to spend."

"And some of the herb that we are wont to use?" she said.

I could not understand why she asked me all the while since she was free to buy what she wanted. She had a strange, uncertain and almost guilty air about her. I bade her do as she pleased and she entered the shop to return with her scenter. I thought no more of it until I returned from the drilling at the mercenary barracks. Then I found her in the room of the hostel, sitting naked on the floor, slumped against the wall. She wore the scenter and made languorous sighing noises.

"What ails you?" I asked, mistaking her stupor for illness. She made no reply, indeed I thought she scarcely saw me. I flushed with anger. By what insolence did my servant lie somnolent and unheeding of me, her mistress? I shook her to no avail. I detached the beak from her head. She seemed completely unaware. Her mouth was loose yet smiling, her lower lip hung with no stiffness, and from her mouth she drooled her saliva which dripped down her chin to her breast. Her body was unexpectedly warm and limp with nipples enlarged and standing stiffly. And her belly seemed to heave with pleasure as she let forth the juice which comes in time of lust. I lifted her hot body and laid her on her bed. Then I took the scenter and her little bag of herb and kept them.

She took several hours to recover. When she did, I slapped her and told her that her service was at an end but she wept and begged, and I yielded to her promises.

"It is mblobe,* the drug that is destroying the empire," she said. "Asg and Kariasg have a great weakness for it, the northern people have not."

"If I were to wear the scenter and inhale the mblobe, would I not become as you were?" I asked.

"No, you would feel just a mild pleasure and speak more freely."

"I shall look after the drug for you, allowing you its use when I do not require your service." For I deemed that if such was her pleasure she had a right to it, insofar as it did not interfere with our contract.

After that, I saw many Kariasg in the grip of the mblobe. It pleased all the senses, so Wanin said, seemingly giving great hunger yet satisfying it, great thirst yet quenching it, great fatigue yet with rest and great lust with its satisfaction. Even, as she told me, the feeling of great bowel movement and bladder relief.

"Sometimes the real feelings are pale compared to those of mblobe," she said.

"Always?" I asked.

"For a few people who never do anything. In my case after a long absence from mblobe, I can have great pleasure for many hours. But after a while I need again the real sensations. It is said that Kariasg are less often given over to the drug than are Asg."

Those words I reflected upon, wondering about the differences of each kind, Asg, Kariasg and Hyperborean, where they came from and why, and how far south and north could understand each other.

* See glossary

*   *   *

Wanin remained at the hostel when I left with the army of southern Wnai, the last remnant of the empire on the Mboran continent. I would return after the battle and with my newly won prowess I should take her with me in the northern movement of the army of the Truth.

I marched with the Weltan two days until we reached a great plain atop a ridge where we knew the Bunnish camped in the woodlands beyond. I sat at night with two warriors, Vogin and Stakern. They had been driven from Weltanland by the Bunnish and had waited seven years for this chance to fight again against the truthless men of Bunedi. They both hoped after victory to move back into northern Wnai–Weltanland, and begin a new life, and they had exaggerated ideas of the beauty and fertility of their fatherland. Vogin was a grim and serious man with black beard but Stakern was a merry companion.

"What then will you do after we conquer the Bunnish and fall upon a town in Bunedi?" he asked. "The warriors will slay all the men and slake their lust upon the women. You will perhaps slay the women and slake your lust upon the men?" His harmless joke had a strange consequence later in my life.

"I am not like to slay women nor rape men," I said, "since both acts are repugnant to me."

On the morning of battle we moved out into the plain which was dotted with small shrubs and grazing animals. It was a bright sunny day and all the regiments who were to fight for Wnai marched into position. We could see our general giving his signals by horns, for the Weltan were to fight beside the Kariasg who stood, proud and tall, their armor sending up a golden flare in the sun. Each wore a gold-seeming breast-plate and apron, and carried a long lune-shaped shield made from metal and wood cunningly wrought for lightness. Their helmets had huge crests and their banners bore the Great Palm of the republic and the Palm Leaves of Truth. All along the line rose the banners of the different peoples, Morton, Namzen, Sunedi, Shambi, Weltan and Kariasg.

We had the advantage of height but as the Bunnish poured across the field like a crawling slime mold, it was obvious that they had the advantage of number. Their rusted brown cuirass and barbaric symbols of magic defense made a poor comparison with our shining armor, all clean and bright, and I felt no fear or doubt of the outcome. Long before any other could hope to strike, I began to loose my arrows, and Kariasg and Weltan alike cheered as some fell in the Bunnish ranks who were still forming up for the fight at what they had supposed a safe distance. I slew a great chieftain, seeing his helmet shudder as my bolt penetrated iron, bone and brain. But even as I did so, a great commotion to our right flank arose. The huge Sunedi army was marching away as had been their treacherous agreement with the Odon and Bunnish, and for which they were to receive parts of southern Wnai. Then we were left with a great gap between the Weltan and the Namzen, and a mocking cheer went up from the Bunnish as they saw our plight. Cax himself rode forward under the flag of parley. I would have as soon slain him but such is not the Way.

He was a huge man in full prime of life, with beard set in waxen spikes, and rode on a skallopen* which feared to come so close to the olligans* on which the Asg cavalry rode. He spoke to us, as is the right of leaders in battle, even those who do not follow the Way.

"Here I see the strange motley groups who would defend Wnai for their Kariasg masters. Strange it be that we, Hyperborean, must always fight a greater number of our brothers than of our true enemies, the Brown Asg (he used the Hyperborean name for Kariasg), as we strive to free southern Hyperborea from their grasp. There are land and riches in plenty for all and I shall grant any man who chooses even now to join us a full share of the imperial booty, provided he be not a Brown Asg. Else I promise him, as is the fate of traitors, a shallow grave. Should you resist me, your wives and women will walk south, naked and chained behind crude and unschooled Bunnish who shall have them for servants and whores." He looked at us, riding slowly by on the skallopen, and his eyes fell on me. "Even the Weltan *women* must needs fill the gaps in your army. I see such a one before me. Say, woman, is it your will to fight in this battle where you must inevitably die?"

"It is my will to slay as many Bunnish as I can and I shall maker greater or lesser success by counting each according to his rank. Therefore beware, Cax, for I would dearly like to

* See glossary

slay you as I slew the chieftain who wore the gray helmet, with my arrow." I brandished my great bow. He stopped, surprised.

"It was you then who slew Fedoniden, my cousin?"

"Yes, I, Cax-who-would-be-king." A cheer rose from our ranks which had closed now on the gap left by the Sunedi, and our general Nbopa spoke.

"It is not the origin of those who govern but how they govern which is to be judged. By your rape and pillage of the whole of northern Wnai, by your scorning of the Way of Truth, by these Weltan who are here from choice and not on your side of the plain, we may see that our fight is a just one." His words were spoken with a weariness as if he had no faith in them. Cax looked at me.

"I shall see you later, lady," he said and rode away on his skallopen.

Then both armies advanced one upon the other. The olligans moved with great dust and amid the mist it created, the Kariasg seemed like a golden host of demons. To our right the Namzen progressed not noisily but with determination, each man eager to prove his worth to the republic. I kept to the fore, loosing my arrows until at the last the Bunnish broke into a run as they charged our ranks. There seemed an ever greater number of them continually pouring from the trees. Well to the left I could see the Odon more disciplined marching against the main body of the Morton. Then the Bunnish were on us.

They had worked themselves up into their berserk fury and our Weltan were taken aback by the strength and fanaticism of their charge, and some turned and fled though but few. I fought with cold fury and soon found myself surrounded by slain Bunnish. Even in their frenzy they began to avoid me, so that I had to seek out adversaries. I came against a true warrior, a great man who stood taller than I and rushed to me from afar after seeing me with his baleful eyes. We fought warily, then furiously, and for the first time in my life I gave ground. I knew from Bonz that there was a time to use the shield and I used mine. Blows rained upon it but by its magical strength it never shattered though dents appeared in it. The first thrills of fear surged in me and passed as I felt his attack weaken. As he had surprised me, so I had surprised him, for probably he had never had his assault repulsed, and his fatigue took him suddenly. Wary of trickery I began to

counter attack and he in turn defended with his shield until
one of my blows shattered it and he had to bring up his
sword. I would have slain him but I was struck in my side
where one of his comrades gave him aid. Although my armor
protected me from a wound, yet I received a terrible bruising
to my ribs, and momentarily stunned I backed off trying to
recover. Then I saw with a glance that things were going
badly.

Our numbers were down by a full half and though the
Kariasg held fast and the Namzen fought well, the thinning of
the line by the betrayal of the Sunedi was a mortal loss.
Vogin had come to my side and together we fought off the two
warriors until my strength was fully returned. With a great
blow I slew him who had attacked me from the side by a
thrust through his cuirass, while I held up my shield against
the great warrior. Then I winged him with a powerful chop to
his shoulder. His arm went limp, his sword dropped and he
fell back so that I lost him among his companions. I too fell
back looking about me.

The Kariasg still stood in a disciplined body, surrounded
now on three sides by Bunnish, like bees swarming on a tree
stump. And the Namzen held their ground and beyond the
Kariasg, the Shambi were even driving the Bunnish backward.
But beyond them, the Morton were falling back before the
Odon, and if they gave way, the Shambi's advance would
become a disaster as the Odon and Bunnish flowed around
behind them. If we too gave way, the Namzen would soon be
outflanked and so would the Kariasg. Had I been the
commander, I should have drawn the Shambi back to strengthen
the line and prevent the setting back of the Morton. And I
should have drawn in the Namzen, so that we would have
formed a shorter curved line with the ridge to the rear. But as
it was, both the Weltan and the Morton were weakening
before the huge number of Bunnish. I regained my breath and
went back to the line.

Stakern was lying dead or wounded, I knew not. Now I
rushed in to the sagging line and fought furiously. Again I
attracted attention from great warriors, this time from two,
and I found myself beaten back, and again fear came to me. I
was tired in my turn and I knew I could not overcome both.
Near me most of the Weltan were engaged with more than
one adversary as the Bunnish pushed forward. Then I began
to wish I had not joined this battle. Had I not given the

Bunnish the chance to kill me by meeting them openly? Suddenly I saw a Weltan beside me turn and run, throwing down his sword and shield. Like a disease his panic spread, and the Weltan ran for their lives. Fear for one's life becomes a physical urge in such a case. I too turned and ran away, terrified that my body would soon be cut to pieces, and wishing only for life and limb.

It is a shocking sight when a whole army runs from a battle, strong men in whom one had great faith, with expressions of total funk on their faces. One's bowels become loose and I saw men foul themselves as they ran, shouting for mercy, shouting surrender but always running. Thus it was that the seeds of defeat were sown. Had we held, perhaps the initial surge of the Bunnish would have dissipated and the Kariasg and Namzen could have moved forward to force them back. But their numbers were very great and ours much less. I have heard since that the Bunnish surged through the gap we left and surrounded the Kariasg who were killed to the last man. The Namzen retreated in an orderly way and escaped to briefly defend the town where we had stayed. The Shambi too were able to withdraw but they came to terms with Cax and left for their own land.

IX

Of this I knew nothing and ran until I reached some woods where I lay, utterly exhausted and ashamed. After all my bold speeches and talk of bringing the light to the north, I had run in panic from the field while the Kariasg, Shambi, Namzen and Morton fought on, betrayed by our cowardice. I was captured as I slept by the victorious Bunnish. I woke with my arms bound and a sword point at my throat. The soldiers had been told by Cax to look for me and bring me to him alive, to gain a reward. Broken-spirited I was led naked and with bowed head into his presence, expecting death. My shame made my face flush, and my fear contracted my belly and made my nipples hard and small. Cax looked at me with a triumphant and insolent expression on his face.

"And did you score well today?" I think he expected some show of defiance but I spoke not. "Come, woman, the battle is over and you have lost, but you yet live."

"For the moment perhaps," I said.

"You disappoint me. I hoped for a greater show of spirit," he said.

"Standing naked where so many sharp blades are in evidence is no great engenderer of spirit," I replied and he smiled.

"Truly spoken. Those who are not afraid to admit fear are the least afraid."

I was in a huge tent laid out for a banquet where all the great leaders and their women lay sprawled before food and wine laid in a great circle. Beside Cax sat a woman, dark and beautiful, with a proud though not haughty bearing. Some cross between Asg and Hyperborean, I doubted not. Next this couple was a man of Odon, quiet and strong, and on the other side another Bunnish man, older than Cax, and wearing robes with bright colors. By him was an empty place set with fine goblets and plates, all of imperial manufacture. The man beside it looked at me with eyes of burning hatred.

"Tie her up in the stocks, let the men amuse themselves with her, then put her to death," he said. Cax spoke.

"You slew my cousin, brother to Enrigras who wishes for revenge." I said nothing, not wishing to antagonize the brother and risk his beginning his unappetizing suggestion anew. "It is the law that he must obtain recompense for his brother."

"Yes, the law. By her death." said Enrigras and began to irritate me with his harping.

"She shall not be put to death tonight. Every man who goes to the field of battle must expect death by another hand sooner or later. Come, woman, share with us our feast, let battle be forgotten."

Enrigras stood up. "I shall not eat with the murderess of Fedoniden," he said and stormed from the tent. Outside I heard the vulgar shouts and drunken rantings of the Bunnish. Cax beckoned me and I sat next to him. He proffered me wine and I did not refuse. The woman by his side looked at me under lazy eyelids. A hint of amusement lay in her dark pupils.

"I have your life in my power." Cax said. "And I would

barter it for certain things." He quaffed a draught of ale which he drank in preference to wine. He looked at the man of Odon whose face remained impassive.

"What things do you propose?" I asked though in truth I would have done anything to save my life.

"First, your word that you will return my gift and give me my life, should it ever lie in your power." Though my war against him would be somewhat purposeless if I could not end his life at the end of it, yet since my defeat and capture I thought much differently about *my* life. It had taken on a greater meaning than a mere vendetta against the Bunnish.

"Second, that you leave Wnai and do not return for two years." A small sacrifice, I thought.

"Third, that you stay the night in my tent and do my bidding." This was a cruel blow to me, since were he to take me to his bed, I should have destroyed the prophecy and could hope no more to be queen. I dared not refuse. Yet I hoped still to avoid the worst when I said:

"These conditions I agree to, since in any case I have but little choice."

"Well spoken. Martyrdom would spoil my digestion. Perhaps now you think less ill of the Bunnish."

"I cannot speak freely in company of so many."

"Speak, woman, you are immune from punishment now that we have our pact."

"Then tell me how you can spare my life so magnanimously, yet allow the rape and murder of so many like me."

As we spoke entertainment was forthcoming. Several women were led in and danced—not entirely unwillingly. As I watched their lewd movements—all had learned the Kariasg dances of mating—I remembered how Arkan had obliged the women of Elling to dance and how I had slain him. How different was my position now, naked myself, beside the conqueror Cax! However I enjoyed the dances of the women since I yearned for bodies of women. They wore naught but the flimsiest of robes and each writhed and turned to the music, taking care to leave no part of her body hidden, yet never letting the lusting eyes of the men feast too long on her charms.

"One cannot lead the greatest army ever assembled in Hyperborea, yet direct them to behave as knights, merciful in victory, sparing life and property. These men are lured on by hopes of money and booty. They act like animals in the cities and towns because they are animals. It is by our number that we triumph, as you have seen. Were I to deny the men their nature, they would lose their impetus and others would try to take the place of Cax . . ." He looked at the Odon. "Do I not speak true, Cudsen?"

"Such is the way of great movements of people, according to the Moshan sages. It is only when people seek to settle that laws are needed." The Odon spoke seriously and looked but little at the dancers. Cax watched all the while, eagerly enjoying the bared charms.

"If you know that the murderous ways of your men are necessary, why lead them in such a shameful war?" I said.

"How old be you, woman?"

"Eighteen since but a week."

"Would you like to be queen, one day, of some kingdom?"

"Yes. Indeed it is prophesied that I shall become such."

Cax smiled, his great beard glinting in the light of the torches by which the tent was lit.

"When I was eighteen, I roamed the plains of Czadac, amid the pine forests and dreamed of small triumphs, to be the head man of the village, to lead the skallopi of the village against the Minden who ever raided from the north. Then after, to be a warrior lord, then after to be a duke, and now king. And lesser pleasures fade until all I see before me is a golden crown laid on my head by the emperor. Were your death necessary for my crown, you would lie dead at this moment . . . and you too . . ." he looked at his dark companion. She looked at me, the smile still in her eyes, and shrugged her shoulders. . . . And so it will be with you, fair assassin, your vision of a crown will lead you finally to the depths. The lust for power exceeds all other desires, and unlike others it strengthens with age." He stopped speaking and tore off a strip of meat from the bone he held. "But let me speak of other things. . . ."

We ate and drank, watching entertainment, and we saw booty being brought in—golden armor of the Kariasg and jewel-encrusted swords and weapons. Finally Cax summoned two women.

"Take this woman and bring her to my tent in an hour."

I was taken to another tent where a great bath had been prepared with water, oils, salts and scented herbs, and my two companions washed me, always laughing. One spoke Moshan—the Old Tongue.

"It is many months since Cax took a woman in his tent. Yet to choose you, a Weltanwoman!"

"Does he not take also the dark woman at his side?" I asked.

"She is his wife, the duchess Vanagund."

I could not understand the situation, for the woman had not looked unkindly at me, and she had seemed but little surprised when he invited me to their tent.

"You are a very large woman, are you not?" asked the same woman. She was using a stick of some dye to make pale green areas on my skin, which the Bunnish women wear when they wish to appear beautiful. In my pubic hair the other tied tiny little garlands of flowers. All my nooks and crannies they rubbed with sweet scents.

"I am larger than all other women, it seems." I answered.

"It is said that you slay men, is it true?"

"So it is said."

Finally they oiled my body and pressed my nipples so that they stood out as they thought fitting for the purpose. As they led me to Cax's tent, I was trying to think of some sorcery that might save me from his bed, though in truth I now expected that it could not be evaded. I wondered if when he saw how little pleasure I got from him, he might become angry and break his word. Yet to pretend pleasure was against the Way.

One woman called and Cax's voice bade me enter. I walked through the tent flaps, expecting dull lights and the scent of incense. Instead there were Cax and Vanagund in full light looking over a great map. They both laughed at my entry and I felt foolish and suddenly ashamed by my nakedness; as Vanagund looked at me though I thought there was a wistfulness in her eyes.

"Sit down and cover yourself with a blanket if you wish. Cax will tell you what you must do for your bond."

I sat and wrapped my body in a silk blanket while they spoke. I saw that Vanagund knew much of the whole region. She was arguing with Cax about their next movement. He favored an invasion of southern Wnai, so that they might make sure that the Sunedin took only such lands as they had been promised. But Vanagund thought differently.

"Let the Sunedin do what they will, Wnai cannot resist. But let them not find us in the lands near to those promised them. They will take more land easily, without fight and become lax and unguarded. Then we shall sweep them from Wnai altogether. If we go now to the south, they will be ready and give us trouble always and defend with vigor, as our near presence keeps them alert. By my way we shall have both excuse and opportunity to take back the lands we gave them. Then you shall be king of Wnai, which shall be called Caxden thereafter."

Thus they spoke for a long hour. Finally they put away their map. Cax spoke.

"I did not bring you here for your favors, woman of Weltanland, but to tell you my bidding. My cousin Enrigras grows strong in the favor of my men. He speaks of there being no city of gold and of their unrewarded service. He is the rightful leader of the Bunnish who came to Wnai. I wish that you shall slay him. It was a favor of the Ice-King that you slew his brother. He longs for your death. He will demand it tomorrow. He knows not what Vanagund tells me, that you are a warrior of demonic strength. When he challenges me to slay you tomorrow, call out that you demand the justice of the Ice-King to fight in single combat with your accuser. None save I know how Fedoniden perished, and I have put it about that you killed him with an arrow fired from a near hiding place. Thus he cannot know that in accepting your challenge he may forfeit his life. And he will suspect nothing since he will have heard of you being brought to my tent in the love-oil to be taken in pleasure. How say you?"

"If it be your bidding. But how shall he believe your pretense since Vanagund is here with you and scarce likely to be peacefully witnessing her husband's infidelity?"

Vanagund spoke. "It has been our custom to take our pleasure together and many women have been brought to us as you were." She sighed suddenly. "But those days seem ended, no doubt for the reason Cax spoke of—he has a greater lust than women now."

"Speak not of such things. When this campaign finally ends in my crowning, then shall our lovemaking return in full."

Thus it was that the prophecy was maintained, even though Cax ordered me naked and oiled to his tent. In truth, had my embraces been with Vanagund, I would have had little complaint. We spoke, Cax, I and Vanagund until late. They heard of my quest, my prophecies and my strange feelings in the matter of sex.

"Now though that I must leave Wnai, I have nothing to do since I may slay no more Bunnish."

"One such as you, so young, must travel the world to see what are the ways of each land. Your fame will gradually spread until you are known through all Hyperborea and as far as the Isles of Rain. And to be queen you will need an Eye of Power made by the ancients who came to the imperial lands long ago. Such an Eye is said to lie somewhere in the far north at the foot of Zee Voshr,* where it was taken by the Boreal Minden who took part in the massacre of the Asg legions in the battle of Upala. Go there and if the Ice-King wills that you will be a queen, then you will find it.

"It was not prophesied by the Ice-King but by a Kariasg sorceress who yet dwells in Wnai."

"If it is a prophecy, then it is in the hands of a god and it is my view that he who we call the Ice-King is the same god as other nations give different names, as different people speak different languages." Cax spoke wisely as do many great leaders of men, as I have found, be they emperor or leader of Bunnish horde.

Before we slept, Cax and Vanagund made love before me because it gave them pleasure that a woman should watch their lewd writhings. I looked ever at Vanagund, wishing that I might be in Cax's place. Her brown body was lithe and convulsive, and she too looked often at me as if to see how I reacted. And even as she contracted her face in paroxysm of pleasure, yet her eyes still lingered on me. Cax too seemed to delight in baring his beautiful wife before me, and he kneaded her breasts until her nipples were huge and swollen and saw that I looked at them. And he parted her thighs and moved her body so that I saw the ripe fruit of her sex which seemed to open and shut of its own volition as her lust increased. And I looked at it because I had not seen such a thing before, and I wished to know how this part of a woman is made and how it behaves when she lusts. I could not see my own, and feeling is not so much able to make a thing out. Their lovemaking was long and violent and at its end they slept quietly. But I lay long, my poor body aflame with desire, a desire that it seemed might never be satisfied.

In the morning I was led to the center of the camp. I was allowed a cloth to cover my breasts and loins, and there faced

* See glossary

the accusation of Enrigras. He was standing in full armor with a group of younger men of his clan—as I saw by their ensignia. Cax watched as the prisoners of distinction had their cases judged, according as whether they could hope to raise ransoms or offer themselves into slavery where they could use their literacy to aid the ignorance of their Bunnish masters.

When I was led forward, Cax made as if I should be sold for a slave, tearing off my cloth and offering me for sale.

"This woman can prove a tower of strength to some warrior not lacking in the power to subdue her. She is strong and can perform the heaviest of labor indefinitely. Also, as you see . . ." Here, he poked my sex, breasts and buttocks with his scabbard. ". . . she has things no male slave can offer. These delights I testify to, having laid with these great thighs wrapped around me and those majestic buttocks pumping as if the earth must give way to satisfy her lusts, which are, I may say, of a power to match her hugeness. And as she is in my property, so I may sell her to any warrior man enough to try his plough in her giant furrow."

Several men immediately began to shout their willingness, but the morose Enrigras roared out his challenge, silencing the lesser men.

"Her furrow has felt its last plough. She must die, as she slew my brother, by suspension." His supporters noisily chorused their approval, and Cax feigned discomfort.

"By our laws I sadly admit Enrigras is within his rights. And as she be but a girl, she has no hope in the Ice-King judgment. . . ."

"Yet I demand it," I shouted. "I demand the right to fight Enrigras, that my case may be judged by the Ice-King."

The warriors all around laughed at my words, a naked woman talking of fighting a great warrior like the count Enrigras.

"Let us not waste time," said Enrigras. "This woman must be suspended, then her body dismembered and given to the vultures."

"So be it, old windbag!" I shouted. "And long will the tale be told of the Bunnish warrior whose knees quaked at the prospect of fighting a girl of but eighteen years. I shall hang happy in the knowledge that the Bunnish counts are nothing but child-rapists, woman-beaters and liars, bereft even of the sinew needed to face a woman if she has the will to defend herself."

Enrigras went white. "I shall take the justice of the Ice-King," he shouted, as many cat calls and jeers greeted my sally, evidently directed at him. He looked at me. "I shall split you from belly to udders," he said in the vulgar talk.

"So be it," said Cax. "May the Ice-King's justice be done. Fetch the weapons of the Weltanwoman."

There was some stir, since not all knew that I was indeed a warrior-woman. I donned my armor, feeling it on me like the truest friend I had, my poor vulnerable breasts, soft loins and belly at last covered by the magic armor of Meon. I put on my helmet, tossed back my long hair and swept the air with sword. A strange sigh rose from the myriad Bunnish, when the sun suddenly caught my helmet, as like Thanda of old, I took the stance of combat. It is customary in all east Hyperborea for each combatant to address the other. Enrigras poured a string of oaths and obscenities on me, dwelling always on how his sword would look ever for my womanly parts. Some laughed, but for the most part the horde was silent, seeing that his speech shamed him. Then he was silent. I spoke:

"Since I have asked the Ice-King for his justice, I shall not boast of my coming victory, lest he be angry at my presuming to dictate his will. Yet I shall fight as I ever do, with Truth at my side, before me and above me. For Truth cannot be conquered; it ever triumphs as the light triumphs over the dark. Stand ready, creature of darkness, for now rises the sun in glorious dawn!"

I drove at him. He was not so powerful as the warrior I had fought in the battle, and soon all his energy was directed to saving his life. His eyes showed a sudden realization of how Cax had tricked him, mixed with fear at his doom. But he asked not for quarter; brave are the men of Bunedi. First I broke his shield with a great blow that echoed around the hills. Then I disarmed him, so that he stood defenseless.

"Thus you stand now, Enrigras, defenseless before me, as my mother stood before the Bunnish. You must go to the Ice-King."

"So be it, demon woman!" he said, defiant to the end, and I beheaded him. Then I skewered him on my sword, and with all my strength I raised his body above my head, arms straight. A great cry of awe went up from all who saw this deed, since it was beyond their understanding and beyond their belief, had they not seen it. I spoke.

"Know this, Bunnish, Truth is not conquered, it over-comes all." Then I went before Cax and laid the body at his feet. I knelt before him, seeking to make a great impression on him, the Bunnish and even the Ice-King who seemed not so ridiculous to me, simple impressionable girl that I was at that time.

"The Ice-King has given me judgment," said Cax. He raised me up and whispered in my ear. "He had but little choice, I think." Then loudly: "Go, woman of Weltanland, and come not near the eastern lands till two winters are past." As I turned to go, Vanagund spoke:

"I hope one day we may meet again, for I know that you coveted my pleasure last night."

"May it be so!" I said, and walked tall and proud, all the Bunnish calling words of praise to me, for men love the valiant of heart, unexpected victors and proud women.

X

I walked back toward Msapa to find Wanin, using the way of the stars to keep always in the right direction. I came on the town after a few days, as it was nightfall, and there were already many Bunnish soldiers smashing the buildings and pursuing the inhabitants. I saw but few Kariasg, chained and led by their conquerors. The Namzen had left and the Shambi too, only some Morton cowered in corners, fearing for their lives. I ignored the freebooters, even though they made ges-tures and shouted coarse words, save one who blocked my path and tried to lewdly fondle me. I threw him off, so that his fall and amazement cooled his ardor. But there was no sign of Wanin, and I grew ever more anxious, wondering if she had gone with the other women or been unfortunate enough to fall into Bunnish hands. Then I thought of the witch-house where the Kariasg worshipped some god un-known to the barbaric peoples, a being not strong, nor clever, nor excelling in anything I could grasp, yet the greatest god for all that, I believe. And an ideal hiding place it would make, for the Bunnish fear to go there.

So I approached the building, but the door was locked, and even with my strength I could not open it. Then I found a window and breaking the glass I climbed in. Inside was no sound, and pitch dark. But I had the strange cup given me by Meon, which magically made little sounds great, and I put it to my ear. And I heard a breathing and a heart beating fast as the wings of a little bird. I knew then that Wanin was hiding within and feared me, thinking me some Bunnish man, bolder than his fellows. And I did not speak her name, rather approached the direction from which her breathing and heart-beat came. Faster beat her heart as I approached, till I stood before a great statue, but dimly visible now to my dark-accustomed eyes. It was a fabulous form with the head of a leaping-cat, and on its top she sat, her trembling now audible to me. I made my voice low, and spoke Moshan but mimicked the accent of the Bunnish.

"Come down, Brown Asg woman, for I know where you sit, perched like an owl. Your life is spared, you have but to part your thighs. I came here for booty, but I am sore in need of woman. If you are the wife of a Kariasg, let me tell you that your husband like all the others was slain. If you think to save your scabbard for his sword, then know that it is wasted. Either enjoy my violation of your body, or bear it with pain, it is all one to me. But come down, lest I overturn the statue and risk breaking your bones."

She remained and in trembling voice spoke: "I am not the wife of Kariasg nor any other man. I am in the protection of a great warrior woman, who will soon come to slay any who ill-use me."

"A warrior woman! Not that great creature of Weltanland who bears the name of Cheon?"

"The same."

"Why, I overcame her myself, and having stripped, beaten and raped her, I slew her even as she begged for mercy."

Wanin began a great wailing at this and I felt pleasure to hear her piteous cries as I conceived that it was for love of me that she wept.

"Is it for love of your mistress or for fear of your loss of protection that you weep?" I asked.

"For love of Cheon, who was a kind mistress and who loved me well."

"Then fear not, Wanin, for it is I, Cheon, who stands before you. Come now to me."

She gave a cry of joy and leapt to me from her perch, and I caught her. Then I felt great happiness, and we held each other, the first time I held a woman in my arms. I think that, had I wanted, I might have done as I liked with her then, but foolishly I thought I could wait till later for my pleasure, and I only embraced her, feeling her small body full of life and movement, hugging me with all the strength of her weak arms.

"I am saved! I thought to die here, since I heard of your running from the battle, and thought you enslaved or slain."

"Yet you waited in hope."

"I waited, but my hope was gone . . ." She wept, and so did I, but our happiness was great.

"Let us leave this evil town and go away," she said when first we stopped our sobs.

"We will, and this night. For I am to go west and north now always."

We prepared our journey quickly, gathering up all our possessions, and we left the west gate of the city, Wanin close to me and afraid, her trembling only making me the bolder. Yet to spare her courage, I kept always to shadows till we were well clear of all habitations. Then with moon bright, we walked ever on, talking as we went.

"I heard that you ran in fear of your life, that you were caught and taken naked before Cax."

"I was not. I fought well in the battle and only left the field when all was lost. And after that, I fought some great Bunnish lord whom I slew before returning."

Later we found a bank of moss sheltered by several rocks, and here, under the sky we lay to sleep. I expected that now, after her words and acts in the witch-house, she would yield to me, and I moved close to her.

"Come close, that our bodies may warm each other," I said, and she did. With hand shaking as if palsied, I took her breast. She made no sudden move, but spoke soft and weary.

"Nature does not change so quickly, Cheon mistress. Though I love you well, yet I am for men, not women."

I ground my teeth in anger but released her breast. "So be it. Let me go over to the rocks, since the feel of my body against yours must be as unpleasant to you as that of a

Bunnish man against mine would be to me." I made to go
away.

"Stay, Cheon. The feel of *your* body is warm and
comforting, and I value it more than any man's. Let us lie
together in peace, as you said."

"Easy for you, but not for me, since I am maddened by
such closeness when caresses are forbidden."

"Then go, if you must."

I sat for a while as my lust cooled and a feeling of
well-being replaced it. "I shall stay." I said at last.

"It is well." she said. Then we lay, happy enough, and
our lids dropping.

"Wanin!" I called.

"What is it, mistress?"

"I ran from the field of battle. I was taken before Cax
naked, as you said." I spoke with shame in my voice.

"It is as I supposed. I know that you fought bravely while
you could. And though you are so tall and strong, yet you are
little more than a child in years, and the wonder is at your
courage, not the lack of it. And in any case, what matters it,
if you ran from twenty battles, since you are here, alive and
safe, a thing I long despaired of in the witch-house?"

On the day following, we walked for many hours along the
damp and dark woodland way which was the old imperial
road to the town of Shawi in the kingdom of Odon. We went
this way because of an agreement we made before we set out.
Wanin feared to go north, since it was ever less likely that she
might finally get back to the empire. But I would have broken
my word to Cax, had I not left the west. And I would not go
south, for I now wanted to find the Eye which Cax had told
me of, at Zee Voshr, the route to which lay directly north.
Shawi however was a great port, where Wanin might dream
of taking ship for the Imperial Lands. Thus we were in
accord, Wanin and I. And then, I might head on northward,
at the same time seeing the kingdom of Odon which was the
pride of Hyperborea, for it had laws, and men dwelt there in
peace, though the armies of Odon were great and the king
feared no man or nation. Three just kings had ruled Odon,
first Magond, then his brother Vira, and now Magond's son
Uldens. All were followers of the Way of Truth, though they
made treaty with the Bunnish who were not.

The lands which we passed were like to those of southern

Wnai—luxuriant and semi-tropical trees crowded the track which was now long overgrown with grass. And they too were abandoned, for they were near to the army of Cax, which yet held in check by Vanagund's will. The few people we saw kept well distant, for my armor was a mark of danger for them, and they did not see that I was a woman because they did not approach. Wanin often complained of her troubles, since she was not used to so hard a work as walking. The rainy season was come and we passed through cascades of water and always through the mist that generally rises from wet ground and foliage. Her clothes were often wet to her skin, and she badly needed some more suitable for the climate. At night we made a fire, using magical materials I kept in my purse, and I obliged her to dry all her clothes, since illness may come to one who sleeps in wet garments. Sometimes I too dried my clothes and armor, and we sat naked as savages by our fire. At such times, Wanin questioned me with a lewd curiosity.

"It is strange, you are so great and you will not lie with men, yet you have the parts of a woman that are meant only for pleasuring with men and bearing children. What use are those great nipples since no child will ever suck at them? And what use your sex, since no man will ever go in, nor child come out? The gods have strange ways of doing their business."

As I had considered the question she asked, I could answer well.

"One is either man or woman, and therefore one's body will have either the male reproductive parts or the female. What use though are your breasts? To suckle a girl-child who in turn will suckle others, or a boy-child who will father sons to father others? And of what use will all these people be, if only to make others by their reproduction?"

"It is they who will do all things in the future. Build cities and fell forests, make laws and plant corn." said Wanin.

"And I may help build a city, fell a forest, make laws or plant corn. And that is my use, which is not arising from my breasts and loins, but from my brain which distinguishes me from a beast." Wanin had no answer to that, and I added: "And my body can give me pleasure, when I can find a woman who returns my caresses, as I know from things that have happened before."

"Such things may not happen again, since they are freakish and unnatural," said Wanin.

"They are as natural to me as your futile attempts to draw pleasure out of a spent Namzen are to you," I said, for women often speak cruelly to one another in these matters. "And I have secret knowledge that there are many women like me, if I can find them." I added, thinking of Meon's words about sorceresses.

Thus we passed many evenings, speaking of matters which interested us both, for otherwise she had no interest in talk of battle and weapons, and I could not abide her talk of civilized times, for she had the habit of repeating the same accounts on many occasions, with many a sigh of yearning to be away from all barbarians, myself implicitly included.

On our fourth day, we determined to obtain a domiden,* since we were not willing to walk more. We went therefore toward a village on the border of Shambi and Wnai, which we saw one night by the light of its fires. And we obtained a domiden partly by my prowess, partly sorcery, and partly by trickery and the power of women to make men foolish in their eagerness to slake lust.

We entered the village by day, and as the Shambi army had not returned yet from the battle of Shruvorga, so there were no warriors in it, only older men, women, children and a few men who by one reason or another had not wished to go in search of plunder. We soon found a trader who had several domidens, of which one looked a fine animal. The price he asked was very great, more than I had remaining in my purse, and guessing as much, he spoke in unflattering words.

"Do not waste more time, ladies. If you have not money, you cannot have this domiden. In these times, one either has money, or one does not, and if one does not, it is not easily come by. I do not wish to be less than courteous, but I must say that the only way of earning money here for such as you is by negotiating to hire out your asses for entertainment. And by the look of you, I would guess that you would need to make several bargains a night for a year, to come near even half the value of that animal. Have the goodness to leave me in peace now."

Although we did not look at our best as women, after the rigors of the journey, we were very affronted by these words, and I felt as if I should thrash him for insolence, but it was against our best interests to alienate him.

* See glossary

"Her ass is not for sale at any price." said Wanin. "As for mine, since I am an imperial princess, it would cost more than all the money that could probably be raked together in this stinking sewer-like place."

"Furthermore we have better means of earning money," I said. "And we will be back to buy that poor creature, if it survives until then, which I doubt, though not at the price you ask which speaks of an unhinged mind."

Then in accordance with my plan, we went to the main tavern of the place, which was filled with farmers. Before entering, I covered Wanin with an invisible cloak—by sorcery I must not explain—and I took an old jug which I had for beer. All looked up as we stepped in, and rumors of my existence having come even this far, I was the center of attention.

"Armor is needed to keep an ass like that from harm," one said, and another: "A skirt of that length is likely to be inconvenient in a field of poker rushes."

I raised my head. "I have come here to sell a very valuable item." I held up the jug. Jeers and suggestions as to its former use greeted my words. "You will soon be vying with one another to buy it, when you hear and see its magic powers," I said. "For I shall pour from it a woman who will pleasure its owner for many hours."

They watched, suddenly interested, and men who had continued with their gaming after a glance, turned to me once more.

"It is some trickery," said one.

"Then behold." I filled it with beer from one grizzled fellow's mug, and poured it over the invisible Wanin who appeared immediately. We had washed her, combed her hair, powdered her and scented her. She wore only a tiny cloth over her sex. There was a gasp of interest.

"There, exactly as I have said," I boasted. No one spoke until one man nodded his head.

"This is sorcery indeed."

"Yet a valuable possession."

"May other women come from the jug?" said one, greedier than his fellows.

"No, this one only. But were different women able to come out, this would be for an emperor and no ordinary man."

"True." Many heads nodded.

"How comes she into this jug?" asked the first man who had spoken.

"She is the daughter of a sorceress, and by her unquenchable thirst for the satisfaction of her excessive lust, she drove her mother to imprison her in this jug, and appropriately to emerge only for her pleasure."

"How may we know that she is as you say? It would be a cruel jest if she would not do our bidding, or had naught but an iron trap between her thighs, as many magical women do."

"As for that, you may see for yourselves, and he who purchases her may try his fortune. Should he be repulsed, I shall refund his money."

"That's fair . . . that's fair . . . Let us then see the minx's purse . . ." For so these men called her sex.

"Show them, Masidazon, the origin of all your shame and punishment." I removed her little triangle, and she sat on a chair lewdly, that they might see her sex and know they were not tricked. They looked curiously like those who buy any goods.

"That's fair. There is no trick here that we can see," they said as she drew aside her flesh to show that no metal teeth lurked within.

"How much is wanted?" said the most bold and interested. I named the sum, and all arms moved in disbelief.

"Why, between us we have scarce so much," they moaned.

"Then you must be satisfied with your wives," I said, and their faces became glum.

"It's always the way," one complained. "We see a desirable thing, and an impossible price is asked."

"Might you not buy the jug together, as common property, to pass each day from one to another?" I asked. "After all, even if your turn came only one in twenty or so days, yet she would satisfy you well, as you will see. And all who wish might try her now to prove her worth."

There was then much debate, all speaking at once, until finally after long argument, a large group agreed to pay the sum I had asked, which was greater than the dealer's price for his domiden.

"But we must try for ourselves whether or not this is good merchandise," said a great bearded fellow who spoke loudest and seemed respected.

"Of course. Try now for yourself."

He looked around, a little foolishly. "It is a thing less easy in the cold light of day, before others, than it would seem if thought on at another time. May I not take her upstairs to a darkened room?" he asked, less bombastic than before.

"No, it is not possible, since you might take your pleasure, then afterwards say that she had not yielded or that the deed was impossible by some sorcery. Then you would have your money returned, even though you had in truth enjoyed the woman," I said with obvious justice. He blustered a little.

"What? Am I called liar and cheat in my own village by a stranger?"

"No, by no means. You may be as honest a man as ever followed the Way, but business, as ever, being business, all precautions must be taken. And you are not forced into this deal, only if you wish to go on with it, you must take the conditions. After all, what man, when buying a loaf, expects to eat part of it first before payment?"

"Aye, Braganzer, this is true, the woman asks only for what is fair. And as we follow the Way, so we must be fair," said his companions. This was a boastful lie, since although the Shambi often claimed to be men of Truth, yet they were not so, as Cax had told me, but great liars and swindlers to the last man. Now aroused by the sight of the shameless Wanin's pouting sex, they wished only to conclude the bargain and obtain the jug.

Wanin watched, large-eyed, with lascivious smile, for as usual she was in sore need of a great staff in her fiery loins. Braganzer made excuses and backed off, unable to do before an audience whatever he was able in private. And so felt many, so that the noise declined. But as is always the case with men, emptily boasting though they often are, yet among them were five, not great men nor specially virile of appearance, rather ill-favored men in truth, with perhaps some sensuality about their poorly shaven jowls, who were eager and thought themselves capable. Without much ceremony and to raucous jeers and taunts, these men in turn drew their weapons and plugged Wanin's itching gap. The table upon which she lay received a great pounding, but she seemed much relieved by the violent flurries of thrusts that she received.

No man took less than ten minutes to discharge his duty, and one seemed to be waiting for nightfall as he thrashed interminably on. As for Wanin, it was not until the second man was nearly done that she took the joy she had been craving. I saw her face twist savagely, and her fingers and toes curl as her breath hissed between her lips. The inn went on with its business as some tired of the sight of Wanin's value being tested. But she tired not and had, as I saw, many tumults of pleasure, till finally the last man drew himself off the now flaming orange flesh, and she sat up. Not for many days did she set up her whining for a man again. At last, with the agreement that Wanin was satisfactory, I poured again and by the simple magic of the Old Ones, made her invisible. Then I held the jug and asked for payment.

"We shall buy this jug," said Braganzer, suddenly finding his tongue again. "But what shall we say to our wives, who will never countenance the woman who comes from this jug, whether she be sorceress, daughter or whore?"

"Tell them that, as well as the jug, you bought the secret of it, so that you can lock them up in it, and pour them out when you want them open thighed, not open-mouthed. And how in the jug they will be uncomfortably crowded together, and how the daughter of the sorceress will have them always as her slaves. Thus will you cow them into silence." Many laughed at this tale, but it seemed not to convince them.

"My wife will never be cowed into silence," said Braganzer. "Nor many others."

"Fools!" I said. "Do you need to tell your wives? Keep the jug here, in an upper room, visiting with some excuse."

"Yes, that is well thought of," shouted the men. And so, with that I scooped up the money and left with the invisible Wanin.

"Try the jug again tomorrow, for she comes out only once a day." I said.

The only trouble we got from the exercise was Wanin having her buttocks all bruised, scratched and stuck with

Note: For those who cannot believe in sorcery, and the tale of the invisible Wanin seems beyond even the cleverness of the tricks taught to the old Asg by the Chzeenyi, another version of this tale seems probable. Hungry and destitute, the two women found a village and obtained food, shelter and the domiden by Wanin's prostitution. Since in this Cheon probably played the role of pimp, she would not be likely to admit the true story. Cheon, while being honest in the main, seems to share with many barbarian peoples the tendency to fantasize, especially where tales of sorcery are concerned. Since she certainly *was* a sorceress, it may be that some foolishness was acted out with the jug in a tavern, and doubtless the crude display of Wanin's charms was an exact account of their sales technique. Sorcery and sorceress are always mixtures of true magic in the shape of unworldly knowledge and technology, hypnotic illusions, drug-induced fantasy, and on the other hand a great deal of conjuring, trickery and simple lies.

many splinters. While she had enjoyed the copulations, she had not cared for that, but now she moaned.

"My bottom is in such a pain, like as if I had sat on a hedgehog," she said. So I took her aside in a copse of trees, and there by my skill in medicine which every sorceress must master, I ridded her brown ass of all the splinters, and rubbed soothing ointment on her. Then we laughed loudly at our trickery and made our way to the stable of domidens.

XI

The dealer of domidens made a bored face as we returned and would not listen until we showed him our money. As I got it all out, Wanin fetched me a sharp kick on my calf, which I understood only too late, once I saw his greedy face.

"The beast is sold only with saddles and fittings, which make a total of twelve hundred palmers," he said with sudden effrontery.

"Five hundred palmers for saddles and fittings? What disgraceful extortion is this?"

"The beast is a fine one, that of a count who went to the wars on a skallopen. Furthermore the fittings are his own, barely used and of the first quality."

"It is against the Way to ask greater than one and three quarter times the sum you would really accept," I spoke, trying to control my anger.

"If I am a liar, then may I be struck down this instant by She Who Knows!" he said, referring to the Shambi goddess (who is not so ridiculous as she sounds) . . .

"You will be struck down, truly enough, by me who knows that you lie. For I may now legitimately slay you and having made reparations to your family in accordance with your low rank, take the animal with its trappings without cost." Here I drew my sword with a flourish. He looked a little uneasy, but blustered on.

"A monkey may imitate its master by blowing a flute, but

no music will be the result," he said, quoting no doubt some Shambi proverb.

"But a large monkey may wring the neck of a chicken, if it takes the whim," I said, and suddenly grasped him by the neck, lifting and squeezing. He attempted to free himself, but my grip was like iron, as soon as he realized, for he could speak no more and his eyes were bulging out. Then I let him down. He swallowed.

"Perhaps the beast may be sold separately as a special concession to your beauty."

I picked up my sword. "Five hundred for the beast with its trappings or your head rolls," I said.

"Certainly, lady, I shall be pleased to so favor a goddess and a princess."

"What of our asses, which you supposed we should hire so cheaply and with such difficulty?" asked Wanin.

"A tasteless joke on my part." He choked on the last words, as I had the sword point to his throat.

"Tasteless indeed, fat wormbag," I said. "Now let us take the beast."

He led out the domiden which in truth was a good looking animal, wholly black, with bright unblinking eyes, long shining tail and large paws. It looked curiously at us, sniffing and cocking its great head to the side. I had merely to frown meaningfully at the dealer, and he found three beautiful saddles with a double sleeping case and excellent canopy which could be raised and lowered with ease. He showed us how to strap them all on, which we did, save the third saddle which we loaded with our own luggage in the carrying panier. Then we mounted the creature and I looked at the dealer.

"Tell me, man, now that we have agreed to a sale, and when it cannot hurt to speak true, what is the real worth of this beast and its trappings? I shall not seek redress even though it be but fifty palmers."

Like all such people he kept up the pretense to the last.

"What? Fifty palmers would not secure a single saddle. It is a wonderful bargain you have struck, since it is only for your great beauty and her nobility that I have dropped from the true price of fourteen-hundred palmers."

As the animal padded slowly away from the stable, I shouted back:

"Had you spoken true, I would have given you the full

seven hundred." He smiled bravely and repeated less convincingly.

"I spoke true, madam."

With that, the animal began to run, and we were soon out of the village. At this moment we realized our mistake, for I had assumed that as a woman of such noble rank as she boasted, Wanin would know how to steer a domiden.

"How shall I cause the animal to resume the correct direction, Wanin?" I asked.

"How? How should I know? I thought such a great warrior as you would know the way with domidens. They are like skallopens."

"Thunderhead! I know nothing of domidens, nor skallopens either. Hold tight, Wanin, lest you fall and I must leap to your aid, thus freeing the domiden which may run off."

I know now, as I have been told by those agents of the Spider with whom I am intimate, that while many animals on the earth are common to those many worlds that are in the sky—(for those who know it not, each tiny star in the sky is in reality as great as the sun, and around it circle worlds, some like ours, some not)—but some of our animals are freaks, so that those who read my tale on other worlds, which they shall, as the agents of the Spider have told me, will not know what they are like. Domidens are such animals. Great long beasts they are, which creep on soft paws, are docile and yet strong and of great staying power. They may carry four people at one time, and they are fitted with saddles, canopies and with long leather cylinders in which some of the riders may sleep. Their gait is a gliding waddle, yet direct and comically singleminded. And skallopens are of the same kind, but smaller and swifter, so they are used by warriors for battle.

Now we sat astride, I to the rear, Wanin to the fore, and watched impotently as our domiden ran along through sparse woodlands in an easterly direction, which I did not intend. We tried pulling at the straps and handles which were part of the trappings, but although it occasionally swerved, we could not see that it was in response to our action.

"We must wait until it stops of its own accord, which it surely must if it wishes to eat, drink or pass its water," said Wanin.

"Yet at the end we must know how to control it, or it will be useless to us," I said.

"I know that! But it is stupid to run back to Wnai all the distance we have walked."

"Did I say that we should? Rather your idea, to wait until it stops, will lead back to Wnai."

Thus we quarreled, for sometimes when I knew not what to do, I could not keep the aloofness which a mistress should preserve before her servant. After that, I remained silent, since I had no scheme for improving our lot. And this was the start of a great adventure, for the beast continued on its way, at last swinging north, after which I counciled Wanin that we should no more try to affect its direction.

"North is not so wrong, and if we try to make it go more nearly northwest, then perhaps we will only cause it to go in some third direction far worse for us," I said. Wanin said nothing, for it was her habit to sulk when I spoke harshly to her, a foolish way of women which I never adopt myself, being nobler than the generality of my sisters. Later, after I ignored her and preserved a silence of dignity for a sufficient time, she spoke.

"Was the way we gained the money for the domiden not a violation of the Way of Truth, since the jug is no more magic than the pains and soreness I now have in my crotch?"

"That is past now and not interesting to discuss." I replied, not deigning to continue the subject, since a lengthy explanation would have been needed to outline the subtleties of the Way to her. For her own part, she had not listened with any great attention when as a child she had been taught the Way, thinking it just one more dullness of the life of adults; and she had grown up, as she was, deceitful, hypocritical and living only for the pleasant feeling she could gain either from mblobe, from overeating and drinking, or from copulating like an animal with any who were willing and able.

The beast ran ever on, its strange gait belying the speed with which it could move, and the smoothness of the ride. Even as dark began to fall, it did not slacken, and we knew from the Moshan proverb—"the domiden may run in the night as well as by day"—that it might continue.

"Let us jump off, and let the stupid creature go, for I am wearied of this galivanting."

"What? And lose our bags and all possessions, not to speak of the valuable animal itself? My money is not thus to be wasted," I replied.

"Your money was earned by my labors. It is not your ass which burns like fire, ever irritated by this saddle."

"You are in my service, and by our contract any money you earn is mine, save for your wage. And in any case you benefit from the creature as I do."

"Benefit?" She squirmed and twisted now, and I felt pity.

"Why not get into the sleep-box? It looks comfortable and is lined with soft material."

"Perhaps that is best. Yet there are things one must do, that seem impossible whilst riding some great beast."

"As for that . . ." I said, knowing what she meant. "I think I have the way." I turned sideways, swinging my leg back over the saddle, and cocking up one thigh, I passed my water, as I had long wanted, squirting over the side, my short costume aiding my necessity. Some went inevitably on the domiden's body, but he cared not, animals being less concerned with cleanliness than are men and women. She did likewise, and we laughed at the foolishness and indignity of it.

The sleep-box is a leather cylinder lined with soft down, held to one side of the animal, and which is so formed that one may relax in it. The one which we had bought had two chambers, and into these we slid, marveling at their comfort. There was an interconnection between them through which one's arm might pass, or a whole body if it were necessary. If it was designed so that a man and woman might caress intimately or copulate, it seemed a curious idea. For my part, I would not feel much pleasure to be so engaged, all the while banging and sliding against a beast which went about its business of journeying, perhaps irritated by the commotion. As it was, our tiredness was enough to make us sleep quickly.

We were wakened by the domiden still travelling, as the crimson dawn filtered through the sparse woodlands where it went. I saw Wanin's face looking into mine, for she had opened her eyes first.

"The air seems cold here. This animal having walked now for near sixteen hours without cease, we are perhaps two hundred miles to the north. Yet look at it, it knows no fatigue, but runs ever on."

What she said was true, and all that day we ran through similar country, sometimes beside a stream, sometimes climbing little hills, coming out into great tranquil vales. We saw villages away from our track and once passed two people not close enough to make out, who watched us in silence. But as the afternoon wore on, we found the world a silent empty place, bereft of villages and people; only great cawing birds cried as we went, looking down from high aeries in rocky cliffs or from the tops of the gigantic coniferous trees which were now all around. A feeling of unease came on us, and with it a greater companionship.

"I do not like this place, Cheon. It has a feeling of great age and death all around."

"I too feel it. Let us hope the beast soon leaves it, for I would not like to be left here to walk."

"Nor I, Cheon. What think you is the cause of this dereliction and desertion?"

"Who knows? There are many bad places in the world, as I have heard, and the reasons are different. Old deeds of great evil or cruelty may leave a coldness and stench of fear; an evil sorceress may have enchanted the land; or a being of another world may dwell near here and its emanations may affect all life."

All day the beast ran, until late afternoon, when we came suddenly on a strange place. An old city it was, for its name is now known to me, the imperial city of Nala-Nama sacked by the Shambi in 432, a hundred and twenty years before. This I knew not at the time. We looked about at the desolation and ruin which was covered by weeds, shrubs and trees, so that only here and there were the buildings discernible distinctly from humps and hillocks. Every so often we saw a great ruined tower or witch-house, moss-covered with cracks and with fallen turrets, yet still beautiful, with ornate carving on every space. Huge idols and statues surrounded some of them, with missing limbs and heads. Once we saw a statue of a woman, better preserved than others, made from some shining stone. Beautiful she was, and larger than life size. But as we passed close, we saw that from the loins sprang a digit, like a man's but more slender and smooth, pointing out horizontally.

"A strange thing," I said. "I wonder if such a creature once lived."

"Why not?" answered Wanin. "Strange women are born . . . You are like a freak yourself. Perhaps you have such a thing, and that is what makes your preference for women, since you cannot use it to pleasure a man."

"Keep silent! I am no more freak than you, and though I

do not brandish my sex organs at every chance as you do, yet they are not different from those of other women."

Later we saw more strange statues, amorphous-seeming things not like any animal of the world, except for many claws like crabs have.

"Some god of the Kariasg." I said. "For your people, though civilized, were said to have enough different gods to fill the land, sea and sky as well."

"It was not so in the beginning, when the Old Ones taught us the Way. Only at the end, when we had lived too long with superstitious barbarians for our servants, did we catch that disease."

We entered a wide square whose paving slabs were still visible among the rank weeds and shrubs. Around it too were great crumbling towers, still ornamented in part. And here suddenly the domiden stopped and stood completely still. We waited for a few minutes, afraid it would run again, but it remained drinking water from a rain-filled urn which stood unbroken.

"I must tie it to a tree," I said, "so that we may walk around without fear of losing it." I dismounted and using the cable as I had been shown, fastened it to a tree. But the domiden showed no inclination to move. After it had drunk an enormous quantity of water it began cropping a shrub, crushing fruit, branches and leaves all together with a lot of noise.

Wanin dismounted, and for a while we busied ourselves washing in a big pool of water, where many dead leaves floated on the surface, stretching our limbs and enjoying the feel of being on our legs again. Where the domiden stood, it seemed as if a great centerpiece had once been, with many fountains and urns, as I had seen in books of the empire. Some flat areas had not yet been overgrown but lay covered in brown wet leaves, where one easily slipped and fell, and I did so, striking my knee with great violence. Wanin helped me to my feet, and we walked toward a building which seemed the largest of the whole place. I limping slightly. It had a pair of massive green copper doors, one of which had almost corroded away, and the other of which was buckled and broken.

"May it not be dangerous to enter?" said Wanin.

"Do not, if it cows you," I replied.

"But I would not remain all alone out here, since it is an evil-seeming place."

I heeded not her whining and entered the building. Inside it smelt old and damp, and the floor was covered with broken shards and bones. No doubt the Shambi had run through it, killing and destroying as they went. There was not much to see, and it was a sad affair, such a great city so dead. As we walked all around the square, pushing shrubs and tall weeds aside, we saw from writing on buildings that it had been called Nala-Nama.

"Let us leave this place." Wanin said, and I knew that she spoke my own feelings. But try as we might, we could not rouse the domiden who had now sat down at some distance from its dung, and was sleeping, having satisfied all its simple needs—unless it wanted a mate. Finally we made a fire which gladdened our hearts, and ate roasted tubers, cheese and fruit. In spite of Wanin's protests, I looked again around the square, telling her to shout if she needed assistance, though I could not see where danger might lurk. Beasts are afraid of fire, and men were evidently afraid of this place.

Then I noticed a witch-house and broke in, hoping to find a small statue of a beautiful woman that I might keep and sometimes stroke to bring me peace, as smooth objects can. But it too had been sacked and nothing but desolation remained within. Suddenly I heard a noise—something crackling like fire, coming from some steps which led down into a dark place. I hurried away, for in those days I was easily afraid of anything that smelt of ghosts or evil spirits, even though I believed not in them. I returned to Wanin, saying nothing since I wished not to frighten her. And I guessed it was some small beast, settling down for the night as we were.

In the glow of the fire we were as one, in accord as always, speaking of the strange city.

"If this is Nala-Nama, it was called once the Shining City of Anala, which was the name of Shambi when the Kariasg ruled," said Wanin. "And it seems strange that it has been left like this, since it was a great capital suitable for the Shambi king—Ojun, Ojurun, Oshojun or whatever he was called at that time. And now no man nor woman dare come within fifteen miles. . . ." Her eyes were large with fear and I drew her closer with my arm.

"Fear not, servant, for are you not under my protection?" We sat thus for a while, speaking of other things—things that were bright and filled with the sun, so that we thought not on the place where we now stayed. As our lids grew weary, we lay back, our heads on furs which covered piles of dead leaves. I listened to the sound of the wind howling through the ruins, and as I listened, so the sound seemed to change, till I heard a strange reedy whining, almost like a melody.

"I do not like that sound," said Wanin. "It is not like the wind."

I said nothing. At first, I too had feared the noise, but now I listened, straining to hear each phrase and cadence, for I liked the sound more as each moment passed. I thought suddenly of my home in Weltanland so long ago, and the mewing of the cats, and my mother singing. What a joy it was to listen to, since it had more power to rouse sadness and happiness than any music I ever heard. But gradually I could no longer hear it, though surely it still entered my spirit, since I could behold the blueness of the sky of Weltanland, smell the cut hay and hear my mother calling me.

"Mallikawna, come now, I have made you a sugarbird for you to take to the carnival. . . ."

"I am coming, mother!" I called, for I had long waited for the sugarbird. I got up from my play and began to walk over the field to our house. At my side Wanin ran, her face afraid, and she spoke.

"Do not go, Cheon, it is not your mother who makes this terrible sound."

"Do not fear, Wanin, for mother always welcomes my friends."

"But it is not your mother. It is great evil of which I have heard. . . ."

"Come, dearest child, bring your friend, she too will have a sugarbird. Your father waits. . . ."

"I am coming, wait for me!" I began to hurry.

"Cheon!" Wanin was pulling me now and speaking in a near scream. "Do not go, do not leave me here, where I will perish."

For a moment I saw the dark square of dead Nala-Nama, then again it was sunny with white clouds and warm breezes.

"Stop, Cheon, you may do anything with me, with my naked body. . . ."

"Do not speak so, it is dirty talk which mother likes not."

Wanin stopped when we reached the house. I went in the

door and saw that all was as always, cool and bright, except that now we had a staircase which led down into a cellar.

"Come down, Cheon, I am pouring some sherbet for you—it is so long since you were here. Come, see the cellar which we have built."

I went down the stairs, the pain of so long parting nearly bursting my heart. The stairs were very long, with many landings and doors to the side. The smell was no longer fresh, and when I came to the door where my mother was, I felt a sudden fear that it was not she who was in the cellar.

"Come in, darling, you must be so tired and thirsty."

I pushed the door and went in. As soon as I entered I saw that all was lost. I screamed.

Before me was not my mother, but a room filled with bones of men and animals, and in a corner some vast unclean creature, not of this world. It had huge unblinking eyes staring at me with urgent desire through the red glow of the room. Its limbs I could not see, but many crab-like pinchers waved and snapped. On its top a mass of whiplike tentacles writhed and spun, and by their swift movement through the air made whining sounds. It was with these that it had lured me down into the cellar where it dwelt. Now that I was in its presence, I could see it for what it was. I would have fled, but it had changed the music, and I suffered a convulsion, my brain being twisted by its devilish skill. My lips were drawn back across my face and downward. My saliva frothed and my legs collapsed, convulsively jerking and kicking. I saw its red-purple mouth open, and the whole bulk dragging itself over the floor toward me. For the thing had suffered long hunger, and saw me as I have sometimes seen loaves of bread, cheeses and wine bottles after long fast. I thought then that my days were done, and regretted that I had not made love to one whom I loved, nor been a queen. Then the convulsion overcame me in an epileptic fit, and I momentarily lost all knowledge of what happened. When I next became aware, the creature's warm mouth was around my legs, so far as my hips, and I felt a mass of sucker-like objects trying to draw me in. In my hand, I had my jewel and as I tore at my hair in my panic-stricken frenzy, all my convulsions ceased. Holding it to my head, I felt its power to overcome the madness made by the creature. Then I put it in my mouth and was suddenly free to struggle for my life.

With both arms I held some kind of bony part, a carapace

or ridge, and using all my great strength pushed to draw my body up from the mouth of death. It was a grim and silent contest, the being seemingly had no other weapon to bring to bear than its mind-twisting sounds, but it was desperate to eat me because of its great hunger. Its life against mine. I could see its huge staring eyes which were intelligent, not like those of the brute beasts. Gradually I overcame its sucking power and drew my legs from its hateful soft mouth. And with the last ounce of my strength I freed myself. As I had only my dagger with me and I had no stomach for further fight, so I ran from the dungeon, up the stairs and out of the witch-house. Wanin was cowering and sobbing by the domiden.

"I have come back! I escaped that death," I said and threw myself exhausted by her. Then I lay tearful while she washed the burning slime of its digestive juice from my body. And I cried, not for fear, but because I had remembered at last my mother and my true name, which I never speak.

"Is it yet alive?" she asked, laying my head in her lap.

"Yes, it lives."

"There are many in this city—an evil plague. Crabs they are called. They live in great numbers in the imperial continent, buried in the forests of night. There they have dwelt since they came from another world. They feast on men and beasts who they call to them in sweet voices. And now I hear their whistling from different directions. Maybe you will again go to one."

"No. For I have my jewel which has power over them," I said and showed her. "If I move again, just hold it to my head and I shall be at peace."

But that night no power of these evil beings which are called Crabs, though they be not crabs as we are accustomed to, could again lure me to their dens. As for Wanin, I suppose that civilized minds are less easy to lull into such yearnings—for we, barbarians, know not how to distinguish dreams and phantoms from things which are real. And Wanin, foolish though she be in many things, had the brain of the great Asg, builders of the empire. And as the Hyperboreans knew not the Asg weakness for mblobe, so the Asg were immune to the spell of the Crabs.

"As I walked to the Crabs' lair, did you not say that I might make love to you?" I asked, though in truth I had no energy for such a thing.

"Yes, but you heeded me not. And I have no pleasure in taking the leavings of a crab."

We laughed, even in our uneasy haven, and slept soon till blessed dawn silenced the whistlings.

XII

After this night of the Crab we again rode the domiden, which continued its journey north. Perhaps in the absence of any direction from us it wished to return to the lands where its fellows are wild. The weather was always wetter and colder, so we sat often under the canopy, scarce able to see where we went for the driving rain and mists. The beast kept to its habit of traveling near forty-eight hours, then eating, drinking and sleeping for twelve hours or so.

One day we came to a village in Soshink, a kingdom hardly worthy of a name, where the empire had been lost full one hundred and fifty years. The people dwelt for the most part in ruined Kariasg buildings of older time, made weatherproof by new timbers added and by using stones of buildings no longer needed. They seemed peaceable enough, their more fiery brothers having gone south generations before. There were many ducks, chickens and goats, some unruly children and dirty taverns. From a youth of simple face and pleasing manners we finally learned the way to steer the domiden. The old rogue had deliberately kept back the steering harness, and the youth agreed to make us one, for he knew the way of it. We paid him twice, for I gave him five palmers with which he was well pleased, yet in the night he lay with Wanin, which pained me but which was a thing to be borne, since I had no cause to forbid it. The deed was done in a barn next the house where his old mother lived, and where I sat talking with her while they did their business noisily, so that we could not fail to know of it. Yet she and I, we spoke as if nothing took place.

On the following day we traveled on ever north, till the

days were always gray like iron, the land first dark and misty, then suddenly clear, and in an hour snow falling which I had never seen, nor Wanin either. It covered the ground and seemed pale violet under the dull but ruddy sky. Though Wanin moaned that we must go west to find the sea and set her on ship for Mnoy,* my foolishness led us ever on, for I thought to reach Zee Voshr and find the Eye. We passed for two days a great water which might have been the sea, but the folk in furs and boots who fished it told us that it was a lake, though vast. I wore now all the fur-lined leather that Meon had given me, and Wanin spent her days in the sleep-box. The domiden was able to find food under the snow, while I shot birds and had to eat their roasted flesh which I liked not. At its northernmost part the lake had become ice, in which men broke holes to fish. Farther north were places so cold and barren that we gave up, fearing to perish there in such a snowy desert. So we turned west along the top of the lake, till we came to a great forest whose edge came nearly to the ice. Then Wanin became silent, her complaining ceased, and I feared for her, since she never seemed warm now, and I knew that through my selfish ambitions she might die. At last, when I thought her lost, we came on a cottage where a family lived, and they took pity on us for Wanin's sake.

It was the poor house of a fisherman who knew no world beyond the village in the wood, where he went once a month on his domiden to sell the chairs he made in the evenings. Yet it was a happy house with wife industrious and good-tempered and two small children who played around me when I felled the trees, and I came to love it as my home, so that my heart was sad at the thought of leaving. They gave Wanin fur trousers and a hooded jacket which they wanted no payment for, and in their care she soon recovered until she spoke as often and foolishly as before.

Then came the time to set out, one morning after a midwinter feast when the sun was at its lowest, a dull red orb in a mauve-gray sky.

"May the Snow-King go with you!" said the man and the woman, for they believed in the Snow-King who was not at all like the Ice-King of the Bunnish, if their stories of him were true. "But do not go to Zee Voshr in the winter, rather in the summer, else you will perish in the ice of Upala

Minden." They spoke with difficulty in the imperial tongue, but I forget now exactly how their speech differed from the true accent, so I write it as if it were normal.

"We will not, for I must take Wanin to the south, as the Brown Asg cannot live comfortably where it is so cold," I replied. "But when I go to Zee Voshr, I shall come again to see you."

Thus it was that we set out for Shawi, the great port of Odon, leaving the northern snow behind us. But I had learned much by this journey. The north is a hard place, and in winter a deadly place. Those hosts of men who have poured from the boreal night, are fleeing a worse enemy than mortal man, the northern winter which was not made for man. My plan to visit Zee Voshr seemed madness now, and I did not expect to go there for many months, maybe years. Wanin however was cheerful as we went ever south and west, soon entering Odon, where laws are made and kept.

In truth Odon, though a fair, just and lawful place, is a dull place too, where all talk is of the Truth and the Way, where faces are long and sanctimonious, and where laughter is seldom heard. Everywhere we went, we found hospitality, strong men who knew the worth of civility, and endless sermons about the Way of Truth. Though it is my mission to take the Truth into the northern darkness, yet it will not be such an affair as it is in Odon. It will be a giver of life, not a heavy blanket of morality. Po-faced and self-righteous as it is, Odon is young and strong, and ready to extend its borders to the south, where Varnax and Shambi are said to be "unworthy of the Hyperborean name" and "Mbora under new names." The Odon have great contempt for the empire, believing it to be completely corrupt and devoid of Truth, and they accuse every nation they wish to attack of being an "imperial republic" or a "Mboric kingdom." In our dealings with innkeepers and traders we found that none cheated us, a thing that can be said of no other people or nation that I ever visited. I even felt shame for some who asked only the true value of things for which I would have paid double. And in spite of all this, I knew that Odon and I would never agree, and in that I was proved right.

In many villages we saw that the witch-houses had been converted to temples to some god, whose sign was palm leaves. This seemed ridiculous to us, since the Way of Truth to which all religions are anathema also had the palm leaves as its symbol. We heard that there was a god called Paten, who was now called the god of Truth, and that priests of the old religion of Odon now called themselves servants of Paten, and had attained much power in some parts of Odon and with the king, Uldens. The old religion, according to some ancient savant with whom I spoke, was a preposterous collection of gods with beasts' heads, spiders' legs, bodies of fire and water, and all manner of other beings to strain the belief of the naivest devotee. Among these was one Paten, a god with the head of an olligan, and he had been chosen to be the god of Truth. Though I believe in no gods in my usual moods, yet there are religions I have found in whose name no evil is done, and which only give their adherents a love of the trees, rivers, seas and the beasts that dwell within them. Such a religion is the religion of Vahahad, where I went many years after. There each tree has its spirit, each mountain and all the things which are important in the lives of the people. And they make images of them, little paintings on wood, and each child has his necklace of gods, with representations of men in the form of all things, even rivers, with a woman formed from swirling waters. But the religion of Paten was not like this. It was a deadly evil.

We came at last to Shawi, a great city which had not been destroyed when the Odon came, since they were never vandals like Shambi, Bunnish and the evil Sunedi. But it was much changed, since buildings that pleased the Kariasg well did not so please the Odon, and they had gradually pulled down all the beautiful houses of the older time, making pointed roofs and long windows, all austere, though pleasant indoors in winter time, as it now was. It had become the greatest city in all Hyperborea, and even though I liked not Odon, yet I was excited by all the bustle and seeming organization. Like many cities, it had attracted men of all nations, because it was a safe place where no pillagers could come; all the strength of Odon stood by it. Stately Asg I saw, black like the burned timbers of their witch-houses, Kariasg, Namzen, Maritimes, men of Pasquery, Boreal men and even Golds. The women wore always long costumes and because I wore a short skirt and drew attention, I too put on a long green dress which I bought in a market where, so the seller told me, it had come from far Peevalx in the Old Lands. I wore it over my armor, for once used to armor it is difficult to leave it off, since one's flesh seems weak and vulnerable.

We soon found, at Wanin's nagging, the harbor where great ships sailed for the Old Lands; like huge scarlet blossoms floating on the water they were, intricately carved, with painted sides and myriad sails of red. On the quay we spoke with the Kariasg who manned them—men of the empire unconquered, unthreatened. Even the Odon, though they had defeated the Wdeni republic a hundred years before, could not stand against the might of the empire, and they attacked not the imperial ships, since the imperial fleet could put more than thirty thousand fighting ships into battle, if needed. Had they not fallen to foolish quarrelling with the Kariasg of Mbora, they might yet rule in southern Hyperborea.

One we found, a tall Kariasg called Snushum, captain of a merchant ship, the Rubumnu, meaning woolwinder in Moshan. On his ship were a party of imperial lords and ladies who took a great interest in Wanin. And though I had hoped that the money needed to secure her passage back to Mnoy might be more than she could obtain, in this I was wrong. They immediately agreed to take her back home, since the sudden collapse of Wnai had stopped all its commerce with the empire, and eye witnesses were very welcome.

We were invited to the hostel where they stayed, a building maintained in the old style by the imperial purse. At first I liked it, since the place where they sat was so magnificent, so large that huge palms could grow within, behind glass windows that stood for walls. All around they lay on silken couches, talking endlessly but with voices so musical, not hoarse shouts as were heard in our hostel. We sat with the group from the Rubumnu, and I said nothing, since I could not speak so easily and cleverly as they at that time. Wanin had no such difficulty, seeming suddenly transformed to another woman, not foolish and simple as I thought her, but able to speak of books, plays and tales of imperial politics, of which I knew nothing. And her stories of the terrible fall of Wnai under the Bunnish horde made her the center of attention. I could have spoken of my deeds, but waited until asked, which I never was, so my glory was not beheld. And Wanin, selfish creature as she was, never told of my prowess, nor my brave deeds, nor how I escaped the Crab, nor how I always protected her. Once, I did begin to speak and all chatter ceased and interested faces became polite and forebearing, as my strange accent and slow and portentous style of speech was tolerated until I stammered to a halt. Thus do civilized peoples ever embarrass barbarians.

"Your friend is not then a woman of Odon," said a young Kariasg, Dnechi. "Her speech is from the east. How came you to take pity on her, since she is so large and with such pallid skin that one is reminded of a chalk statue draped in green for a mourning. . . ."

I would have thrashed him, had I not been so awed by their civilized way. I knew that if I did, it would only bring greater scorn upon me. But Wanin knew my mettlesome temper and quickly spoke.

"Do not speak ill of her, for she has served me well," she said, and I denied not the lie, as I had promised her that I would not reveal her humiliation at serving a barbarian. I felt the whiteness of my skin so anemic compared to that of these beautiful brown-limbed people. And I knew that my presence cast a gloom over them, since I was a barbarian, unpredictable and dirty as they thought, though I bathed as often as Wanin.

One morning as Wanin made ready to go to her friends, I did not rise from bed. I hoped she might make much of my not going, and perhaps stay herself. But she seemed not sorry, and when she returned to find me eating in the tavern, she said words that brought my tears.

"I am leaving your service now, since we are to sail tomorrow. Only think of it, Cheon, to return to civilization, where I can be always with other civilized people. You cannot know how it is, as if I am born again!"

"Is my company ill then, after so long that we have shared suffering and joy together?" I said, for I had not learned that to beg for love is useless, and bad for self-respect as well.

"I served you well, so do not complain. But it was agreed that I should leave if chance came to go to Mnoy. And it has, and so I go. What is there to complain of?"

I said no more till I lay in bed, and she for the last time by the door, as she had on that first night so long before. Then I spoke my plan, which I had formed.

"Let us reverse now our roles, Wanin, so that I might be, as they think, your servant. I am strong and able to always protect you as before and also serve you. For I cannot be parted from you, and if you will not stay here in Odon with me, then I would like to come with you to Mnoy. And I too would like to see the empire, which is the greatest nation of all the world and all time, as Meon told me." I waited, thinking how we would rejoice that both purposes could be served, our friendship and her journey to civilization. But she stung me with ill-considered and cruel words.

"Do not be foolish, Cheon. What do I want with a great white creature to ever remind me of the depths to which I sank once? Go, find men and women of your own sort, for no civilized woman will ever return your love."

"You have then no sorrow, no feelings for me, now that you know we shall be parted forever?"

"None, Cheon. It is best to speak true, so that you entertain no false hopes."

"What then of your words in the witch-house of Msapa? You wept for me, who you said you loved well."

"What use is there in bringing up old words? Do you imagine that I will suddenly remember that I love you well? That I have forgotten? My words were spoken from relief at your return since otherwise I must be slave again to a Bunnish man."

Foolishly I wept, so that she sighed with anger at my noise. I could not bear to think that we should never again lie together under the stars and discourse as of old. When I slept at last, it was a terrible sleep filled with dreams of Wanin, the smile of Wanin, the laughter of Wanin, the naked body of Wanin that I had caressed so many times with my eyes alone. But in the morning I watched the red-sailed golden-prowed ship sliding out of the harbor, and I ran on the quay as it creaked along, the wind billowing out the sails. Wanin gave one wave only, then was gone below. I saw it till it was but a speck on the far horizon, leaving the world empty and worthless. I returned to go to my bed and sleep, so that by losing consciousness I might lose the pain of it. I wept, even as I went to the wooden stairs. But then, under the door of my room, there was a letter with Wanin's writing on it, and I took it with beating heart and read:

"Cheon, I loved you well enough, but I am for men, not women, so it is best that we now part. My hard words were necessary, else I had never left. Come in two years to see me, for I will send word to the Kariasg hostel where I dwell in Daidym. You will soon lie with women as you wish, for many women are partial to their own kind, though not always exclusively as you are. When you come, you shall tell me of it, as we drink palm wine under the stars in the warm happy lands of the south. And know this, Cheon, if ever woman lived who must be queen of all Hyperborea, it is you, who must rule, not serve. Your servant, Wanin.''

Thus did I lose Wanin who I thought never to see again. But I did, as you will learn if you read all my tale, be it ever so long.

XIII

I spent many days lying in bed like any silly girl whose lover has left her, treasuring what small things Wanin had left behind and weeping over them. And I reread her letter many times. But young as I was, I became bored with this life and began to walk about the town, gazing often out to sea, wandering along the quays looking at the ramshuners drawn up on them in great numbers. Big square-sailed, sharp-prowed boats they were, and each had a name which brought to mind the northern regions from which the Odon were supposed to have come: Driving Snow, North Wind, Polar Darkness, Singing Voshr, or Horned Shark. And each had some hideous figure at its prow, demonic gods heads dreamed up in the northern night, when spirits lurked abroad. These ships fascinated me, as often the sailors remarked.

"What look you for, woman? Some lover who told you he would return from the sea? Or seek you passage to the Isles of Rain, or Ohohora?"

I sat too in waterside taverns, and it says much for the restraint and lawfulness of the people that none ever interfered with me, beyond a few ribald words. I drank the fiery Izden* spirit, which is the favorite strong drink of all western Mbora. When I felt a little more ready for merriment and conversation, I began to speak with others, especially at one waterside tavern, the Emperor's Palm, which boasted a great palm-tree made from wood and leather by its door, and a

* See glossary

painting of some emperor, Bazezym, Imba or another, I know not who. There I fell in with a group of other foreigners, as foreigners often do for companionship. One was half-Asg, half-Rainish, from the sacred land, Bhoumer—a small cunning-looking fellow, yet pleasant and full of words to make me laugh. Another, Dandus, a man of Varnax, serious but always eager for gaming, with brown hair and clipped beard. And last, he whom I favored most, Klune, a Pharn from Kukajull. Also there were two women, she who lay with Dandus, and Theela of some people unknown to me, the Canedi, who lay with Klune. She was older than he, and sensual and lustful, and they often retired from a game of seventeen with the duodecahedrons, because they were inclined to sex.

"I feel me a great desire of thrashing your ass on the bed, Theela—what say you?" he would say without shame.

"Brave words to impress your friends, Pharn." she would say. "But if you last long enough for the smoke of the candle to disperse, I shall count myself lucky, and doubly lucky if it be cool enough to take your place." Such rude banter was their usual habit.

I learned to play mzum,* wherein small armies of bone make combat by unvarying laws on a rectangular field divided into many small parts of different shapes. At first I lost every time, even against Theela who disliked the game and played only when naught better offered. But soon I became able to hold my own, and at the last I could defeat even Dandus who was the habitual winner. Yet I bored them all with my long thoughts by which I plotted their defeats. From them, I learned also two things, both of which had great significance for me.

I learned that the unruly people of Odon, who did not like the lawful life that had come of late and who itched for battle and adventure, became by one path or another ramshuners. Some by choice, since they wished to visit foreign lands and win booty, land and women, but more usually by punishment for rebellious and troublesome behavior. The ramshuners were the seagoing pioneers who took the language and arms of Odon to all the lands of the world. They went as mercenaries to fight for empire against pirate or empire against itself, or Rainish against Bergian, or as conquerors of some land where an Odon was rightful king—by any imaginative claim.

* See glossary

Or as simple adventurers to explore where few had been, and find even new lands where they hoped to take the unsullied gold from the virgin soil. And from this, I could begin to understand both the lawfulness of Odon, and why its seed spread over the globe. It was not a comforting thought to imagine all those sanctimonious speeches being repeated so far from the dreary origin of the sterile Odon view of Truth.

The other matter of which I learned concerned more immediate things. As I am a woman and have the body of a woman and many of the thoughts of a woman, yet am I also in some measure manly. For my very way of life is that of a man, and so are my lusts which I have noticed are like those of a man. I have read foolish tales of the great women heroes who are common enough in the myths of the north. These tales are written, as I am sure, by women who are not strong as I, but weak and feminine in all things save an overactive imagination. I am sure, because their heroines after leading bands of desperate men through all manner of catastrophic trials, and who ever defeat men in combat, are always prone to yield to some burly hero of handsome appearance. And he is always at the last greater than they in the combat, and more knowledgeable than they about the world, its lands and its ways. And in their love-making, the heroine becomes docile and groveling. And ever after the man is near and while she again leads her band of desperate heroes, this man looks on with no role to play in the tale, only to smile kindly, never overruling her decisions though if it were a true story and he as wise as he seems, he would surely not always fall in with her plans. And the tales are written thus because the writer believes in her heart that all women must have a man who eclipses them in all manly things, and she includes wisdom and strength among these. And she cannot imagine a lover who is not so, and wishing to make the tale pleasing to herself, adds these preposterous scenes to her book. But they are foolish tales.

My power as a warrior rises in me in the mind as well as the body. One could not set out to battle with men believing that a well-made man must always triumph. One must believe only in one's own power and strength, and this I do, and I need no strong shoulder to rest on, nor wise counsel to depend on, but only my arms and my cunning. And whether this be because I am thus and have no need of men and therefore crave my sisters, I cannot tell. But thus I be, and like a man my lusts rise fiercely when I gaze upon a woman's flesh, or am by chance standing close or touching one who is comely. I shall not describe what things happen to me at such times, since they are well known to women of spirit and men of red blood, but in Shawi after Wanin's leaving they came oftener and oftener as the days passed. Even Theela's warmth became a source of frustration to me when we were seated close. And because of this, I took to roaming the town and tried to meet some woman of like mind whom I could befriend and caress in any manner I pleased. But I was not successful and had many embarrassing and humiliating moments when great misunderstandings arose. Twice I invited women who were comely and friendly to my small room at the Emperor's Palm where I stayed, but as soon as I made a gesture which clearly spoke my intention, all went amiss. The first left hurriedly with few words. The other called me an Odon word—Schuntendey—which the Pharn told me meant literally "dirty cat," but was generally used for women of my type.

Nowadays I have long had many women friends who are like me, and we have a saying: "A man may have difficulty getting a girl to his chamber, though if she once enters, her breeches will fall easily enough. But a woman may easily lure a girl to her very bed, yet her breeches will cling as if glued to her ass." And though merrily expressed, it is not far from the truth.

I became sad and depressed after these failures, and one evening when I had drunk a deal of wine with Klune and Theela, Theela asked me my trouble.

"What ails her, Cheon, that she is so silent and hears not the music of reed players which is her particular liking?" Theela often spoke thus, because the Canedi language has no word for "you," as other languages, and she would relapse into the grammar of her own tongue.

"Yes, tell us, Cheon, for you are a merry companion usually, when drunk, as when you drank from the malm-glass held between your toes, and when you sang the Weltan song of the Snudberander, whatever that be, while dancing on the table before you fell." He spoke true, for I had done these things, and as they were good friends to me, I began to speak.

"Well then listen to what I say. For I am a freak of nature, as you can see, and know by my strength, as when I threw the Kariasg poet through the window. But I am freakish too in another way. I do not wish to have men as lovers, as other women do, but hope for women." I guessed that these two were not like to faint from shock at any sexual deviation, since I knew that one of their pleasures—a strange one—was for Theela to pass her water on the Pharn in their drunken raptures. So I went directly on without waiting for them to give any opinion. "But in this hope I am thwarted always, since I cannot find any woman who will lie with me. And I am in great need, my loins aflame for some relief."

The two crudely laughed as I expected, but soon settled to consider my lot.

"We had already supposed this to be the case." said Klune.

"We have watched her eyes nearly leave her head when the Asg dance, and seen her trouble at the touch of women. But since she might be offended by any remark, we did not tell her. Even Klune asks me to sit close by her and see her heart beat."

"It is so easy to divine then?" I said, for I was surprised.

"Simple," said Klune.

"Did she lie with any woman?" said Theela.

"No, none," I replied.

"It is a sad thing, since she is a ripe enough woman. She must be accommodated somehow."

"If Morwern were here, it would have been easy, for she would lie with anyone, man, woman, child or even animal if any could be coached to the task." said Klune drawing his pipe.

"Do not speak so, Klune, since Cheon is not to be likened to animals, nor must we mock her for these problems are very painful and she is but eighteen."

"I joked. But answer me, Cheon, that I may be better able to help. Are you, as many women, set upon finding someone with whom you will act wife and husband, some woman you imagine perfect in your mind? Or have you lust like a man, satisfied by a night or two of wrestling in bed with some suitable though quite imperfect partner?"

"For me, any woman, not ugly, nor ancient, nor diseased, would be like water in the desert. When the great thirst is satisfied, then speak to me of fine wine."

"Then I can solve your problem, since though Odon be a holy place by its own boast, yet here are brothels not different, I suppose, from those of Wdeni (the name of Odon in imperial days). For mouths may speak as pure as mountain dew, yet asses are ever asses. And I shall take you to one where the girls are clean and comely, and management honest. And you shall lie with a woman all night at my expense.''

"And he will have to stay too, I suppose, to see that all is well?'' said Theela. I thought she addressed me, but he flushed and answered.

"I do but aid Cheon and you may come with us, if it pleases you.'' She would have quarrelled but I interrupted, wishing to avoid an argument.

"Surely, no strumpet would lie with a woman? Are they not all for men?''

"Money is their desire and we have enough of that, since I won from the three Namzens what they had gained in payment for their arms.'' For Klune obtained much money by gambling on the duodecahedrons. And in this I was a useful ally, since I could cow losers who turned to resentful complaint.

"Klune, do not laugh, for I am sure Theela would understand, but I would not feel pleasure if I knew that the strumpet was striving to conceal displeasure, in order to gain money.''

"Ah, such niceties. . . .'' said Klune. "Difficulties arise.''

"She is only right. We women are more sensitive than men on this point, needing more than a knot-hole in wood to fulfill our dreams.''

I made a vulgar oath, for I had picked up that way of speaking in the Emperor's Palm.

"Do not worry,'' said Klune. "I shall arrange it to your satisfaction.'' And thus it was, and as the tale is amusing and perhaps stimulating to lovers' palates, I shall tell it.

Klune took us to a brothel in the southern quarter of Shawi, which was the older and more civilized part. It was a great tavern, with erotic singing and dancing, where many men went for gratification of lust, and couples for the thrill which can add spice to lovemaking. There I sat, watching two girls, one a black Asg, and one white, dark-haired Sunedin with great breasts, who danced naked except for tiny cloths over their sexes. And I became aroused, and even Theela watched, since the women were very skilled in the art of kindling lust. Klune had left our table to arrange for my strumpet, and he came back with the proprietress, an Odon plump and merry, unlike the generality of Odon.

"Your friend has explained your requirements. I have told my girls that any who wish may take you for the night, with only the normal payment. So you will know it be from choice. Come then into this chamber, where they may take the opportunity to see you—a strange reversal of the usual roles."

We entered a room with rich carpets, a bath set in the floor and a bed laid with silken sheets.

"Now that they may know what they are to accept, you must undress, at least to your shift," the woman said. I had not expected this, but my lust was too great for me to argue. I had put on my finest gossamer shift of palish blue, through which nipples and hairs could be seen and as I took off my leather clothes, the woman nodded encouragingly.

"Under all your grim garments, you are as soft and shapely as any of my girls." she said, and lifted my shift right to my neck to see me more clearly, looking professionally at all the parts she had bared. "There are some rich men who would pay a fortune to handle you. For there are those whose taste runs to women of strength and power who are yet nubile as you are. They are often men of words, not deeds, and their desire is as incongruous as a buck-rabbit which lusts after a she-wolf. But as I hear, you are not likely to require or desire such employment." She touched me with her hand on my soft hidden flesh and knew then how great was my lust. "You have been enjoying the show with some anticipation, it seems?" she said. My head whirled and I nodded, seeing that she knew in any case, and that this was not a place to pretend innocence. She let down my shift and bade me wait, after warning me not to be offended if I was not to the girls' taste, for it was I that asked for a partner who desired me.

And she was right, for several girls as she brought them in in turn, would not approach and shook their heads diffidently, not wishing to displease me, yet afraid. I blushed to be standing there, near naked, all bathed and perfumed, while so many would not have me. And I would have gone, but the proprietress would not let me. And at last came a girl, not bad looking, dark-haired with pale olive skin but with nose a little too long. She wore a glittering skirt about her waist, all red sequins, and her breasts were covered with a pale green band. And instead of hovering by the door, she came to where I stood, her face curious but not frightened. Her brown eyes looked at me, and she suddenly smiled at me, though I wore a long face of disappointment. She turned to the woman.

"Yes, I will lie with this woman," she said, and I was pleased and smiled too, as the proprietress spoke.

"Do you wish to lie with Ocea?"

"Yes," I said. "Since she is beautiful and in any event no other has chosen me." I called her beautiful to please her, which it did.

Then the proprietress left, and suddenly I was afraid. My lust disappeared in a flash and I knew not what to do nor how to begin, so I sat heavily on the bed, lost and trembling. So many times I had yearned to caress a woman, yet now when it was possible, I thought that I was not skilled in caressing, and I felt only impotence. But she saw my trouble.

"You are afraid now, Weltan woman, even though you are so great, and a warrior as I have heard. But do not fear, for many brave men are like that, and I have cured them." She approached me and bade me stand. Then she threw off my shift.

"You are beautiful, Cheon of Weltanland, and I am glad I chose you for this night, above all those who are patrons here." She stroked both my breasts, making the nipples rise again to swollen attention. "Lie abed, where you can be at ease, for I am your slave tonight." And I lay on the bed, and my trembles ceased.

"It is your first time with a woman, I can see as much," she said. I nodded. "Then I am fortunate, because you will one day be famous and a queen and a savant. And you will always remember Ocea of Shawi, and write of me in your histories, and I shall ever live in all times." She rubbed my skin now with a soothing oil, lifting my arms and legs to aid her. "Is it not so?" she asked.

I nodded again, too moved to speak.

"I am half Odon, quarter Kariasg and quarter Weltan, so we are in any case cousins, fair giantess," she said, and I rejoiced because she was of my blood, even a quarter. Since she lay my thighs open, she soon saw that my lust rose again, but by her art she tantalized me.

"Roll onto your stomach, Weltan, for I must rub your back." I did so. "What an ass you have, giantess!" she said and we laughed. She lay then on my back, and I felt that she too was naked, her breasts warm on my skin, her belly-hairs coarse on my buttocks. After that, it was easy and natural.

And we did many things, some I had expected, some I had not, but all were good, and I spent my lust first once, then twice, and at the end eight times in all. She marvelled to see how I never tired and to see my arching back again and again. And in the morning we slept and none disturbed us, since Klune paid for all and the woman of the brothel had a romantic heart and had taken pleasure in our pleasure.

And though Ocea yet worked at the brothel, she came with me in many evenings, and we became notorious for our open and, so it was said, unnatural love.

XIV

One night as I sat with Ocea in the Snapper's Head—the tavern being known by the skull of an ichthyosaur which was mounted outside—I was disturbed by a sudden entrance to the room. A man clothed in a long green robe with palm leaves hanging all about him burst in, accompanied by two youths of fanatical appearance.

"Here be the sinners!" said he who wore the palm leaves and who I knew to be a priest of the but lately invented God of Truth—a blasphemy, if ever there be, since Truth needs no god. He pointed his sinewy hand at Ocea.

"Woman, you have sinned against Our Lord Paten, who decrees that woman shall not lie with woman, nor man with man. Though your life as whore was not a good one in the eyes of Our Lord Paten, yet it was a thousand times less sinful than the foul and disgusting deed which you have perpetrated against the Lord's will and which outrages all men. You must be flogged and thrown into a dungeon until the Lord sees fit to release you."

Ocea began to whimper and cry for mercy, since she believed that this Lord Paten really existed, and that this man spoke true. But I did not.

"Hold your tongue," I said with annoyance. "Let the Lord

Paten speak if he can, which is not likely since there is not such a god.''

''She blasphemes against Lord Paten, she must be slain!'' the priest who was not an old man, rather a feeble but cunning one, called out in fury of zeal.

''If I must be slain, let it be by Our Lord Paten, who so decrees.''

''I am the instrument of Our Lord Paten, and through me seeks your death.''

''A weak god who trusts in a man to kill those who speak against him. Yet I say this, priest: I have no quarrel with Lord Paten, but rather with you who wish to slay me and beat my companion. Is it not by saying that Our Lord Paten, or some other god, orders this or that, that in reality priests such as you achieve their own ends, thus gaining power by cunning that they cannot have by strength of arms?''

I have noticed that this kind of speech is never answered by priests, rather they speak more frenziedly of the blasphemies which are committed against their god. And this is not strange, since there is no true answer to my question. Such ways arouse in me a burning hatred which I can little control. Thus when he again screeched out his charges of blasphemy and sin, I sat silent for a while, speechless with rage, for I knew that of all dangers to the Way, his was the most evil and the greatest. Since the Way of Truth had but lately come to Odon, so the priests of older times, angered by it, had sought to change it to a religion, that they might command others as before. But one of a group of seagoing men of Odon had been listening, and he spoke now for me who sat mute.

''The words spoken by that woman are just, and I too have long noticed the way in which shifty cowering men, having bedecked themselves in strange raiment, strut like kings, ever forbidding those things that are pleasant, so that at the last only groveling before these men is held to be a commendable act. They cannot bear the sight of simple folk taking pleasure at carnivals, feasts or in each other's arms, unheeding of their sanctimonious whining, since they feel then a weakness of their power.''

''You too, a low man of the sea, now challenge the glory of Our Lord of Truth!'' said the priest, perhaps less certainly. ''Vengeance will not be far.''

''I challenge nothing but your insolent power to order us like children in the name of an invisible god who speaks not to us, but to you in private, where we cannot hear him. It is like to the Kariasg who made the republics, where all was done and orders cast in the name of the People, by men like priests in guise of council men. Yet when people are so many, they become like Lord Paten, invisible and speaking not, except through lying mouths of counselors. Maybe there are gods whose will must be done, and because of this I speak not against them. But hearing the words of this woman, I must not let it be thought that she has no allies in this place, and others too in all lands.''

"The king shall hear of this," said the priest, calm now, his face filled with angry contempt. "You will not speak so brave when you are hurled from the Moaning Head to the rock below. For the king holds Lord Paten's will sacred and blasphemy punishable by death.'' And he made to leave. The seagoing man looked ill at ease, having spoken in righteous anger but now realizing the consequences. Yet I was not afraid.

"Hold fast, priest, if you value your life.'' I drew my dagger. "If we are to die because of Lord Paten's will, then you will die first, in spite of it." The priest and his two deacons looked at last cowed.

"Do not commit further blasphemy." he said in shaking voice.

"Is not one blasphemy enough to be hurled to the rocks? For two am I cast twice?''

"Perhaps the king will be merciful.''

"Tell me, priest, are you the true servant of Our Lord Paten? Speak true, only truth, for your life depends on it.'' My limbs trembled with fury. He looked about him and saw no help, only the fascination all men have with a quarrel turning to violence.

"I am his true servant.''

"A master must defend his servant, is not this the Way of Truth?''

He shook, his legs unsteady. He spoke not, but others nodded and murmured assent, for it was the Way and all knew.

"And since our Lord Paten is the God of Truth, thus he will act?''

The priest was shivering now. He had but to deny his pretense to be servant of Paten to save himself, yet he would not. Such is the way with them—it may be he believed his own lies.

"He will defend me," he said, his voice a long throw now from the pompous tones of his entrance.

"Our Lord Paten!" I shouted. "Defend your servant, since I am going to slay him!" And I did the deed, an unpleasant thing yet not against the Way. Nowadays I would not kill a priest, even though my reason were just, since I know that for each that falls, others come to take their place and that priests under one guise or another will never disappear from the face of the earth.

"You will be imprisoned now, at the least," said the seagoing man who had spoken in my support.

"So be it," I said. "Yet he would have killed us all three, so I have lost nothing."

"I am Megridon, captain of a ramshuner; we sail tonight and you may sail with us," he suggested, though others of his group seemed less pleased.

"What! A woman to make trouble during months at sea?" protested one great blond bearded fellow.

"If she lies with women, not men, then how shall she make trouble?" said the captain.

"Who will sit at her oar with her, since all women are wont to smell foul at certain times, and certain women all the time?" said the blond man.

"We can ask all. We are short three hands in any case. Would you have me leave her here to face her death as likely as not?" The blond man considered this argument.

"It is not our affair . . ." he mused. "but the slaying of a priest can be no bad thing, since they kill all joy . . ."

"Then silence your carping. The woman comes with us, like it or not. And let us make haste, since the deacons are gone to tell the tale to the bishop."

I turned to Ocea, but she was nowhere to be seen, doubtless having flown away in panic as things turned to the worst. And I hoped that she could go into hiding, though in truth I know not what became of her. Yet there was no time to find out, and indeed I must have left her there in any case. So we cleared out of the tavern and hurried along the misty quay, till we found the captain's ship, which was called Windwolf. There, the rest of its crew sat around the decks, gaming and idly passing the time. When they saw me, and caught up with the events, there was much discussion since these wild seagoing Odon did not behave as slaves to their captain, rather he was a chief of a like-minded band of men. Some agreed with the blond man's point of view, though he now accepted my joining them, but the tale of my slaying of the priest weighed heavily in my favor. And one broken-toothed fellow of scarred features agreed to let me sit on his bench and help wield his oar.

"For you look strong enough, and as for your smell, at sea it cannot trouble me much, since in any event few who sail in Windwolf exude a fragrance of roses. Besides I enjoy a conversation at my oar, which may touch on other things than war and women, and the captain's report of your words shows that you will be able to discuss such matters as I like."

So it was settled. And with ten other ramshuners we slid out of Shawi that night, as the rain poured on us, and we pulled in time with our oars. Thus did I become a ramshuner on the Windwolf.

XV

I sat watching the dark waters, as we made ready to sail, for I was of little use, knowing nothing of ships or the tying of ropes, and Fidzer, the man who had invited me to his oar, thought it better if I kept away now from the maneuvers, so as not to be a hindrance, but during the voyage, I would soon learn of the ways of the ships.

All along the quay, the ramshuners were preparing for the expedition to far Aday* in the Isles of Rain. There, duke Anderman was rightful king through his betrothal to Pat, known as the Flower of Aday, daughter of Queen Ulla lately dead. But now she had been taken by Morden of Athyssen who proclaimed himself king. In fact, as I guessed, all claims of rights to this and that throne were open to doubt, and arms

* See glossary

must settle the issue. Duke Anderman had raised a great fleet, many of the house of Anderman, his kin, who were to receive land in Aday, once he was on the throne. Others like Windwolf, he had promised a share of booty, as much as they could carry off.

The harbor was lit by great flaming torches and leading lights, with each ship bearing blue beacon to the fore, yellow to the rear, and red and green on either side. As we pulled at the oars, Fidzer showed me how by keeping the two red lanterns one upon the other, we could row safely clear of shoals of rocks and out into the open sea. All around the voices of the men of Odon were raised in song, for the pulling of oars is greatly aided by tunes special to the purpose which are sung in the rhythm of rowing. It was a sight to rouse the blood of any true daughter of Thanda, and I felt in the vastness and depth of the ocean which heaved in that night, at last a gigantism to match my own. And my whole spirit soared with expectancy like the gulls that flew around us, as we set out to win land or booty from shore and riverside all over the world, for none were safe from us, the ramshuners as we were called in Odon, meaning the riders of the north wind.

The winds were against us and no use was likely for the sails until land was far behind, when by cunning changes of direction we could proceed to windward in zig-zag motion. Like stars slowly moving in their courses, the whole fleet single file crept out through the castles that stood on each end of the harbor mouth and out into open sea, where I soon discovered the water rose and fell with a huge swell. We did not cease for four hours, when the shore was but a thin line of lights on the far horizon. Then at last the ship was put under sail and when the helm was manned there was but little to do, save sleep. The ship had two decks, one covered, one open on which we sat when rowing. Below deck there were hammocks where the men slept but it was decreed that I might not sleep in this place, rather in a deck-house used for stowing extra sails and ropes. Here Fidzer and another man of pleasant manner, Conderan of Emden, slung a hammock for me.

It is difficult now to remember the order of events as I learned the ways of the sea. For many days I was seasick, rowing when it was necessary in a nightmare of pain and discomfort, since my buttocks were much chafed by the continual rubbing back and forth as I swung the oar. At night my skirt was stuck fast with congealed blood from the burst blisters of the day. I mourned this hardening of my flesh, since it is not womanly to have the leathery skin that men take pride in. Fortunately Fidzer saw my trouble and found silken cushions stolen from a tavern in Shawi, and on one of these between my skirt and my skin I could row in less discomfort. But still I was sick, so that I neither ate nor drank and often leaned over the side and retched painfully. None laughed at my plight, rather I gained respect since I did not whine nor ease in my efforts, but always pulled my hardest with the rest, because it was my duty to be manly in this endeavor.

As my sickness subsided I found greater and greater pleasure in the gray-green white capped waters of the Zoic sea. Sea birds always followed us, calling, and swooped to pick up what scraps they could, even when there was nothing but what I had voided from my stomach, for they were not particular in their taste. There was often great merriment in the ship, and the captain allowed beer on some evenings, and we drank it by the light of the lanterns while all boasted of the deeds they would do in Aday.

"I shall get me a woman as great as Cheon who will never tire of my assaults." said one, Aganzer.

"I shall find one, small with long hair, as long as the hair of a weeping-tree," said another. "And she will serve me in all things, even when I lie with another woman."

"Mine shall be with great bosoms, hair black as an Asg, with an ass so comely that it will be a braver sight than the face of Fidzer," said a third, and all laughed.

"You will have naught but an old harridan whose face is not better than my ass," said Fidzer. "But as for women, they are but little important if we can have great riches. For then, when we return to Odon, we can buy women in plenty."

"But we may not wish for prostitutes, rather women who will be our wives, when we have lands of our own," said one strait-laced fellow.

"I do not mean to buy in the sense of prostitutes." said Fidzer. "Let me tell you that women, when they see a man able to produce gold coins from his purse, are not wont to refuse any offer he may make, be it marriage or the satisfaction of a whim of curiosity to enter her with an old wine bottle."

"Those words are not just, Fidzer," said the strait-laced man, Gordom. "What say you, Cheon, does he speak true?"

"Far be it from me to give any man of Odon the lie, the more so since he is my oar-partner," I said.

"Speak, Cheon," said Fidzer. "For we value your words, seeing that you are woman and must be better able to know how your sex may act."

"As for that, no amount of gold would persuade me to accommodate a wine bottle, nor any other thing that such an affluent man may offer. But I am not like other women, as I well know, and I have seen that riches are wont to wet the loins of many women."

"As I said," said Fidzer, "she backs my words."

"But of what use are such women more than prostitutes, since any man with greater riches may lure them away, even though you be married with them?"

At this all shouted that they would disembowel any man that thought to steal their women, little considering whether as well as richer, such a man might be greater in fight.

Once I became accustomed to the rise and fall of the sea and the pitching and rolling of the ship, I liked it well. The endless gray-green waves at our sides, the whitecaps blown into froth by the wind, and the crying of the following sea birds became a source of great tranquillity to the troubled spirit that lived in me. And as we sat in the cabin to the fore when we went under sail, to shelter from the wet westerlies, I liked the rough comradeship that united all. I have heard that on some ships there are many quarrels with rebellious sailors, bullying captains and ill-suited men thrown together for long duration on the sea. But we were not quarrelsome nor rebellious, nor was Megridon a bully. Rather all had high hopes to gain riches, princesses for women and even land if such was their fortune. And the oppressive reign of Paten was lifted once we were under way. There was no priest aboard Windwolf.

Often Fidzer, the captain and I would discourse upon matters which were not of interest to our shipmates. We agreed all three, that religions were generally mere kingdoms within kingdoms, where power was kept by threat as by earthly kings. But I and the captain both held that there were gods, not unlimited in their powers, rather beings like us who had come to the world from other worlds, which as I have said, are many. This I had from Meon, though I preferred to unfold each idea as if it were my own thought alone, and I knew that, from this, I gained the respect of all those on board who thought; for I was young then and sore in need of some admiration. Fidzer held that there were no gods of any sort, and that one must act only as one pleased and not in accordance with any other's will. Since he was a kind and honest man, his theory brought no ill to any. Those men who cared nothing for my theological powers yet respected me, for they marveled at the feats of strength which I performed to amuse them. And the fellow who had boasted of capturing a woman as great as I, was inclined to second thoughts.

"For if I do/find such a woman, may she not flog me when she pleases, if I were to commit some small indiscretion with another woman, or have a mug or two of ale?"

"Well, she might," I said, bending my great bow while staring wild-eyed at him.

"Cheon is a good shipmate," it was agreed. "Since she is fair of speech and comely, yet likely to be a good link in the battle chain, and with all we may enjoy the sight of her great bosoms when she washes, thus whetting our appetite for the women who we are to have in Aday."

I weep even now for those who found nothing in Aday but poor unmarked graves. Yet such is a warrior's life, and many fulfilled their lusty dreams and as I know, yet live.

We sailed at last one misty morning in sight of the coast of Aday and moved up Blackwater Sound, between Aday and Roden. Each ship raised its pennant, and my heart swelled to see what a proud sight we made, our great figureheads scowling ahead, each little flag fluttering in the breeze. We were to sail up the river Andumic to Thondalm where Morden lived falsely as king of Aday. A day we sailed, and all on the shore were folk looking at us, some cheering, some still and fearful. We cared not for secrecy, since the power of Morden must be broken in a great battle, and we wished that he have time to gather his men.

At dawn we furled sail and sang our rowing chanty, "North wind, north wind, cold north wind, from the darkness"—simple words but as we chanted, so we summoned up strength for battle. On either side of the Andumic, were snow-covered winter trees whose leaves were fallen and which held their myriad bare branches against the magenta dawn. The shores were now deserted, as the people who dwelt near ran for their lives into the interior, afraid of the ramshuner. We drew up to the haven of which Anderman had heard from his spies, four miles from Thondalm, and I saw the water growing a forest of masts, as the boats disgorged their men who leapt for the bank, their number ever spreading. A dozen crew men were left on each boat, to move it nearer or farther from the shore, according to tide or weather. They were men not overeager for battle, and there are such even among the ramshuner.

One ship, Ouroubouros, had like me, a woman warrior of the Sunedi, and as we ran through the icy surf, we passed near. She was a powerful creature, no doubt, but not so great as I. We looked at each other curiously, jealously also, yet with sudden smile as we saw how both tied her hair around with the green ribbons of Truth.

"Good fortune to you, Sunedin!" I said.

"And to you, Weltanland woman!" she answered. I heard later that fortune was not so good to her, since she took an arrow in the belly and another in the neck. But she lived, as I know, since I have seen her with her sons and daughters in Aday where she stayed all the years.

On the top of the beach we assembled and had but little need to wait, since the armies of Morden were in the field. When north fights north, it is not a time of long speeches, and neither duke Anderman nor the so-called king chose to address his enemies. To us the duke spoke but shortly.

"I choose to fight now, as soon as we come to Aday, so that we may finish with the difficult business at the first. Had we landed at Kasdak cape, we should have camped two days whilst Morden marched to meet us. Here he stands at a time of our choosing and before his town. He is no king, nothing but an abducter of women. Queen Pat does not like him, and though they are married, she does not lie with him, and the consummation was by force. I am the king of Aday, and those who come with me as my kith and kin are the true lords of Aday and shall soon have the castles and estates which we shall win. Those who come as adventurers will have the booty of Thondalm and what they can collect by two weeks' pillage of Aday, after which they shall depart in peace, taking in no case more than one woman to each. As for this fight, there are none in Aday who can stand before the ramshuner in such numbers as we have. To battle then, and good fortune to all!"

Our army advanced upon the Rainish armies and soon battle was joined. They had the air of men but lately come from warmth and peace; we were like devils from the sea, and at first they gave before us and we drove them ever back, through the trees, toward the crest of a ridge where they made a stand. The hill was bare of trees except for a few and some fallen trunks. We could not approach them, since they had the advantage of the slope, and their arrows rained upon us. I took one which hammered against my helmet, another against the breastplates of my armor. But I loosed many, and since no armor could withstand the power of my arrows, many fell hit in the heart which is where I aimed.

I knew nothing of the strategy of battles, though I think we tried vainly to draw them from the hill by making pretense to run away. The Rainish people were too cunning for this however, and they held fast, jeering at us, women's voices mingled with the men's, since Rainish women ever fight with their men. I could see no way that they could be displaced, and it seemed to me that the battle was lost. But Anderman had a plan and as I know now, it was this: The whole army was to thin out along the bottom of the scarp which they held. A group of two hundred—the best warriors from each of the ships—was to remain together though seemingly merely a random part of the line. When the Rainish stretched out along the top, which they must if they were to avoid us outflanking them, we would begin an assault. Yet at the last, all but the two hundred would hold their positions. Then the two hundred would suddenly coalesce from the line and in a body charge up to the scattered and weakened Rainish defense. By their power they would hold for a few minutes, until behind them as quickly as possible, our whole army would follow. By my boasting in the ship I had convinced the captain that I was a Thanda reincarnated, and with Conderan of Emden I joined the two hundred.

"I am glad it is you, Cheon," he said. "For I know that you are strong since I have seen, and that you are fearless since you slew the priest."

At first I spoke not since I was afraid. It is a shocking thing to be suddenly selected for a task which may result in one's own death. But then, thinking that if I lived, he would report my bold words and that if I did not, it mattered little what words were uttered, I said:

"Fear not, Conderan, for I think we shall easily scatter these Rainish jackals."

He smiled, and we began the slow advance, separate at first since we wished not to arouse their suspicions by presenting a denser part of the line. At our center was Bornkynd of

Minden, a great and fearless warrior whose bright armor we were to use as a meeting point when we made the charge.

At last Bornkynd raised his sword, and with shields before us we charged up the slope, knowing that now speed was our only safety. This had the advantage of alarming the Rainish, since it seemed a desperate endeavor, nearly insane. And many of us had painted white skulls on our faces and made an eerie sight as we ran upon them, howling the ghoulish wail of the ramshuners. I took an arrow in the knee which stuck fast and pained me, but I kept on, sensing their wavering. At the top their men remained, the women retreating down the slope since they fought only with bows, not with swords. As we gained the summit, Bornkynd fell, and had I not shouted to all to follow me, we might have turned to retreat. But I made for the great Adayman who seemed foremost in the defense and screaming in the high unearthly note of a woman, smashed my sword on his helmet and though his armor did not split as I expected, the blow knocked him senseless. It was but a few moments then before the Rainish men ran down the slope, and the white skulls soon stood victorious. But even as we cheered and heard our army approaching from all directions, we saw a fell sight. For a whole cohort of Namzen in the hire of Morden were now running up the slope, just as we had done and just as boldly. We had not expected to meet Namzen, and the word itself was enough to spread unease amongst us who had stormed the hill. I heard some who stood by me speak of running.

"We must escape while we yet live. Our ships are near."

"If we turn, the others down the slope will block our running and we shall all be slain like dogs," I said.

"Aye, Cheon is right. Hold fast," others agreed, and so we stood.

But the women archers who had seen me rally the men, and partly for this, and partly because they were women who were jealous of my beauty* and my power, began to pepper me with arrows. And although my armor deflected most, I received one through my cheek guard that penetrated my upper jaw and I felt it stuck firm in my mouth, its head emerging from just above my incisor teeth. Thus it was that

---

* It is difficult to see how the civilized Cheon with a white skull painted on her face, and hair in waxed battle spikes, green ribbon or no, gave such an impression of beauty.

we were in sore straits. Yet I saw suddenly a chance that might halt the eager charge of the Namzen which was rapidly bringing them close to us, since the slope on their side was much gentler than that on our side. I shouted to a ramshuner to raise a fallen trunk from the ground.

"For I may use it to repel the Namzen by sorcery," I said. In a moment, forty men were raising it high, since I had an air of leadership which lay easily on my shoulders.

"Wait until I shout, then hurl it down the slope and you will see a great magic!" I strung my bow with the special arrow which Meon had given me. And when the Namzen were close, I shouted and the tree trunk was hurled, and it half rolled, half leaped down the slope, banging first one end, then the other on the ground in unstable flight. And I loosed my arrow which entered the tree. And a few seconds after, with a great flash and boiling luminous smoke the trunk burst into a myriad burning fragments, each of which stuck firmly to a Namzen, so that all were in great pain.

"At them, now!" I cried, and we ran down the slope to strike the confused soldiers. I head shouts of "Sorcery!" or a word like to it in their Rainish tongue, but we crashed into them and laying about us, slew men who scarce knew we were there, so dazed they were. And gradually they gave backwards, not running but by many falling, and pushed by the weight and power of our charge. And behind us now came all the skullfaces howling the death chant. Namzen, though mild of manner—some say soft—and polite of speech— some say hypocrite—are the bravest warriors of the northwestern Isles—that is the Rainish Isles and Bergian Isles—and they fought bravely but vainly.

I was engaged in one battle with a great Namzen but I had wounded him sore and he staggered away. And as I watched, too long, from the side I just glimpsed an axe that swung for my head. I raised shield and took it, but it was the hardest blow I had ever felt, and for the first time in my life, I fell from the force of another's arm. And I dropped my shield. "Here then must I die!" I thought, and looked up to see the young face of the largest man I had ever seen. He was fair and with gray eyes, and he looked down at me, raising his axe. I made ready to try a parry with my sword, but had he struck, my head must have rolled. Yet he did not. He only looked momentarily.

"I do not wish to slay thee, though I could." He spoke in a

graceful dialect of Moshan. "For I took thee by surprise, and it be not just. And thou art a comely woman, and full of spirit, put there by Umbdon, Lord of the Clouds, and not for me to still. Take thy shield, woman, and fight on, for I must go back now as the day is yours." And he walked unharmed away from us, for none would strike down so noble a warrior from behind.

Then I gathered my shield and we stood, of the two hundred, watching the rout of the armies of Morden who, once we had gained the ridge and when the Namzen could not hold fast, gave way and ran from the field. I sat, spent, swallowing the blood that poured from my wound into my mouth.

"Cheon has won the day, by bravery and sorcery," said Conderan of Emden, and none disagreed. Several of the two hundred filled pipes, and then amidst the sounds of the retreat and pursuit, we drank spirits from our flasks and smoked. For as often happens, it was not the boldest and finest warriors who like best the pursuit and capture of a vanquished army. Rather it was the lesser men who did not run forward with any great speed when the Rainish held the top of the hill, or when the Namzen appeared. Bornkynd had not been killed, but his wound was bad, and he could not speak nor properly understand where he was, nor what had happened. And he made a gruesome gargling noise in his throat. It was known by experience that he would not live, or if he did that his spirit would not remain in his body. And his cousin Ornilden slew him, and many wept as we buried him there, where he fell. And his armor we buried with him, for the ramshuner who believed in older gods than Paten, thought that he would need it on his journey to Vahahad. I wept, for I knew that he would never again need his armor and I felt weak and feverish, my heart beating fast, because so much of my blood had poured into my stomach. Conderan of Emden cut off the shaft of the arrows in my jaw and knee but could not remove the stubs, since they were barbed arrows, and a sorceress or physician was needed for that. And as we walked toward Thondalm, the victors of the battle of Thondalm which decided the future of Aday, he held me, that I might lean always on him, and thus we entered the town.

As we were the last to enter, it was full of ramshuners. In principle, there was no killing, since the people were deemed to be Anderman's subjects and under his protection. But their goods were forfeit and any ramshuner could enter any house or shop and take what he wished. And since it was quite likely that much had been hidden, so bad feelings soon erupted, and blood was often spilt. And any ramshuner could take any woman he wished, either permanently for his own, for a few weeks or merely to pleasure himself on the spot. This is not a just thing, and any man seeing his wife, sister, or as may be, his mother, so used, would be inclined to violence. Thus there was much noise of quarrelling, squeals and cries of women, as we walked to the place where the captains were to wait to account their men.

"I like not this cruel time," I said to Conderan, my voice weak from loss of blood.

"Nor I, Cheon, but it is necessary."

There were some fires burning, and the sky glowed red. In the taverns shiploads of ramshuners caroused with pipes and jugs, while frightened servants attended their wants. Music of many kinds came from all sides. There was mist and bitter cold, and I shivered from it. There were many wounded who sat and lay in the streets, untended by their comrades, groaning, mostly Rainish who had returned in their pain to try to find shelter, not able to face the march north Morden made with the remnant of his army. And among them were women whose wounds made them of little interest to the ramshuner. Yet we could not help them, since I was not in much better condition, some great vein having seemingly been cut in my jaw.

"The blood seems never to stop," I said, my alarm rising a little.

"Never fear, Cheon. I know from many battles that your wound will not be your death." And he was right, as is obvious, since I lived to write so many words.

As we walked, I limping and slow, dependent at last on another, and a man, which I never expected, I felt perhaps as ordinary women feel, such a welling up of ndowna. This Moshan word means a thing not expressible in northern language, a mixture of gratitude, a feeling of vulnerability yet safety, and sudden admiration of the bold and strong man on whom I relied. Both sensed this turn of feeling, and his hand stroked my long hair, though it was not smooth or shining, since it was stiff with black wax which I put on it for the battle, to make it spiky and fearsome. I feared though that he might misunderstand my feeling, and I understood at last how

Wanin had felt, how I loved Conderan well enough at that
moment, yet knew that I was not for man. But he was wise,
Conderan, though he could not read nor write, and knew not
that the world turned around the sun and not the contrary.

"It is a pity, Cheon, that you be as you are, since of all
women I have known, I never saw one I coveted more. And
though you be weak now and cling to me, like the daughters
of my sister in Emden, and bear my caress, yet no sooner will
your strength return than you will be as likely to slay me as
lie with me."

I laughed, looking at the red light that glowed on his
scarred yet gentle face and into his cavernous eyes.

"I will not slay thee, Conderan, nor do thee any ill, since I
like thee more than any man I have met." I used the language
that the Namzen had used, who spared my life, since it
seemed so soft and fitting for such a time. "But neither will I
lie with thee, so thy words are true, and thou knowest things
that I have not told thee, which is often the way with men like
thee, who have not the learning of books as I have." And we
spoke no more, but stopped in a doorway, and weak as I was,
he kissed my lips and I kissed his, and his leathery hands did
stroke my buttocks, and I allowed that, for I knew that he
would do no more.

"Come, Cheon, for you must be laid to bed, and I must
find one, not half the woman that you are, who will lie with
me and quench the thirst that you have roused in me." And I
was not angry that he spoke thus, for it was the Way of Truth
in purest form. And I envied neither him nor the woman he
would find, for when the Truth is in the ascendant, all
jealousy melts away.

In the square we found the captains and all those of Windwolf
who survived. And I was surrounded by cheering and smiling
faces, for my fall had been seen and my death feared. "Cheon
lives!" went the cry, and as I was the hero of the battle, we
soon were at the center of a circle of ramshuners, captains
and men, and duke Anderman himself came from his banqueting
table which was at the center of the square to see me. He was
a very handsome man and not old, and his eyes were wise
and just. And he smiled when he saw me.

"Cheon, what a birthday gift you were to me, since you
turned the battle atop the ridge when Bornkynd fell. And
what a strange trick of nature that you are woman and comely
too. For the generality of women warriors are not beauties.

Yet you, greater than any even amongst the two hundred, are but for your size, the perfect type of young womanhood." His eyes suddenly changed as he saw my weakness, and they became soft like Conderan's had been.

"Yet you are wounded sore." He called to his adjutant. "She must lie abed, yet I would have her close by me with her comrades near. Bring a litter in which she may lie, with her head and back supported, for such wounds are dangerous where the head is laid down. And draw her close to the fire, cover her with skins until she be warm. And bring to me a physician, an Asg only, since they are the only true physicians. And you—" he addressed my shipmates—"come to my table and be near Cheon, since at a time of injury, familiar faces are best."

So I lay while an Asg physician and his assistant, a lovely black Asg girl, attended me. With great skill he cut free the arrows that were embedded in my bones. And since he could make each part of the body numb with his ointment, so I felt only small pain. And with his waxes, special cloths and thread he made my bleeding stop, while all the time the Asg girl soothed my brow and whispered words of comfort in my ear.

"Fear not, woman of Hyperborea, since your face will heal, leaving no mark to mar your beauty. And your knee will be as before, and you will be able to run again in battle as you have done today."

"Spare me that, it does not tempt me." I said, and she laughed, little knowing that were I strong as usual, I would have been hard pressed by her nearness, and apt to steal my hand beneath her robe.

As it was, I lay near sleep with the duke Anderman on one side, Fidzer to the other, who tried to tempt me to eat though I could not. Conderan and others had slipped away to find more sultry pleasure. Before I slept, I saw the leading in of thirty of the comeliest Rainish women warriors who had been taken prisoner. They wore their armor still, but one by one each was obliged to strip naked and walk along before the tables, turning sometimes so that her buttocks could be seen, and at other times facing the tables. Most had legs and arms painted in glaring and discordant colors, but once their tunics were off, we saw that they had not troubled to cover their bodies with this paint, so they seemed to wear long bright gloves and socks. But in between were their white bellies with darker triangles of pubic hair and quivering bosoms. Their faces were dejected and their shoulders bowed.

I marveled at the great variation in their private parts and their bosoms. For the former were sometimes thick and matted, sometimes sparse and straggly, hair sometimes growing all around their inner thighs and near up to their navels, others but a tiny clump not greater than a rabbit tail. For the most part they were in dull brown colors, though occasionally there was a golden fleece or a black impenetrable thatch like mine, and it was these I looked at most often. Some bosoms were large and wobbling like wineskins, some were small, others barely daring to exist. And the nipples too were randomly distributed, since sometimes great dark circles the size of large onions surmounted flat barely swelled bosoms, and in other cases tiny little buttons were incongruously set atop veritable mountains of cringing flesh. I preferred best those of middling size with large nipples. Mostly the nipples were hard and stiff, as if in lust though the true cause was their fear and the cold.

I was too sleepy to know exactly what happened, but every so often a prisoner was called, and she went to a man who either bade her sit at his feet or took her directly to one of the streets that led from the square, no doubt to find a warm quiet

Note: The battle of Daycalx, as the action described by Cheon is called in history books, sees the first mention of her by scholars. Mintenather of Mubble writes in his "Origin of Hyperborean Power":

"The battle of the Ridge was settled by the bold charge of the two hundred and an account told by a Rainish warrior to a contemporary scribe is in existence: 'As we stood in triumph atop Daycalx, so we slew many ramshuner with arrows, and we watched them begin to disperse. But with guile they had made a plan, and on a sudden, many of their strongest ran up the slope in a body. We were well pleased when their great leader Borkin (Bornkynd) fell by an arrow, but then fortune turned from us. For a mad warrior—a woman stronger than an olligan—leaped on the body of Borkin, screaming oaths in a mixture of Moshan and some Hyperborean tongue (probably Weltan). She was daubed all over in white and crimson paint, in the fashion of a skeleton, and her hair was set into great serpents around her head, and foam bubbled about her lips. And by her strength which we thought demonic, she struck down all who stood before her. Our archers, (the women of Aday) hit her with many arrows, one sticking in her face, another in her thigh, but it availed nothing, and the ramshuners began to follow the two hundred along the slope. And even the Namzen but lately arrived on the field, fell back before her, as she hurled fires of death on them. At the last she fell exhausted by her frenzy, and struck by a glancing blow from Gambervil, who would not slay her . . .'

"This story accords well with Cheon's account but adds interestingly: 'After the battle, it is said that Cheon became pregnant by a ramshuner, one of her shipmates, but that she miscarried the child only two months after.' Certainly Cheon never mentions this event."

place where they might copulate. The bitter wind on the naked flesh was cruel, and I doubt not many were pleased to find warmth, though it meant parting their blue goose pimpled thighs for a perfect stranger with a skull painted on his face; some still had such, though I had washed mine off after the battle.

Such is a woman's humiliation after defeat, for she knows that just as the softest and weakest part of her army gave way and opened to the invader, so surely her softest part will be parted again to one or more of the invaders, in miniature imitation of the battle. And as I knew, to stand vanquished, baring one's body to a conqueror, is a moving experience which a man may never know. Although I did not know it, my litter was taken to a great home confiscated from an Adic lord, and there with the Asg girl to watch, I slept many hours.

XVI

It took me a week to recover from my wounds, and this was bad for those of Windwolf who wished to find women and booty, since on the fourth day Thondalm was declared purged of its guilt, and no more looting was allowed. We had but ten days left, at best; afterward before by Anderman's command, we must leave Aday. Yet so loyal were my shipmates to me that they would not go without me. But Anderman came again when I was strong and spoke with me.

"Where will you go now, Cheon, since you are well again and can do as you wish?"

"I will go wherever Windwolf goes, since I am bound by promise to stay with that ship until we return again to Odon. And even after that I will go on Windwolf, because the captain will sail south toward the Old Lands, and these I wish to see because they are the wonder of the world and because I have a friend who went there, who I have a mind to see again."

"And what of the distant future, Weltanwoman? Will you become wife and mother in some land of your choice?"

"No, I shall not marry nor bear children. But I am to be a queen, so it was prophesied by a great sorceress." Anderman smiled.

"So may it be, and I doubt not that you will be queen, else many must die in the prevention. But I am obliged to you, Cheon, since it was by your courage, strength and sorcery that I took the ridge, turned back the charge of the Namzen and won the day. Therefore I ask you to desire some boon, which will in small measure discharge a great debt. Speak, if you will, and I shall make all effort to satisfy any whim that you might have."

I thought for some moments, then answered.

"That my band of the Windwolf might stay a month and take their fill of booty, and find fair women because by my resting wounded they have lost a great chance."

"It is a just claim, and I shall make a great charter to give you, which will bear my seal and may be shown to the clerk of any town you visit to be read to its mayor. And there is a great town of Aday farther west than here and on the coast. And if you go there, you will find women a plenty and gold enough to sink Windwolf." And then he left. But not long after, he returned again with a strange idea that he had.

"Before you leave, Cheon, what say you to some merry sport, wherein you may wrestle my champion who has never been thrown by any man? For he is an arrogant fellow and I would be pleased to see him thrown by a woman and by your look and your reputation I dare to hope you may succeed."

"I will do it gladly, but not if it is to be a bloody contest, since I wish for peace now for a time."

"The contest is a sporting one and it is governed by rules of imperial making. And I shall have it stopped if harm comes to either contestant. For though in war ramshuners are dealers of death, and in peace often drunkards, tavern brawlers and gamblers, yet in sporting contest they are always looking to fairness and good humor."

Thus it was agreed, and we were to fight before a banquet which was held in the Great Hall of Thondalm, and a feast was laid out on tables surrounding the wrestling ring. Since I was guest of honor, none could eat until I ate, and as I did not wish to eat or drink before the contest, we began early, that hunger might not be too great. I wore a tight garment like tiny scarlet breeches only, since clothing is of assistance to an opponent if he may grasp it. And I liked to stand bare-breasted before so many, since a woman's breasts are always covered in ordinary time, and therefore many gazed eagerly upon mine, and I was proud. I did not fight naked, as the sight of the lower parts is reserved for other times.

Their champion was a great Kariasg whose muscular body shone with the oil upon it. He too wore only a garment at the loins—the skin of a leaping cat*—as if to proclaim that he was accustomed to slay such beasts. He walked around showing his muscles to the audience with the pomp of a strutting bird. I too oiled my body and we approached one another in the center of the area where a carpet had been laid to protect us from grazing, if we struggled on the ground. The room was lit by great arrays of torches on the walls, and the light reflected off our bodies, so that the Kariasg looked like a man of brass. And as we closed, I heard Conderan's warning.

"Take care, Cheon, for you be but half-healed." For he had been against the foolish contest from the first. But the rest of Windwolf's crew cheered for me, though their cheers soon died away, for I knew nothing of wrestling and the Kariasg was a master.

When I lunged for him, by some cunning move of his body he contrived that the force of my arm was turned against me, and I fell heavily to the ground. And at each encounter I was thrown and struck my head or back or knee to the ground, and as I am larger than ordinary people, so was my fall heavier and more disorienting. And my knee suffered an opening of the wound of the arrow, and I was less able to be agile. At each fall I became more angry, flushed and confused and an easier prey to the wrestler. And he made me fall heavily on my buttocks which was painful but humiliating too, for it made me appear foolish and impotent. And worse, because I am a woman, my tears are easily drawn forth and I felt them welling up in my eyes. As I got up from one throw, I let out a childish sob which I would have given much to retain. And many of Anderman's party gave sniggering laughs. I looked through tear-misted eyes at Anderman who was impassive, but at his side was a face distorted with mocking laughter and contempt. It was a woman whom I had never seen before, and of all the faces of the Hall, it was the most evil and sneering. And as I went again to the wrestler, I was conscious that she awaited my fall with eager lust. And I

* See glossary

rushed angrily at the Kariasg who threw me higher than he had done before, and I crashed down and my head struck the carpet and a flash of sparks came before my vision. I staggered up, the world seeming dark and vague, and would have been easy prey for the wrestler. But as he moved to finish me, Conderan jumped to his feet and drawing sword leaped toward us. I saw a man of Anderman rise to stop him, but Fidzer held him back.

"Stay, friend, if you wish to drink wine rather than your own blood," he said, and the man sat down, for when Fidzer spoke other than in jest, few disobeyed him. Conderan pointed his sword at the Kariasg.

"Do not throw this woman more, for see you not that she be stunned and not able to reply?"

"It is the rule of the contest that I may throw her till she cannot or will not rise." said the wrestler.

"Hark, Brown Asg! Cheon will never lie down if she can stand to fight, though she be nearer death than life. But is it not the rule also, as I have seen in such contests, that there is a time for rest?"

"Aye!" shouted all of Windwolf, and not a few others.

"So be it," said the Kariasg. And I was led to where my comrades sat. And water was poured upon my head, and salts held to my nostrils. And Conderan spoke.

"Do not go on with this foolishness, Cheon, for I know that one can be slain by the breaking of one's neck at the hands of a skilled wrestler, and he means to do it."

"He shall not and I shall slay him," I said, but my voice was still broken with my cursed sobs. And though all wished to stop the fight, I would not.

"We shall easily explain your difficulty by your recent battle wounds," said a youth, Ooman, of noble countenance. "And we wish to rejoice, not mourn."

"You shall not mourn. Let me back to the fight." I said.

"Then heed my words, Cheon. I have watched well the way by which he defeats you," said Ooman. "It is by your own strength and the violence of your attacks. He knows some crafty trick by which he always contrives to trip or lever you, so that your force goes to the ground. But approach him by stealth, slowly, like a fur-serpent of Minden, till with gliding movement you seize him. For I am sure that if you once lay hands upon him, he will succumb to your strength, as all must. And rub your hands in the dust of the floor so that the oil will be spent and he shall not escape." Thus spoke Ooman who was a youth of brooding temperament, who thought long before he spoke on matters where newly seen phenomena were concerned. And I trusted him.

When I went again to the arena with my face washed and hands dusted, I walked only slowly toward the Kariasg. And as I did, he watched like a hawk always ready to throw me if I lunged, but I did not and he saw my purpose for he backed off, not wishing to feel my great arms around his waist or neck. And I followed him, and silently we paced around the arena, I forwards, he backwards.

"What? Do you not throw her, Brown Asg?" shouted Fidzer, and my comrades began to taunt him.

"Take care, Brown Asg, lest she strike you down with her Truth-wallet!" (This is a little bag carried by the Given Women of the Way, in Odon, full of little palm leaves to remind them of their chastity, and the yellow juice which marks their forehead as Given Women.) "Or grasps your loincloth to snatch it away, to see if you be man or no."

"Or steals your wife, for she has a liking for brown girls and can likely plough her furrow with greater vigor than it has felt of late!"

Even in spite of their vulgar suggestions he yet backed off, and while he did I could not catch him for I dared not make a sudden spring. But then one of his own people, a Kariasg, shouted out in shame.

"If you be afraid to stand your ground, Wrabnan, then yield now and let us eat, for I be hungry and we are like to starve if the end of the fight depends upon your boldness." Wrabnan's eyes were afraid because he could see the great muscles that lay just under my womanly fat, and guessed that I was not of ordinary strength.

"Yes, stand fast, brown man, for I tire of following you and we seem foolish like bold suitor and cringing maid," I said, and for some reason these words made him angry, and foolish too, for he did stop, and I seized his waist, and he seized mine. And for a moment we struggled silently, he finding my embrace too loving and feeling difficulty in breathing. He twisted, letting go of me, and tried to dip out of it. He used all his strength and cunning, and turned away and tried to use his body to throw me over his shoulder by leverage. But now I had him round the chest, my hands locked to my arms and drawing them ever closer over his sternum. There was a sudden hush as a groan escaped Wrabnan's lips, and I knew he could not breathe since I held him in a grip the like of which he had never before imagined. His knees buckled and he would have slipped to the floor, but I took his weight and then suddenly drew every ounce of strength that I had in my murderous arms. And there was a great sound as of a thick branch of tree breaking, and then another and another as the Kariasg's ribs snapped one by one. I let him fall, crushed mortally by my power, for he died later in the night, and I regretted the deed.

But as I looked to Anderman, I saw the face yet beside him, the eyes so mesmeric they seemed to glow blue like the midnight sky in Weltan summer. The face had now lost its sneering cast and stared out at me. But I was angry and strode over to where she sat, my face, as Anderman later told me, contracted into a beastlike fury. And I reached for her throat and caught at nothing. Anderman looked at me in amazement.

"What ails you, woman? Has your fall addled your brain that you strike at ghosts?"

"I mean to kill your companion, for she has the face of the great underdevil who looses the arrows of evil." My words trembled out, a babble of confusion.

"What companion do you speak of? See, there is none here, and I saved this place for you, Cheon."

Conderan had followed me, afraid that I might strike Anderman and so sign my death warrant, since he was surrounded by armed men in the shadows.

"He speaks true, Cheon, for this place has been empty as he says, though I think he did not expect you to live to occupy it." He added the last with meaningful looks at the duke.

"Do you accuse me of treachery then, Conderan of Emden?" The duke spoke quietly but there was steel in his voice.

"Not treachery since she went willingly to fight, but not hospitality either, when a woman barely risen from her sickbed is matched against a master wrestler who can kill by breaking necks, as I have seen before."

"You speak unjustly. Cheon against my will begged that I might let her fight my champion and used my gratitude as reason for overcoming better judgment. I understood it not then and less now."

"You lie, false king of Aday, for it was your request that I fight in sport, and your intention to intercede if blood stood close to being spilled, which you did not.''

When I called him false king, men moved out of the shadows, and it would have come to a short fight, but Anderman did not wish it and motioned them back.

''I know you, Cheon, and I see by your eyes that you speak from righteous anger and believe me to have acted false. But hear this, as I shall not again be called false king and liar in my own court. After I left your chamber yesterday, someone who was like you in every detail, great and beautiful and mild and fair spoken, such a one did so speak as I have said. But as you say you did not, so I know this was not you, but some demon or sorceress who sought to make us enemies. And if you doubt my vision, doubt your own, for none but you saw the woman at my side, though as you say she was there, then so she was, and it chills my blood to know that a specter sat by me so long.''

These words were fair and just, and I knew then that the being who came back into my chamber had been not Anderman but the same demon who had spoken to him, and surely she who sat by Anderman.

''This is sorcery, king Anderman. And I do regret my words.'' I said, and so it was mended, and I sat by Anderman for the feasting and Conderan sat near also, and we three were at peace though we feared the demons who walked in Thondalm. But later we learned a greater mystery, for Anderman asked that I describe the phantom that had sat at his side. And I did, and because she had so impressed my mind I did it well in many details.

''She was beautiful with black hair like mine, with thick red lips and green eyes like emeralds. And at her neck she wore a great shining blue stone in the likeness of a spider. And her hair was held by a band of blue—like midnight. And her face was evil with a malice that cut through my flesh and bones, and penetrated my belly like a blade fashioned from ice. Who she is or what, I cannot tell, only that if I meet her one day, it will be her death or mine.''

''And what gown did she wear?'' asked a woman who sat near to Conderan.

''A pretty gown it was, with appearance of the heads of beasts in palest blue with mild eyes, all on a ground of darkest blue. And atop her head she wore a crown with an eagle. And at her left cheek she bore a scar, a round one like

the scar of an arrow." And not till then did I realize whose
face it was that had mocked me.

"Such a face as yours." said Anderman.

After that I was silent though not surly, and ate and drank
in deep thought as to the meaning of the vision. And I
watched the woman who sat with Conderan, a fair creature
with cool northern eyes and without the passion that we of the
south are slave to. She looked also at me, for she knew that
Conderan liked me, and she wished to see what kind of rival I
was. Once she spoke to me.

"That scar that you have; it is so bad to have a scar on the
face in a woman. Though perhaps it matters little to you."

I was angry yet said nothing, thinking Conderan would
reprimand her, but he did not. Neither I nor Conderan asked
Anderman why he had not stopped the contest when blood
seemed about to be spilt, for we did not wish to cause more
anger. I could not guess whether he had enjoyed the fight too
well to spoil it, or whether the shade that sat at his side had
cast its power on him.

XVII

As we left Thondalm, we traveled up the coast to the town
of which Anderman had spoken, Miden it was called. We
were not to attack it, but present our charter to the mayor, and
then take our choice of gold, jewels and women. For it was
necessary for ramshuners to find women in foreign lands
because the women of Odon would not marry them, as they
had the reputation of drunkards and pagans who would not
follow the Truth. And in Odon so many women were "Given
to the Way" that there was a shortage for all men.

What happened in Miden did not add to the glory of
Windwolf's expedition. It is one thing to sail ready to do
battle and having risked life and overcome one's enemy in
hand-to-hand fight, then to take his towns, his gold and his
women. It is quite another to enter a town with some charter

enabling one to take booty and women from it when battle is far behind.*

We rowed into the harbor and none came to resist us, for since Morden's defeat all armed men were with him in Athyssen in the north of Aday, the part called Amzzen. We made headquarters at an inn, where the innkeeper and his wife were obliged to feed us, give us drink and smile at the drunken excesses of our crew. I stayed there, not venturing forth since I disliked entering shops and houses, making peremptory demands that had to be obeyed, and seeing blood spilt unfairly and cruelly. Conderan also did not go. The stealing of gold was bad enough, but obliging women, maids or wives, to leave what they had known and come with rough strangers on the wild spring sea was even worse. Yet since it was my fault that my companions had had to wait until the noise and sound of battle were far away, I wished not to say what I truly thought when they gathered more and more weeping creatures in the tavern. And I did not want to take the part of the women openly, for I was a ramshuner and must behave as they, else my position was a foolish one.

Some of those whom the men brought in were not displeased at all; wives of bullying and aging husbands, girls who wanted adventure, as women do, not less than men, those who had seen one or other among our crew to whom they took a strong fancy; those who were excited by the feel of violent abduction and some who were nothing but whores who saw a chance to become wives of adventurers who might end their days as lords. But others were tearful, trembling and piteous to see. Some of them had been raped before being brought, though one or two seemed to have had enjoyed the experience, and no doubt hoped that all their lovemaking might be so violent and so fiery. In this I dare say they were disappointed, since men often start well but go on badly in these matters, as I have heard. Yet there were those who could not cease from weeping, and I was saddened and sickened by it. Some had been virgins, gentle girls who were shocked near senseless by their new circumstances, poor creatures having but lately abandoned their dolls. Others were wives of kind husbands whom they loved or had loved, since some had been slain. Others had been taken from children by

*It seems likely that this time brought Cheon's first experience of pillage into her mind with roles reversed, and she did not like it.

men of Windwolf. And though many jokes were made, yet there was a bad feeling amongst all of us. And many eyes were on me, sensitive to any censorious thing I might say. And though at first I said nothing nor intended to, yet in the end I did, and this was the way of it.

One of our crew, a young man though above a youth, named Jujak of Bera in the north of Odon, had brought in a tearful woman of great beauty whom he had taken from her husband, a sick man. Like many of the men, he acted thus only because he had heard that this was the way of ramshuners and feared it to be his last chance. He wished to make her cheerful, that he could be merry as he had hoped with jug in one hand and woman in the other, and young as he was, did not see the futility of it.

"Why do you not drink with me, woman? For I will not harm you and am ready to give you a house and land. And I am not a worse man than another, and have taken you as fair spoils of war. I cannot see why, since I have won you, you are weeping and will not be merry. A man must win a woman or have none."

"It is not by taking a woman away from her home that a man wins her, Jujak," I said. "It is a law of war that a man may take a woman in a defeated town, but it is not thus that he wins her. Only a true man can win a woman, whether he come on the icy winds of the Minden Voshr with frost in his hair and the gray boreal sea in his eyes, or from the warm waters of Weltan with hair burned black by the sun and the hot wine of the south for blood. And it is by his look and his words that he wins her, and thus you must do, else you are not man, only cruel boy cutting legs from frogs for his pleasure."

Jujak began to cry when I said this, for he was a man of simple nature and saw the truth of it.

"It be not fair," he said. "A woman went willingly with Ooman, and two wished to go with Judson, yet all turned from me. If I let her go, I shall return without woman."

"Hearken to me, Jujak. Let this woman go, and I shall get you a woman who will go with you and willingly if you wait, and I will do it before we return to Odon. For I know the way of it, and where to find them too. And I shall help all who wish to let the weeping women go, and my promise is always kept."

"I shall let her go," said Jujak. "If you can find a woman

like this one, with such long hair and with long fingers and the shining nose." For he thought that beautiful, since he had no knowledge of what is true beauty, and he was not wrong, for why should not long fingers and shining nose be as beautiful as black skin and large nipples as I like? And other men already sick of their whining women said the same, and all agreed it was good.

"For the sound of weeping all the time is a dreary thing," they said. Two only would not let their women go, and these came with us. One never became cheerful though the other, after weeping many tears became a merry little thing and said one day that she was glad to have left Aday.

"For they were a morose company, my mother, father, brothers and sisters, as like to eat porridge only, drink water and talk of the leaking roof, as to joke as we do and drink wine."

Thus I saved many women from being abducted unjustly but made heavy promise of which I was daily reminded by many men. To myself I thought that in extremity of failure, I could leave the ship on a sudden and hide on the shore, or threaten to slay one or two if their complaints were too loud and insistent.

Yet on the ship many of the women who had wished to come made pretense of their anger at being stolen from their homes, because as they told me, they could by this means ever after persuade their men to do their bidding to make up for this deed, and they seldom ceased from complaining and demanding. And though some men were well pleased with their women, others wore a look of unease and often told one another what a good thing it was to have a woman at last, while looking eagerly for land. Perhaps they hoped to excuse themselves from their women and the company on shore, and on pretext of going to fetch wine, tobacco or other item, make escape and settle down in some land where they would be at peace again.

The whole aspect of Windwolf changed from that time, because once accustomed to their new home, the women were not at all satisfied with it and began to pay great attention to things that had gone unheeded before. The deck had to be cleaned, the cabins also. There had to be a place for washing and drying clothes, and below deck by ropes and canes they made for each couple a form of bedroom where they might copulate with some privacy, though Fidzer and I, who often drank and talked late on deck, heard all manner of strange sounds coming from below. Sometimes it would be like a struggle with grunting, panting and heavy thumps. At others like a rhythmic dance wherein the woman let forth piteous sighs at each measure. And Ooman's woman made a sound like a cat may do when it invites a fight with another.

All this I liked not, for a ramshuner is not a ramshuner when he sails on a ship full of chattering women; though I am a woman myself, I still say this. And whereas before I had been a center of attention, now I was but a freak again. And the women made sport of me, calling me "the ogress" and "Thundermouth" for my great size and deep voice. The woman of Conderan especially led them in this, for she always feared Conderan loved me, but he did not and allowed her rudeness, which is a measure of the shallow nature of men. Ooman's woman, however, who was younger even than I, and plump and red-haired, was not inclined to follow the others, and I struck up a friendship with her. She would sit listening as I taught Ooman to read, and being young and alert, she got the way of it. And later in the voyage I was glad of her, because I became ill with a great evil and lost much blood and would not eat of the usual food of the ship, which was biscuits and salt meat, from weakness. And in this time she looked after me as Wanin would have, and prepared food that I could eat, and kept my deckhouse clean and the clothes I wore. And though Fidzer would have helped me, if I needed it, but at such times another woman is a much better thing. She was always asking about the ways of Odon, and whether Ooman would have land. When I told her of the dreary and sanctimonious atmosphere, she pulled a long face.

"I shall not like it in Odon, for I hate somber people." She had picked up a deal of the Odon tongue in the month we had been at sea, for neither she nor any of the women had had a word of it before. It was a great surprise to me how quickly they all got hold of it. Women seem more adaptable than men to me, and to see the ease with which they had all settled to the ways of the ship was proof of it.

Windwolf made slow going, always with the oars, around the coast of Aday, then along the shore of Bhoumer,* the Sacred Land, because we could not sail in open waters for the icebergs that were floating south in the spring. And as we

* See glossary

were in the ship seven weeks, those who had no women were longer deprived, so they became less pleased with me. When I was ill, some left me alone but not all. And as I lay there, I considered how I might satisfy them, as the ship pitched and tossed and I rolled from side to side, not strong enough even to hold fast in my hammock. I could hear the pleasant sounds of men and women jesting and the cries of the gulls that followed Windwolf, but for me it was no longer as it had been.

It got warmer and warmer as the spring approached and as we were headed south, and I was able to come on deck again and take my seat beside Fidzer. When we reached the part where the sea became blue and the shore white and gold, I wished that we might land, since I am of the south and it was a homely sight to me after the northern winter. We had rowed nearly fifteen hundred miles now and would soon begin to sail across the Zoic sea in these sub-tropical waters. All sweated at their oars, and the women who had angered me before, now did good service, shading the rowers, bringing water and always good humored, since they liked the sunny climate, the like of which they had not seen. Some discarded many garments and lay in the sun, that they might have the novelty of seeing their skin turn brown. But the captain made them cease this, since their flesh made men slack at their oars, forever peering at the breasts, thighs or ass of some woman that they thought with optimism they would see. And many of the women, being pale creatures of the dark north, turned a bright red in the sun, like the crabs we boiled, and were in pain, which made me laugh. I am a white-skinned woman, as I have said, but of a southern kind whose skin turns a golden brown and makes me beautiful in the eyes of others, and I had no trouble with the ever brighter sun.

On the equinox, we held a great feast in the ship, and drank our fill all night, waiting to sing the welcoming song for the new coming of the sun, as he rose crimson in the east. This song is similar over all the north lands, Bergia, North Rainland and all Hyperborea, and we took each a partner in the singing, for the woman must be the earth who calls back her lover who is the sun, and he answers, and thus it goes until the real sun rises. From far places where the sun never shines in the winter this song has come, and thus we know, all the peoples of the north, that we are brothers. Even so I hate the Bunnish and am not partial to Shambi nor Sunedin.

But Namzen, Weltan, Morton, Odon and all the Rainish folk are my kin.

I was partner to the captain in the song, which was an honor for me, and for him also. My voice being so deep added a pleasant sound to the women's voices, and being moved by simple things, I felt tears in my eyes when our entreaties brought up the sun, and with it a myriad birds and butterflies. And at this time, those men who had no women felt their plight most strongly, so I hammered my brain to think of a solution, which I did. For I remembered a book I had seen about offices where women went to find husbands in the empire, where there were often a greater number of women than men. And I knew that the coast near where we now sailed was an imperial domain, for Meon had taught me the use of maps, and because we often saw the beautiful imperial galleons like birds floating on the breeze. And also because the captain told us it was so. I made as if it had been always my plan to be revealed on equinox and spoke suddenly in portentous manner.

"Now we must enter port, and there I will find women for Jujak and the other men who lack women." The group all cheered loudly and began capering about the deck, talking of the fine women they were to have, but the captain was not pleased with me.

"Why did you not say this when we were beside Wtodan which is the only port nearby? Now we must row back again; otherwise I intended to find water near here, then strike across the ocean. Did you not know of Wtodan?"

"I did not," I said, following the Way though I was tempted to lie.

"So much then for the great education of which you tell us so frequently," he said, which was an utter falsehood, for I had told them but once, or at most not above three times, and then only because it was necessary for one reason or another. But I answered calmly.

"Let us then put ashore and take on water with all speed, and I will pull at my oars the harder to aid those who must row only because of my error."*

---

*The naive pride with which Cheon always recounts what she calls her "fair speech," suggests that she did not always speak so, when aroused. And indeed a courtier who met Cheon later has the following to say about a somewhat bawdier form of communication.

"When king Umkrun asked Cheon how she would repay him for returning the lands north of the Eltiping river (which she had forced out of him in any case), she

We put ashore in a bay amid barren rocks of palest gray and beach white as chalk. The sea was calm and blue and the tide was low, leaving a great flat plain of wet sands with tranquil pools in which creatures swam idly around, little knowing that their home was drying up. The party of us who were to land waded through the white breakers which rolled over onto the shore, dragging the boat which bore our water tank. On the shore I threw myself down and lay on the warm sand and others did likewise. Those who suppose that ramshuners be fiends not men would scarce believe the peace that came upon us on that balmy day. But it was soon interrupted, for suddenly we heard shouts and a scream cut short from over the dunes.

We leapt to our feet, swords in hand and made up toward whence the sounds came. But barely were we halfway when several of the party appeared running for their lives, as fast as men can run, faces overcome with terror. There was not long to wonder at what had put them to flight, since but twenty meters behind came a terrible set of beings, green demons ten feet in height or more. They were not all of a kind, as I saw even in so short a time, for the larger and darker green had flatter faces with straighter backs, and of the ten demons, eight were of this kind, and terrible though they looked, as will be related, they were not to be feared. But two others were quite different, with pale green skins with bold patterns of black and gold, and great green tooth-filled maws, one still filled with blood from poor Fentid who had been bitten in twain. And they ran with forward inclination and very quickly, for though their hind legs on which they stood moved less

made a great belch, for she was able to produce them at will, and sounded it under his very nose. And not satisfied with this, she went on: "My gratitude runs over and would speak for itself," and puked stale wine upon him, for this too she had the knack of."

This sounds a less than courteous way of conducting delicate diplomacy. But more amusing is the account which has come to scholars, it is said from the daughter of one of the women who sailed in Windwolf.

"After the captain scolded Cheon, she shouted that he should find the new women himself unless he wished to 'lie with Jujak and Jujak be agreeable.' Then she sat angrily in the stern and no one dared speak to her, until Fidzer took her a mug of beer."

In fairness it should be said that all sources are agreed that she was generally a fair-minded and ladylike speaker, preferring to calm troubled waters. But she had a quick and fierce temper especially when she was young, and even though she was often ashamed later, she could not always control it.

quickly than the ramshuners' legs, yet by the great length of their strides, they were quickly overhauling them, and all had large tails held out behind.

And my heart did leap with fear when I saw that one had singled out Conderan for its prey and was gaining rapidly even as its comrade seized Huzen, a man as great as Conderan, in the white surf. Huzen swung with his sword, but the creature's hands lifted him, and though the sword crashed against the bony skull it made little impression. Then the demon bit off Huzen's head, and spat it into the foam which turned red, and hurled his body like a doll's high in the air where it spun to earth still spurting blood. Why the creature was so angered I could not guess, but I had no time to wonder, for I did not want that Conderan be slain.

I strung my bow and fired an arrow into the demon's neck, which it did not like, for it stopped and turned to see who had so challenged it, and Conderan made a great distance from it, and speedily he did it. But the demon saw me and began to run toward me, fearing not my arrows, which was stupid of it. For as it drew nearer, so I found it an easier target, and I pierced its eye with an arrow, which enraged it, so that it screeched. It came close to me, and I was sore afraid, feeling the ground shake with its weight. But its eye was greatly troubled, and it turned its other toward me, that it might see me better, and I shot an arrow straight into this good eye, blinding the creature.

And even as it blundered about, I fired an arrow at the other monster which was far distant. It turned and saw that we had wounded its comrade sore, and could not understand how we had done it. But it soon learned, for I loosed an arrow at its eye, which missed but stuck in its head near to it. Then it began to shout to the injured one in a strange voice, the like of which was not to be imagined until we heard it. But this too was a waste of its time, because I hit it twice more and found its neck, which made it screech, and it moved away, followed by its docile companions; and I shot at them also, since they had watched quite calmly as we were like to be killed one by one, and were therefore our enemies. They ran off with comical speed with arrows in their backs and tails, for I aimed at where their asses would have been, had they had them, but they did not or not ones that I could see.

We then attacked the creature that ran wildly around, un-

able to see. Its strength was fearsome, but we knew that it
could not see us, and thus we were emboldened to our task.
Even so, another man was badly hurt by a sweeping blow
from its tail, before our constant hacking and thrusting brought
it down and I could strike at its neck. I severed the head and
kept it for my trophy. Then we returned cautiously to the
dunes, and saw that over their top was a village of sorts, made
up of holes where these creatures spent their nights. But they
were afraid of us now, and as soon as we appeared they fled
away across the barren sand, calling to one another in their
weird voices. We used their well to get water, and after, we
fouled it so that they were even more punished for their
evil-doing.

At the time, only *I* believed them to be beings as we are,
who can speak and act in cooperation, but later we found that
I was right. They were reptiles who had lived in that land
since the land itself was young, and who could speak and
make plans like men. But they are stupid, and not able to
discover even the simplest things for themselves. They cannot
make fires, they cannot make ships nor weapons, and they
cannot make houses to live in, only scoop out holes in the
sand. Yet they can speak to one another, and can understand
the speech of men, if taught. And they can cooperate and help
each other. All this I heard after in Wtodan. There are two
kinds who live always together. Those of the dark green type
who eat only leaves and those of the pale-green-patterned
type who eat meat, even men if they can get them. And worst
of all, they eat the dark green kind, so that in exchange for
protecting these docile ones, they also eat them, which is an
abomination in my sight.

This incident had a great result, because the place where
we landed was part of the empire, and since the weakening of
the imperial armies, these fierce reptile-men had been used to
defend the shore from ramshuners. The Asg had among them
men who could speak with these reptiles, and they had in-
duced them to attack any who came from the sea. This could
not be achieved by any pact or exchange, since the reptiles
could not grasp such an idea. Only they had been told that
those who came from the sea were bad people who wanted to
eat them all, and in their simplicity they believed them and
attacked all such people with a terrible ferocity, thinking that
they must kill them as quickly as possible. As it happened, no
invader had ever been able to slay a reptile before this, and

therefore it was a terrifying thing for them when I did. Thus the reptiles left the shore and went into the desert, telling their fellows that men had come from the sea who had killed and eaten their companion, for they could only imagine that we ate it after blinding it. When this news spread, the reptiles emigrated from the shore where the Asg had persuaded them to go, and went to live in the desert. And after this, many ramshuners came to land there, and settlements were set up of fishermen and hunters of lizards. And the Asg could not dislodge them, for the desert was difficult to traverse, and by sea the ramshuners were usually victorious in battle, since the empire would send no help from the Old Lands. So in killing that reptile, I began the process which separated the imperial domains in Bhoumer to two parts.

This was not a good thing, though I did not slay the beast for that purpose, but to save Conderan of Emden who did not, as I hoped, praise me loudly before his woman on account of my courage and skill. In the boat there was great sadness, since both the slain warriors were good shipmates and also they had brought women from Aday who were now alone and mourned pathetically. I said nothing to them, because I knew not what could be said to cheer them. All my life I had been alone as they now, but this was not a time to speak of that.

XVIII

The entrance to Wtodan was a sight to stir the memory of all of a life. The town was built all of white stones which seemed glazed, so shiny they were. The harbor was made of two arms with castles on each, carved in intricate detail, so that they seemed like porcelain. And in the center of the wide bay was a great statue, made also from the shining white stone, many hundred of feet in height, of the great palm of Truth. And along the jetties were moored ships of the empire in myriad numbers with sails of every color of the rainbow, and with brightly painted and finely carved hulls and superstructure. And all around the jetties, were Asg and Rainish folk who busied themselves about the ships, with great flowing robes predominantly white, but of other colors too, so that it was like a painting with so many hues against a sky blue as skystone. From the sea, the city made a scene like the paradise pictures I had seen in Odon, a great hill of beauty filled with trees and parks.

And there was such an atmosphere of peace and love, that we, ramshuners though we were, fell silent so that only the splash of our oars was heard mingling with the melodious voices of the folk in the harbor, on that hot spring afternoon. I saw at once why Wanin could not rest until she had returned to her beloved empire.

"What a city to plunder!" came the voice of one more foolish than the rest.

"Speak not of such a thing, for this is the sacred land," said one of the women.

"Sacred or no, it is made of marble and gold which could be carried away," he said.

"And we are made of flesh and blood which may be spilt," I said, and pointed to the four imperial triremes which moved slowly beside us, filled with Rainish warriors.

"I only say that it would be a rich fruit to pluck, were it possible," the man repeated, but his new woman silenced him.

"So may a stupid maggot speak of a jewel in the emperor's crown which he takes for a fruit. But if the emperor sees him, he will be flattened, so he best hold his tongue."

Yet I know by sorcery that one day Wtodan will fall to the Hyperboreans, though it will rise again in the distant future.

I left my oar and ran to the prow where Megridon stood, and I raised my arm in a gesture of peace to the Asg triremes' captains. And by waves from them and the rowers, I knew that they understood. And I shouted, loudly as I am able, to the nearest which was but three oarlengths distant, in Asg speech.

"Mtona bni, Mtona nimba. Mtona bni, Mtona ikani-namdi," which meant: "We come in peace. We come to barter. We come in peace, we come in small number." For their speech is a rhythmic thing wherein one must repeat often to give a poetry to the sound, and I have been well taught by Meon who said that I had a gift for language, poetry and speech which conveyed meaning well.

"Come then in peace, but let only few leave the ship, and without armor or weapons. For your kind are habitual drunkards and troublemakers, even when they think themselves to be coming in peace. We are not patient latterly with ignorant men who, seeing much that they do not understand, fall to noisy laughter and boisterous pranks."

"He speaks insolently," said Megridon for my ear alone. "But since we are greatly outnumbered we must accept his authority, if we mean to continue."

"We shall do as you say, ship captain," I said. "Though it would be more noble to await our foolishness before speaking of it so freely. It is my intention to find a number of women who will take husbands among this crew, for we have nine men who have been disappointed in some earlier negotiations." I spoke not of the violent form of the earlier negotiations, for I did not wish to aggravate the unease which we caused, though probably they cared little for the defeat of one set of barbarians by another, if it was outside the imperial borders.

We rowed on in silence, our men saying little in the face of the Asg's inhospitality, which did them credit. We passed several smaller statues set on the rocks, which were near to the surface of the sea. One, a great olligan with Asg rider, we were close enough to see in detail. It was old and dilapidated with no trace of any attempt to refurbish it.

"This is a sign of the imperial sickness," said Conderan. "And wherever one goes in the empire or these paradoxical republics, it is the same story of degeneration and the approach of ruins. Were it not so, the Odon would yet shiver in the northern forests and pray to the spirit that dwells in the Voshr, that he holds his ground."

"It is not so in the Old Lands," said Fidzer. "For I have seen them."

When we moored at a jetty, we had to speak with the representative of the mayor of the city, who waited with a huge contingent of soldiers. It was agreed that we could go ashore in a party of a dozen, but that we should be immediately arrested if we behaved as vandals, and the ship made forfeit until we paid a large sum of money. Yet all could see the town and spend money if they wished, by going ashore by turns. I was to be in each party, since I was a Companion of the Empire, having been born in Wnai and having the imperial mark on my hand, which cannot be forged nor obliterated.

As we were not familiar with this city nor any so big, we

set out with a guide—a Beldan* who are the true inhabitants of Bhoumer. He was a small, dark, wiry man, helpful but asking often for money which he said was needed as some form of bribe. We first went to a shop to buy clothes, for I wished that the men appear civilized and not rough. And as they were overawed by so much power and glory, they were easily persuaded and they strutted naively around in the fine costumes we bought. Each wore a color suited to his personality and looks. And we visited also a bath house, where they were attended on by servants who shaved them and cut their hair. I was amazed to see how good a figure they made, shaved, trimmed, washed and well dressed. Jujak and Andible especially were like young gods, fresh from the Minden Voshr, where the northern gods are thought to dwell. Fidzer though was the most surprising by far. In a lavender costume he seemed like a true Beldan, an artist perhaps or scholar. And when they saw how fine they looked, they wished to behave well also, for they were like children, open to any suggestion, and I had told them that only imperial seeming men could hope for women.

"You must not bellow for wine," I said when we sat at a tavern. "But wait until a server comes, which she will. And you must not drink from the flask, but from the glass, and not too quickly or in too great a quantity. And because of this I shall be responsible for pouring your wine, where I can ration it, to your advantage."

Of course they were not really like to men of the empire, doing many things which distinguished them from the citizens of Wtodan, belching and breaking wind, discussing too loudly the personalities and physical attributes of the women they were to have, or those they said they had known before, though in this they mostly lied, judging by the preposterous tales they told.

"Shall I have a black woman?" said Andible. "Who may perhaps have a greater ass than a white, if my eyes have not deceived me. And it will make a change to tell truth, for I have bedded only with white-skinned women, in great numbers in the town of Drandain, where I lived before I was a ramshuner. There, I was in great favor with all the women of the town, for I piss farther than any man, a thing which women all prize, as they do a man who can bite open a

sweetnut without using the pincers, as I can, even if it be
fully black.''

"And I can juggle three duodecahedrons and can read the
time from the clock in Shawi, and these are skills beyond
combat which Cheon says is not enough to win women.''

I did not ridicule their mistaken boasts, for they had known
so few women that they had but little idea of what pleased
them, and spoke in hope more than belief. But I counseled
them.

"Your skills are not to be boasted of, but talk of the
beauties of the woman to whom you speak. Speak soft and
politely, do not mention her ass, bosoms nor any unseen part
of her. Look into her eyes and tell her that you wish to go
with her all through the world, until you find a land of your
own where she can be queen and you king. And if she seems
even a little interested, then carry on with ever greater look of
love . . . like this.'' And I took Fidzer so that all could see,
and made a face of love which I knew from books and which
was comical, I dare say, but which they all imitated eagerly.

"Maiden, though I be but a simple mariner from a land
over the sea and cannot hope to be as an Asg or High Beldan,
and can offer naught but material riches, a pleasant home and
the modest hope of lands won by my courage, yet I dare to
hope that one as beautiful as you might dignify my dukedom
as duchess, that we might bring the Truth of the south and the
burgeoning strength of the north together, in trust and love.''

"Unhand me, filthy scavenger of the sea,'' said Fidzer.
"For I detest the scent of stale smoked fish which ever
heralds the entrance of a ramshuner.'' All laughed at this, but
I gave each a speech to his taste, which might move a maiden
of Belda.

We walked through the city until we reached a great mansion where the guide led us to the gardens. A woman approached and seeing us, spoke.

"What can I do to serve you, good people?''

"We are ramshuners who wish to find wives in civilized
fashion, having spurned many chances to seize women by
force,'' I said.

"I take it you yourself do not seek a wife, seeing that you
appear to be a woman, and seeing that it is customary even in
these times for a woman to take a husband rather than a
wife,'' she replied. "And in that I can serve you too, if you
will.''

"No, I am not looking for a husband. Rather let us meet some women who might not be afraid of traveling to a distant land on a ramshuner ship called Windwolf. You can see for yourself that these men are no ordinary barbarians, but men with the will to learn a higher way of life. Is this not true?" I turned to the men, and by a sign of my face made them all bow as they had been shown.

"Yes, Cheon, it is as true as the return of the sun," they said in moderate and restrained tones. The woman who was not young, nearer her middle life, yet comely enough, looked at the men.

"It is as you say, though they are still barbarians by any measure." She looked long at each. "Yet they are fine men with some spirit about them not often seen in Belda now," she said. At this, the man who held himself an expert juggler produced the duodecahedrons that he had meant to use in wooing his choice. Fortunately Fidzer took them away and spoke quickly.

"A custom of Odon, whence we come, where a bride-groom symbolically hands over his dice as a renunciation of the frivolous pursuits of a single man," he said. When the man made to argue, Jujak, who was quick of thought, bade him keep silent.

"For the woman is not to be made to wait on us so long," he added.

"I shall send out messages to bring many women here that may be bold enough for this strange purpose. Meanwhile wait on the terrace and rest, taking fruit juices or wine in the shade of these cypress trees." she said.

"Not wine, I think." I said, and added hastily. "For it is the custom in Odon whence we come, to await ladies before drinking wine." The woman looked at me.

"Many are the customs of Odon whence you come."

"Many indeed." I said.

"Come with me, woman, for life here is somewhat dull now, and you are an unusual seeming person who may, in exchange for my hospitality, bring a diversion to me." She led me to the house, where by the use of strange pulleys and ropes, she did send the messages of which she spoke. For on the roof of each important house was a great system of wooden arms which could be set into certain positions which could have certain meanings, and thus messages could be sent over long distances by relays from high places. She told me the name of this system and it was called telegraph.

Then she took me to a dimly lit room, where water ran always into a bath, cool and sweet. "Bathe here while we talk, if you will," she said.

It was not easy to undress before her, but I did, since I wanted the cool water on my body. When I was in there, she gave me a cool drink made of aromatic fruit with ice, which she must have got by sorcery in that climate.

"Tell me then, woman of Odon, what is your story?"

"First, I am not of Odon, but Weltan."

"A place of which I never heard tell."

"It is in Wnai."

"Ah, poor Wnai! . . ." A cloud passed her face. Then I told her from the day of my birth till the arrival at Wtodan what had befallen me. And she laughed loud at some of the things, and at others she fell silent, and her eyes widened. At the last she shook her head.

"You are a woman of Vortex, the god of unrest," she said. "And you will ever be. And you are strange also in your preference for women, though such a thing is not unheard of in Wtodan either. And tell me, pray, since you look for women, am I pleasing to your eye? For although I am not myself able to imagine taking pleasure from a woman, yet I am mightily curious to know if I, old as I am, can still please a woman who loves women."

I lay back with my hair flowing out into the water.

"My inclinations are not to be exposed for idle curiosity. For those who wish for my love, there is an end to curiosity. But for those like you, men's playthings, there is none." I answered thus, for I do not like to be treated as a freak whose desires are to be measured and recorded. She smiled.

"You are young and proud. But you are also marked by Cheeroneer, for it was him you saw in your fight with the wrestler. And he can only appear to us in some other guise than his own, which is too terrible to see. And he has some dark purpose for you—so take care, woman of Weltanland!"

I had never heard of Cheeroneer, so I asked her, "Who is this Cheeroneer? Some fell demon of the ice?"

"There are no demons of the ice, fair giantess. They are foolish tales dreamed up in the ignorant discomfort of the northern winter. Nor are there any true gods, save Cheeroneer.

And he sees all that happens in the world, and he has seen you, and seen that you are a wonder of the world, for though you are a woman, you are greater than men in combat, yet with the mind of a woman and the body of a woman. And he has some purpose which he will show you in due course. And as I am a sorceress, so I feel a great power within you, and I feel the great purpose that he has. And it is an evil purpose, Cheon, beautiful dealer of death. Though you be not evil, yet evil you will do.''

And she spoke truth, those who read, since I have done the greatest deed of evil in all time and all space, yet I still live, and I am not evil.

"You are a sorceress then?" I said, surprised that she would speak of it, if it were so.

"Yes, and I know that you are also, though of little power as yet. But come with me to my chamber of sorcery, and let us try to see what will be the great evil which I feel in you. Dry yourself and with the towel about you, come through to the inner sanctum, where we can burn the necessary herbs.''

I wore the towel like a short robe, and we entered her tiny witch-house.

"None save other sorceresses know of this room, Cheon, for we live in troubled times and such knowledge is to be imparted only with caution.''

It was completely dark save for a window whose glass was azure blue, casting a cool and evocative light in the room. She too undressed, and we did certain things which are necessary for sorcery, which are not told. Neither must I say in what manner the herbs were burned or by what means we inhaled their smoke. Nor how we did obeisance side by side and naked to the presence which came, for it sounds a foolish thing when spoken of outside the potent aromas and mystic light of a witch-house. Then we lay in strange stupor on our bellies, only hearing the deep sighing breath of the other, as our minds floated clear of our bodies.

Then I was in a dark palace in the presence of a goddess who sat on a great throne of crystal, which was in a vault higher than the ordinary sky, with stars and nebulae twinkling more brilliantly than can be imagined without seeing. And all about the room was gossamer and foliage and running water and small tame beasts. And She who sat on the throne looked at me, and I looked at Her, and I wept because Her face was more beautiful than the starry vault where She sat. And Her eyes were glowing with a light that was like to be truth so strong it took real form.

"Come close, Cheon, for is it not just that I should see her who will slay me?"

I went closer, trying to speak.

"I shall not slay you but serve you in all things, and my life be forfeit now, if it be your will," I said.

"Nay, my life be forfeit, not yours. But there is time yet to live and love."

I stood now before Her, and Her strength poured over me like the music of a waterfall in the time of rains.

"Who be you but the true god?" I asked.

"I am not the true god, Cheon, nor Cheeroneer nor the Ice-King, for each being dwells in the sphere of some greater. Some call me the Great Spider, and others the Witch-Queen, still others the Goddess. But who be you, who comes thus in spirit to see her prey?"

"I be Cheon of Weltanland," I answered. She looked long at me, till my body trembled from Her silence. Then She spoke.

"You are a great monstress, Cheon, for in all the worlds that I have seen, I never saw a woman made like you. It is a sure thing that, as I manipulate the universe with my web, so some greater being has made you for his purpose. Yet a turn of the crystal will show all differently, like a game of chance wherein you be but the result of a throw of some mighty duodecahedrons, wherein each face shows a palm leaf against all odds. And you will slay me, and my body will fall as lifeless as that of a bird shot down by an arrow, and for many hundred years none will come to take my place. And if I could, I would escape that fate and be instead of the Great Spider, some simple girl in some far land, for no life is given willingly. But die I must."

"I will not slay you, though I die for refusing," I said, weeping. She laughed then.

"You speak so nobly, great child, yet slay me you will. Forgive my laughter, for I cannot contemplate you without merriment, even though you be my doom. For your voice is so deep, yet it is a woman's. And your body is so great, yet it is a woman's, and you weep like a woman, as if a leaping cat were to squeak like a mouse."

Then I lay again beside the woman of the marriage office, and I was not weeping and she too was again conscious. She looked at me and her eyes were wide.

"What say you, Cheon?" she asked.

"I saw a goddess," I said, "who said I should slay her. What saw you?"

"Naught but blood and a demon with your face. Yet you are not a demon."

"I am not and I shall not slay Her, so Her prophecy is wrong, and She be not called a goddess, but a queen only, though of great beauty," I said.

XIX

Later the women who thought to see what kind of husbands the ramshuners might make appeared dressed in their finery. In truth they were not great beauties, and it was for this reason that they had to make use of the office. And perhaps they had been here on many occasions only to be disappointed. But they had for the most part good-humored faces, and the manner of women who would accept a rough and ready existence in the hope of better things to come. And the men of Windwolf who were not accustomed to the arts of make-up could scarce believe their fortune, since they took them as the finest fruits of the empire. Had they been captured women, no doubt many would have been raped on the spot or carried off to the ship. But because the ramshuners knew that these women would come by choice or not at all, they were silent and bashful, not knowing how to begin a conversation. So I went to one woman—the least good-looking and not exceptional for her youth either—and led her forward.

"Are you then brave enough to go with these rovers of the sea? They are fine men all and have but little time for the niceties of courtship, since they are eager to buy lands with the prize of their campaign. But you seem the rarest prize to me, and must have first choice among them before your friends.''

"I am brave enough certainly. Yet these men seem tongue-tied and awkward, not what we expected for ramshuners.''

No doubt she had hoped for a desperate assault, and she now contemplated the suitor she might have between her thighs that very night.

"I think you are wasted here, for I know that the captain would take you if he were here, and bid you wait while I fetch him,'' I said.

"No,'' cried several men. "These women are for us, not him.''

"Aye.'' said Andible. "But may we not see her stripped of her garment? For we are making a decision of importance and must see all.'' I made as if to be greatly shocked.

"These are ladies, not tavern wenches to flaunt bosom and buttocks for your satisfaction. You must forgive these men, for they are of red blood and little schooled in courtly manners. You would, of course, not dream of exposing your naked body to that man's lustful gaze?'' I added the last with a slight hint of a question.

"Why . . . no, I would not . . . not wish to do that . . .'' she said in comical pretense that the idea had not sent hot liquid to her loins.

"You may see nothing but her legs,'' I said, and turned to her saying: "With your permission,'' and raised her dress very high, so that I could see her hairy thatch, as I knelt, though the men could not. She had, as I had suspected, a comely pair of calves and full sensual thighs. Andible and the others looked eagerly, making complimentary remarks.

"I like this woman,'' said Andible. "I am of a mind to choose her if I be to her taste.''

"What say you?'' I asked the woman. "And what be your name?''

"I am called Camden, and I like this man well enough by appearance and speech.''

Thus I saw that the first bond was to be struck and saw a chance to amuse myself.

"Of course, so that Andible who is a shrewd man, be satisfied of his side of the bargain, I shall assure myself that your body is all that a woman's should be. As I am a woman, so you will not object.''And I ran both hands under Camden's robe, feeling all her flesh. I grasped and stroked her hot fat buttocks, and took the breasts, one in each hand, feeling great hardened and swollen nipples, for she was in full heat. And between her thighs I kneaded her sex which felt like a putrid mango with a cleft in it.

"You are not wanting in any respect," I said, as she breathed heavily with anticipation and the animal pleasure of the rubbing on her, who perhaps had not lately felt such a sensation, though she was no maid, as I had made sure.

"Let us then be married, right speedily, if that is the law of this country," said Andible. And by the offices of some official who was in the mansion, they were married. Since Andible could not read, I had to read for him, and let him make his mark where a literate man must have signed his name. It was the usual custom to have a great ceremony and feast at such a time, but I told the woman of the office that it would be better not to have such a time-wasting function, nor run risk of the men becoming drunk and causing trouble. And the bride and groom were in a great hurry to get to the consummation chamber and did not care to wait.

"And after, we can go to see my mother who yet lives . . ." said Camden as her hips twitched with impatience. And they went up the stairs in an unseemly hurry, and though I have no proof, I warrant that whatever Andible did, he did it soon enough for him and too soon for her. But they remained in the chamber, and no doubt she brought him back to life for a more leisurely combat more to her taste.

By the time I had made a check upon the essential aspects all of the merchandise, and the couples were all ensconced in their consummation chambers, I was in a fiery state of lust. And since Fidzer too was not immune to the effects of seeing so much furtive groping, we went together to find a brothel of which there are many in Wtodan. We bid the woman let the men be kept in the mansion until we returned to take them to the ship.

"Let us take our pleasure together," said Fidzer. "For I have never seen woman love woman. And I believe it would add much pleasure to the act, if I could see you in your ecstasy."

To this I agreed, for when I am in lust, my pleasures are often in the way of watching others copulate, and of knowing that others' eyes are upon me as I writhe naked and desperate.

"But perhaps we shall not find strumpets who will agree to

lie with us, if we are not shielded from each other's sight,'' I said.

"We shall have whatever we wish," said Fidzer, ''since we have much money. And as your desires, as you have told me, are for lecherous women who enjoy acts of lust, we shall go to the Sounding Sea, for the guide told me of this place. Here women too come for satisfaction, because in the empire there are many women who cannot find husbands, and others who have them but are not satisfied. And both men and women pay a sum of money to the management, that they may use the brothel to meet partners and lie with them.'' And this we did. And we found satisfaction, as I shall recount.

The brothel was a great lake on which barges floated, surrounded by tables and chairs where the guests sat, having paid a large sum of money to do so. They then had to find their own partners, and no claim could be made against the brothel-keeper if they found none, but they could stay until the morning if they wished. And there were several young men and girls in the employ of the brothel, who were to make up the numbers if either sex was too greatly preponderant. Here we sat and looked around till we saw two women at a table, one a black Asg, tall and slim though with large womanly parts. The other was a squat creature with rough face yet sensual and wicked eyes ready for any perversion.

"These seem a possibility," said Fidzer. "For they sit close, and the short one's hand often rests on the belly of the Asg. They may be pleased to attend to your furrow.''

"Let us approach." As we went to them, both looked up with lecherous smiles, not the least surprised by my sex.

"We wonder if you two might join us on a barge," said Fidzer. "For we are looking for adventurous partners, and we are much attracted to you. Cheon is a lover of women, as you may guess.''

"Why not, Knilmon?'' said the Asg.

"I agree. What of you, woman? You are a veritable freak in size, but if you have a snatch, I shall find it without the help of an atlas.''

"You will not need to go looking for it," I said, pleased with her brothel-speech, ''since it lurks in the shadows waiting to seize a woman like you, and having drowned her, devour her.''

Both laughed at this, and we entered a barge which an

attendant pushed into the middle of the lake. Among the rich tapestries and hangings we made a great battle, all four. Fidzer began quickly with the small creature, and I and the Asg watched, for we were of like mind; our sexes were twitching with excitement, yet since we knew they would have their fill, we did not hurry, but rather increased their hunger by what we saw. We each slid a hand on the other's hot flesh, and did nothing more than look at one another when we felt a great contracting or pouting. The other two rolled over and over, sometimes near, sometimes far, having no regard for us, so great was their sensation. I liked best to see the woman on top, when her white ass would pump like a sail oscillating in a gale. She was never satisfied, and having made Fidzer give his first energy, she turned to me and she and the Asg tore off my garment, and it pleased them to discuss my body.

"Why, she is like an olligan, so big are her thighs. And what is this that seems like a quagmire in the forests of Whynne?" And this talk, though vulgar, excited me at that time, though I cannot tell why.

Then they fell to licking my body with their lewd tongues, the Asg at the upper part of me, the little fiend of lust at the other, where she was not afraid to forage in the quagmire of which she had spoken. Fidzer watched, his face curious, and knew that he was adding one more experience to his memory, of when he saw the three women engaging one another with their tongues, because I did likewise to the Asg. It was not long before my strangled scream proclaimed my satisfaction. Then Fidzer took again the little she-devil, he being not lacking in stamina. I satisfied the Asg, and for a while we lay in an embrace, for thus do women feel inclined after their climax. But we watched in admiration as Fidzer served his partner.

It is a strange thing that in those days, though I was as now stronger than all other people, yet in this matter of sex I had no greater energy than many others, and had less than some, like this furious creature who seemed to gain in the ferocity of her desire. I watched her twisted feature as, like a suffering animal, she twisted and convulsed with the intensity of her sensations. As I am a giantess of physical strength, so she was a giantess of sexual energy, and drew Fidzer's sting again. And in turn we satisfied her again with fingers, lips and tongue, and still she was not quenched. At the end, we did what was necessary with a big candle which we extinguished, and at last we made her quiet. Then I lay with the Asg, and Fidzer went to smoke his pipe and drink wine in the small cabin to the fore. As the virago slept, I spoke with the black Asg.

"Have you enjoyed your visit to this brothel?"

"Truly I have. For though you are greater than a Namzen berserker, yet you are gentle and know the way of love with a woman. And though Knilmon likes a style of love more like battle, I like well enough your way, soft and kind."

"Do you then love with Knilmon?"

"No, before tonight I never loved with a woman. But I will do it again if the chance comes."

I looked often at her black face, for it was pleasing to the eye, and it roused a great curiosity in me. For the Asg are like no other people and seem to know some secret of which they do not speak, but which renders all the world an irony, and all other folk fools. Even though the Hyperborean star rises to the ascendant, yet still the Asg see us as but children.

"What is this secret of the Asg, black beauty, that we can never know? Tell me now, and I will forget again, and none other shall know. For I have given you pleasure tonight and you may tell me this in return."

"Have I not given you pleasure, white barbarian?"

"You speak true. Then let us exchange secrets. I shall tell you the secret of the white peoples, you tell me that of the black?"

She laughed, her lids lazy, and massaged the great muscles in my back

"The white race has no secret, or if it has—and I make the suggestion from politeness between peoples, tell it first, that I may be proved wrong."

I laughed and felt her hands upon my neck.

"You speak true again. We have no secret but a pugnacious nature and a thirst for riches."

"Yet perhaps you have some secret. For you are a preposterous creation. Here is the neck of a leaping cat, with muscles like taut leather thongs, and the rest of your body to match, even though it be made round by womanly fat. Are you thus from sorcery? Or did you grow like this, only as one tree may outgrow all the others of the forest?"

"In truth, I know not. For I asked it as a gift from a sorceress when I was but a child and she granted it. Yet she was a Kariasg, and by the mockery in her eyes and what I have thought since, I know that she cast no spell. For I know now that even as I asked, I was the greatest child of thirteen winters who ever trod the earth."

"So it may have been. But let me tell you, Cheon, not the secret of the black Asg, nor yet the white barbarians', but the secret of one such as you. It is that those things that happen by the greatest improbability and most unpredictable chance are at one, and at the same time, the things of greatest design and flawless purpose. And that is your secret. And you are both an enchantment and a fortuitous freak."

And that Asg, strumpet though she was, spoke the greatest truth of my life. And it is the way of even the simplest and least elevated Asg to speak truths which we can never find, who are not Asg.

We lay thus speaking until near morning when we left the barge and ate a hearty meal as the sun rose over the lake, and with many other tired pleasure-seekers around. And on the return to the ship, Fidzer told me a curious and incredible thing, that the small woman whose name was Knilmon was the priestess of a college of chastity, wherein men and women spent periods abstaining from any intercourse in order to reveal to them the Eyes of Truth, which were said to be blinded by lust. And as I was utterly incredulous of this, we visited the college a few days later. But it was true, and she delivered a fine lecture to a great many serious people who wore robes of chastity.

". . . If you will only allow it, by rejecting your lust, Truth will enter your bodies, as it has entered mine," she said in a bold zealous voice.

"Followed, it may happen, by a candle and the great palm tree itself." Fidzer said to me in a voice loud enough to anger the collegians, who bade us leave, which we did.

I debated with him why she could speak such hypocritical falsehoods, but we could never agree. Fidzer said it was because she gained her power from the college of chastity, though she could not suppress her nature. But I thought she gained sensual pleasure by the very outrageousness of her hypocrisy.

We remained many days in Wtodan, for all the crew

wished to see such a large imperial city. And though they
would have liked better to enter as conquerors, they neverthe-
less eagerly visited its gardens, taverns, brothels and markets,
wasting large sums of money on foolish purchases, because
they knew not the value of things, and were too easily
tempted by bright colors and glittering glass. Despite the
agreement that I should accompany all of them, I did not, for
there is something shameful in walking with rude and ignorant sailors in a city of civilized people. And though I am also
a barbarian, for so the Weltan are called, I am much more
cultivated than they. Therefore I and Fidzer ever parted from
the expectant groups at a tavern near the sea, where we told
them to meet us again at some simply determined time, such
as dawn or dusk. Then we went our own way, speaking often
of the chance to live in such a place, as Fidzer looked at it
ever more longingly, for he was made for the delights of the
south.

"Why, for you, Cheon, it is a simple thing. You have the
mark of a Companion and by this you may go to the Old
Lands, where the cities are even more splendid. And there
you may easily take service with the Hyperborean Guard, or
some other group, and live all your days in comfort and
splendor."

"Yet I wish to see many lands before I come to live in one
place. And I am to be queen in the north, by prophecy."

"Perhaps being queen in the north is not such a fine thing
as to be an ordinary citizen in the south. For in the south one
may see a hundred beautiful women in an afternoon stroll
. . . See there!" He pointed to a group of girls who played
with pet dogs under a tree of orange blossom in the gardens
where we sat. "Each one is a paragon of beauty to my eye. In
the north are hard-faced, frost-bitten creatures with colorless
hair, who be either maids guarded by jealous brothers or
wives hidden away and obliged to wear shrouds lest any see
their beauty and steal them. And the only other kind of
women are harlots or dirty grease-covered tavern wenches. To
enjoy one is to struggle with a bacon joint fresh fallen from
the frying pan."

I seized him then in pretended jest, though I was not
pleased by this speech which was an insult to me.

"Which kind then be I? Frostbitten maid or scullion ready
to lard you with my greasy body? Speak, else you will have

your wish never more to leave the empire, be your life ever
so short.''

"Why, you are none of these, Cheon, for there are too
princesses, and queens in the north, and you are one of these
who escaped my mind. But no ordinary man can hope for one
of these, of course.''

"Indeed he cannot,'' I said, leaving hold of him. "And
likely enough he will obtain only such favors as he pays for,
even in such a woman-infested city as this.''

Though I visited several brothels, sometimes alone, sometimes with Fidzer, I did not find so great pleasure as I had
with Ocea nor with the Asg. And I began to yearn again for
some girl like Wanin to be ever at my side, as she had been.
And in this town there were many such, always with pleasant
families, handsome male companions or with foolish friends.
And when any looked at me, it was only for amazement at
my freakishness. Once, in walking along the great thorough-
fare of the town, I saw a long switch of dark hair that bobbed
and weaved before me like a fisherman's fly, till I could bear
it no longer and seized it. But the girl turned fearfully and
called to passersby.

"There is a barbarian woman, like an olligan, who has
caught me. Help! Fetch the watch!'' So I let her be, for I had
not hurt her, so soft I had been.

"Get on your way, little fat goose, for I took your plait
only in sport, since you wave it about so much,'' I said. She
looked at me then for a moment, then gave a merry laugh and
ran down into a narrow way full of shops.

Before we left Wtodan, I and Fidzer went to see a drama in
which actors pretend to be people who they are not, and
quarrel and make speeches as if some event were happening
which it is not. It was amusing to see it, as the women wore
very pretty costumes, which showed most of their bodies. But
halfway through the performance there was a great disturbance in front of us. On the stage, one who played the part of
an evil man who had slain his brother was denying his guilt.
And it happened that two of our crew with their women of
Aday had come also to see the drama. And one of them,
Haden, stood suddenly and shouted to the man on the stage:

"You speak false, for I saw you do the deed with my own
eyes, and so did many who are here. Is it not so?'' He turned
to the audience, who hushed him, but he would not cease.

For he believed that all that happened on the stage was real, and he wished for justice to be done.

"If none other will aid me, I shall slay you myself. For I am a man of Odon, a witness to Truth." Many people spoke behind and before him.

"Be silent, for we wish to enjoy the play," they said, and he turned, confused.

"It is not right to stand by and watch such knavish deeds," he mumbled, yet sat. The woman who was with him well saw that the play was a pretense, but it amused her to see Haden's behavior. Probably she was bored, since she could not understand Moshan, as all the Odon did. As the play continued, the unfortunate actor committed a further deed to stir Haden's anger, when he obtained the favors of the heroine by a series of lies. At that time, I too was unused to plays, so I could understand why Haden behaved so. He leaped to his feet and pushed his way to the stage, jumping on it. He had no sword, since we carried no weapons, and was as near drunk as makes no difference. He seized the actor and hissed to the woman.

"Do not listen to these lies, for he slew him who was to be your husband, who was his own brother."

At this point I and Fidzer left the hall of the performance and went laughing to a tavern where we ordered a great flagon of wine to be put before us, and we drank it all amid the scents of a refined southern town on a spring evening. Then we saw the priestess again leading her followers along the street, so that Fidzer called to her.

"Priestess, come here, since I would speak with you and will leave on the morrow."

She turned and bade her followers proceed to whatever foolishness she had planned. Then she came to where we were. And Fidzer immediately spoke words that amazed me.

"What say you to being my wife, who am rich, clean, lusty and yet of better intelligence than any other ramshuner? And of greater strength and power in battle than the enfeebled creatures who dwell here?"

"Do not speak of it, insolent baboon. I am the high priestess of chastity and have much work to do in this city. And were I to choose a husband, it would not be an evil marine-smelling oaf, who knows naught but thrusting oars and swords, unless it be how many bones he must offer to some preposterous god in the arctic night."

"I know of thrusting other things," said Fidzer. "Why not a candle, say."

"Keep closed your foul mouth. Those called to greatness are often those most sorely tried by nature."

"Speak not so fierce, small priestess. Drink with us now, since tomorrow we will be gone from Bhoumer."

She calmed. "Why not? You are interesting folk—though rough and crude."

I called for another goblet and filled it with wine. But she drank only a little and spat it out, screeching to the server.

"What is this piss you have served these visitors? In the land of Truth, do we steal from strangers? If he brings not a better vintage, good Cheon, take him and drown him in one of his wine barrels, and I will justify the deed to the watch."

"That is not necessary," said the Beldan server, a dark youth with olive skin and brown eyes. "It was the orders of the tavern-keeper, but I shall disobey him and bring you the best." He went off and returned with another flagon even larger than the first, and Knilmon poured us each a goblet.

"You shall learn what it is to drink the wine of Bhoumer, ramshuners. Here, drink . . ."

I tasted mine and I liked it well, for it was like the summer sun of Weltan with the rains of autumn all of a piece. And we passed the rest of the evening drinking there. We called the server and I made him sit upon my knees, so that I was not without a partner, for Fidzer and the priestess soon fell to intimate caresses, even while she droned with words of chastity. I caressed the serving youth and asked him of his home, and whether he had laid a woman, and he told me of his few conquests. But he liked well to sit upon me and some woman-ish side of his nature gained the ascendant, so that I fondled him and he giggled like a young girl. It was the first time I willingly touched the hidden weapon of a man. And I felt my power waxing by this reversal of roles. The priestess being so small could not hold her wine and passed out at last. When she had, I let the server go. We sat silent for some time.

"Do you really wish to take this woman for a wife, Fidzer?" I asked.

"Yes, I do. Because she is all that I could ask in woman. Lusty, civilized, with spirit and cantankerousness. For it will be my pleasure to defeat her with words and to enjoy her body even as I do. And as a priestess, she must be a mistress of sorcery, which will be a great advantage in the land I hope to have. And since it is to be in the south, which I like well, it may as well be here, or the Old Lands, and therefore a woman of the empire is my choice.''

"So be it. And your mockery of the other men for their desire of women before riches was but a pretense.''

"Not so. It was not until I beheld this priestess that I thought thus. I spoke true of the thoughts I had then.''

"Let us then carry her to the ship and take her with us when we leave.''

"Nay. I can have her by fairer means. Wake her if you can, Cheon, and let us see.''

I rocked her and poured on her a magic potion which I had in my pouch, brought to deal with drunk ramshuners, and she woke.

"Come then, priestess, bid farewell, since if you will not take me for husband, I must leave now.''

"Take you for husband? I would sooner marry Mathemus the Great Reptile, who lifts the great loads from the merchandise cart at my house.''

"Then so be it,'' said Fidzer. "And good riddance to you, pestilent harlot!'' The priestess looked at me with an amused expression.

"If you speak with such silver voice, how shall I refuse? Let us then go to the office to wed this morning. But you must take the vow of chastity and become the high priest of chastity from the far north. Though I shall exempt you at certain times,'' she added, again looking at me.

Thus it came that Fidzer never left Wtodan, which was an unhappy thing for me. Drunk as we were, we staggered to the office of marriage and the deed was done. As often happens, this bond made in a miasma of alcohol at short notice was a lasting one, for I saw the priestess again many years after, and Fidzer too in Wtodan. And they had many children, and Fidzer spent his days as he had ever wanted, sitting on a terrace overlooking the blue southern sea, drinking wine and telling the bold deeds of his ramshuner days to all who would listen.

But Windwolf was lonely for me with Fidzer gone, and we went more slowly for the slain men's absence and his. I am a woman often sad for those gone for any reason, and it was many weeks before I was cheerful again.

XX

As we rowed east, I became again sick though from a different cause, mayhap some southern fever I got in Wtodan. And I was melancholic too and at night I had dreams which troubled me. All the ship was a merry place with the new women always keeping lively and teaching the Moshan language to those of Aday, that they might be understood in many lands. "For though you are of the distant north," they said, "your men may take lands or service in a more southerly region, where this language is spoken." But I sat moody at my oar, left out of the celebrations, with no Fidzer to speak with, Conderan besotted with his shrewish wife who bore malice to me, and now the captain spent his time with Conderan too, because she was always fair-spoken to him and encouraged him to sit with them when he was idle.

"Why do you look so over the blue waters, Cheon?" asked Ooman's little ginger girl who still favored me. "Your eyes are so hollow, and your hair wild and unkempt."

"It is nothing, a passing melancholy, that is all. Go about your business, I am better alone," I replied. Thus I spoke even to her.

One night I slept badly for thinking of Fidzer and his new wife happy in their civilized home. I dreamed it was I who dwelt there, and the priestess was my wife, then after she was Fidzer and I was she, and I was always arguing with him, and my head was a buzz of meaningless complex thoughts. I woke up and went out of my deck house, where I still had my berth. I sat in my oar and the lookout saw me but said nothing. The cool wind blew on my face, so that I felt better. And I looked at the moonlit ocean and saw distantly a great disturbance of the waters. I turned to the lookout, but he saw it not and gazed beyond it. Yet over the waters a woman came to me, large and with blue fire around her. She was like to the woman who I saw in the witch-house, yet I knew it was not she. For I could not look at that woman without trembling, whereas this one I looked at without emotion. And when she spoke, her voice was not like the voice of that woman.

"Cheon, come soon to do your work, for I weary of eternity."

"Who be you?" I asked, for now she was beside the ship, striding on the water.

"She whom you love, Cheon."

"You are not, for She makes me weep, and you do not."

"It is because you do not do your work that my radiance no longer bathes you."

"It is not. You are not She, and I know it. You are some evil water spirit come for a soul, whether mine or another's, I know not. But I see even now that you lose your form."

For the woman dissolved and descended until she was but a strange creature that emerged from the dark water. Part fish, part frog, part monkey, it had great eyes like eggs of pale green with brown yolks. And bubbles were around it, and many gases escaped from the water near it, long gray streamers also filled with bubbles. And about its head more bubbles grew, great congeries which becoming round parted from it and flew away. And its head had a high crest of spines with a bubble at the end of each. And as it spoke, so bubbles gurgled in its throat and emerged like fireflies in the moonlight. And it spoke now in its own voice, which was like the sea itself.

"You see me as I am, Cheon, a thing few ever have or will. For I am Cheeroneer, god of all things, who dwells in the abyss."

Now I was afraid for I saw that he was Cheeroneer, and that real or not he might slay me there as I sat.

"What would you with me, god of the waters and lands? I am but a woman, lonely and lost."

"You are the chosen one, Cheon. You are soon to do the deed that will dim the stars of the galaxy by its brightness."

"I shall not slay Her, for She is good."

"She is not as you saw her, Cheon. She is the Great Spider who sits bloated with the substance of a trillion beings at the center of her great web, which shivers at each breath, to bring her swinging through the filaments to suck blood."

"She is not, and I shall not slay Her, for it would be an evil deed."

"What is evil, Cheon? Good is but the will of one god, evil the will of another. And all men do the bidding of gods, so all are good or evil. But the gods do not speak of good and evil when they speak out of the hearing of men, for they know what is the Truth."

"And I know also of the Truth and that Truth is good and falsehood evil."

"Truth is not good or evil, Cheon, it is above them."

"If you say that good is but the will of one god, say you not that Truth be but the word of one god, and falsehood the word of his enemy? May not your words be neither true nor false?"

"Truth is not the word of any god, Cheon, nor is any god's word the Truth. Soon you will know what is your destiny. Yet I come not to tell of that but warn your life shall be in danger. Look to the north, for lurking close are the Black Death who have followed your ship from Shawi."

"Who be the Black Death? And since I see them not, how can they be so close?"

"Ask not. Do what I say, if you value your life and those of your shipmates." And as he spoke, Cheeroneer dissolved into a swirl of bubbles. And I scanned the horizon but saw no mast.

I know now who are the Black Death—mad Asg who attack on the sea in the night, for they have lost homes and riches to the ramshuners or other Hyperborean invaders, and because of this they hate them. And they follow by means of magic eyes which see not the ship but the heat of the bodies in the ship. These eyes they have had since the Old Times, when they received them from the Old Ones. And they swallow a drug like to mblobe, yet different because it makes each a fearless and berserk warrior.

I still stayed upon the deck, which was a good fortune, since an hour after, I caught sight of the Black Death of which Cheeroneer had spoken. It was low on the horizon, but I watched long enough to realize that it was coming up with great speed. The lookout was dozing drunkenly at his post, so I began to ring the bell, and gradually men came on deck, sleepy and staggering.

"What ails you, mad Cheon?" they asked. "Can you not settle in your berth but must wake all?"

"Look, yonder, fools! Here comes a great ship which I

have been warned of. It bears death." And all looked at the ship which was now much closer. And as they ran to collect weapons and armor, I went to the prow with my bow. The captain ordered that we unfurl sail and fly, which was a wise thing to do, since we were only half awake and had women aboard, and the Asg ship was greater by far. But it was of no avail, for the Black Death closed ever more rapidly, and we knew that it was our lives or theirs.

As it approached, we heard the drums of the Asg in insane rhythm and loudness, which disheartened our crew, for they echoed with the very wrath of those who beat them out. The ship's sails were all of black with no banner or insignia. And then the Asg appeared, clamoring like devils along the gunwale, waiting to grapple. Men who are usually brave are often less so when lately wakened. On all faces save Conderan's, I saw fear, and this was worse as the women came on deck though they were told to remain below. And now we heard the chants as well as the drums.

"Death is coming—Death is coming—Blood of the north— To grow pale in the sea."

"None ever survive a visit of the Black Death," said one old warrior. "We are doomed men. The riches and women which we have won will never profit us now. It is as the Lord Paten says."

"I shall survive," I claimed. "And if Lord Paten says I shall not, he lies, and his name of lord of Truth be itself a lie." But few were cheered by my words. And I went to the stern and stood where I could see now the white teeth of the mad Asg in the moonlight. Then I drew my bow and began shooting the grinning faces.

"Blood of the south shall be the breakfast of all the fish of the sea!" I shouted, but my voice was answered by high-pitched yells and curses of eager men who were not cowed by the deaths I brought to their number.

Now the ship loomed over us and I watched in fascination as they grappled us by cunning irons at their lower deck, which opened in the side. Then like a plague of black demons, they poured upon us from all sides, their faces set in convulsed smiles, foam at their lips. And like demons they fought. Our force was swept back and half a dozen of us were slain at the first assault. Whenever we killed them, so they threw themselves at that place and drove us back. But I was in the mood to kill or die. All the anger I felt for Conderan, Fidzer and Wanin was inside me, and I liked the feel of my sword as I hacked and thrust. The Black Asg saw how I slew them, for all my experience of two great battles and many single combats came to my aid, and my great strength never failed me. A sudden thrust . . . thus for Fidzer, whose friendship was worth naught but the ass of a dwarf priestess. And an Asg laughed no more. A great sweep . . . thus for Conderan whose love was worth naught but a cold north maiden with icicle for tongue. An Asg's head flew, its eyes yet staring with mad hatred. A mighty hack . . . thus for Wanin, and thus, and thus, and thus. For she whom I loved, loved me not, only yearned for a soft bed and glittering jewels. And an Asg already twice dead died again. And still greater came my anger, rising like the howling wind from Minden Voshr.

"Die, filth!" I shouted, and like a whirlwind advanced into the thickest throng of the black drug-frenzied warriors. "Die all demons, for I slay gods and men with equal hand. Thus dies the Lord Paten with sword in his throat . . . and you, you be Cheeroneer who thinks to use me like a doll . . . die then, bubble god from the deep . . . now hold fast, Ice-King, for you too shall die . . . ah . . . thus, your crown falls with your head. Now die all, since I have lived without love, thus shall all die . . . Another Ice-King? Another Paten? What is this but sorcery? Yet greater than sorcery be my power, for I am come on the fiery dawn. . . ." My voice was now a scream with words that were in my head but could not be understood from my voice. "Die, Ice-King, and die again if need!" And thus I went on in a frenzy the like of which I never knew before. Again I slew the Ice-King, and again Lord Paten, again I killed those who had wounded me. Then on a sudden:

"What, is this the true god Paten, for your skin is white, and by my power you have let down your disguise as black Asg? . . . Now die too!"

"Nay, Cheon, he is a ramshuner." I heard Conderan's voice at my ear and held my arm aloft. For I was frenzied but not mad. And I saw then the true case.

The deck was piled high with bodies and parts of bodies, and blood swilled around three inches deep because of the blocked scuppers. No sound now of drum or Asg, and the black ship was sailing away, those in it were its crew who had remained sober and were afraid now in their turn, having seen the slaughter I had wrought. I lowered my sword and sank to the deck. Around me in a circle all those remaining stood silent and awed, men and women alike. And suddenly one, Andible it was, sank to his knees, head bowed.

"Tell us thy bidding, Cheon, for thou art not woman but goddess who cannot be slain." Immediately many did likewise. I looked at them and anger was in my heart again. So eager are men to make gods and goddesses, yet so feeble in honoring friendships.

"And if I bid you to jump over the side, that my sister the Sea be propitiated, what then, fools?" They said nothing. "I am not goddess but woman, and want not worship but wine and bread, that I may regain my strength."

One of the women then spoke. "You are woman, Cheon, but not woman as we are, who wait in fear at such a time."

"And you are not man as we are," said the captain. "For though we fight as bravely as we can, yet there is no likeness to you, as we have seen. By some reason you are not as we, and as we know of only ordinary men and women, so this man thinks you goddess. But I know that you have been sick, that you weep like a woman and yearn for love, as other women do. So you are woman, and this we must believe. But though any man or woman here lives to be a hundred years, he shall never see the like of what you have done this night. For you have slain more than fifty men, and saved our lives, who were driven back in fear, so that we waited only for death. And we were given back our courage, so that we aided you and have slain the grinning Asg to the last man. And because of this, the ship will never more be called Windwolf, but Dawnwind after you, Cheon of Weltanland, bringer of dawn. And at its prow I shall put a carven likeness of your fell head, as it was in this battle tonight, to go ever before us, whether you sail with us or not."

I was moved by this honor but did not wish to appear so, and therefore I said:

"Put my ass on the ship prow if it pleases you, but bring me wine, else I die now of thirst." This brought laughter and a better atmosphere to the vessel.

As I drank direct from a wineskin held to my lips by the ginger-haired girl, the other women took off my armor and gave succor to my wounds, which were many but not deep.

They pleased themselves too, by looking and touching parts that were no concern of theirs, to see if I was indeed a woman like them, which they had long wondered.

"She be woman just as I," said one, "though she has some parts so large, none but an olligan would dare venture there."

"Hold your peace, insolent creature, lest I tear your garments from you and beat your fat ass." This made them more circumspect in their talk. But I spoke only in jest, since I would not have harmed them, sluts though they were for the most part.

The Asg corpses were thrown over the side, a job which took longer than the making of them. Our warriors—thirteen of them—who had died were launched in a funeral boat which went toward the rising sun as it slowly sank. Their women of but a few months wept and cursed the day they had set foot in Dawnwind.

"Fear not." the captain told them. "There are many rich men in Odon who will be pleased of wives in that woman-starved land."

"Do not speak of us as if we are cattle to be sold to any who wish for them," said one widow. "We are women who must find husbands whom we love, and that is not like to happen so soon."

"Live then like priestesses, you have much money which is yours from your dead men, since you have not sons," said the captain.

"There are some of us who will have sons or daughters ere long," she replied. "And then we will be in distress."

"Because you are with children does not mean you will bear them," said I cruelly, but none spoke after. And Conderan looked away at the distant horizon. The dawn had come and we sat in a bloody ship where many human parts still lay, hands and pieces of scalp which could be seen when the sun rose. And while they were thrown over the side, Conderan called out:

"Land, yonder! An unknown land!" And truly we were near land, which we knew by navigation was one of the islands of the Zoic sea.

"Let us land here and repair the damage done to our ship by the great ram of the Black Death," said the captain, and this we did.

I felt now disgust in my arms, for slaying men is the work of evil, and though the cause may be good, the deed is not. And I knew that many hearts were stilled forever by my sword, many voices would never whisper again in loved ones' ears, many eyes would never again open to the blue sky and songs of birds, because of my deeds. Thus I allowed the women to dress me as they wished, in white silk like a great doll to amuse them, for they were simple creatures who forgot the blood more quickly than the most hardened warrior, though they had screamed the loudest at its spilling.

We beached the ship, and those who were skilled in carpentry got to work on the smashed wood. Others, with me and many of the women, wandered inland over green grass which grew everywhere. There were no trees by the shore, but farther in, protected by great rocks, there were flat meadows flanked by forests. We saw no men, only sea birds and animals of common sort which looked at us from afar, showing they had seen men if we could not. It was mid-summer and many flowers blossomed in these meadows, which pleased the women who bedecked themselves with them, and so cunning they were that each seemed a princess when she had finished.

I sat alone amid tall grasses, and watched those insects which spent their days going from one bloom to another. And I said to myself: This place is a peaceful and pleasant one—a demi-paradise. Yet if I were to stay here to have peace now all my days, it would soon be a center of war, sorcery, lust and jealousy, for these things all follow me, as if I were a mother-duck and they my ducklings. Therefore I shall not stay but enjoy this moment, for it is a gentle time, following that fearful battle in the night.

As if some god of trouble had overheard my words and planned to cut short my rest, I suddenly discerned distant shouts. I got up and went into a wood from where the sound came. But I was too late to see what occurred, for I heard a great scream and a cheer from voices I knew. And I came out into a clearing to see that a man, Ruthzen, had slain a woman of middle-age, dark-skinned whose hair was shot with gray. She lay stabbed to the heart upon the mossy ground before an ancient tower whose door was open.

"What has happened?" I asked. "Why has this poor woman been slain?"

"She is no poor woman, she is a sorceress who came in the guise of a demon," said Ruthzen. "And I slew her even as she was yet in the likeness, for she was very evil, as all saw." The other men and women nodded and murmured agreement.

"A demon thus she seemed."

I guessed the truth, that the sorceress had been visited by ramshuners before and used some art to put them to flight. And now she had appeared in some magic guise to do the same, but our victory over the dark forces of the night had given the crew confidence, and thus had the poor woman died, her sorcery of no avail.

"This is a bad thing," I said. But as I spoke, so another demon emerged from the door, a terrible one, red and black, with eyes like ice-holes and teeth of a leaping cat. And I thought it real for a moment. But Ruthzen—no doubt wishing for the title of demon slayer—strode forward with his sword at the ready, and the demon seemed to waver. And I rubbed my eyes till I saw her, the sorceress who made the appearance. Not sixteen summers she seemed, thin and unwomanly and quaking with fear. Her eyes were red with tears and her hands, in which she held her incense burner, shook like leaves. Yet she tried to concentrate on her task of frightening the men. But Ruthzen was bold and he raised his sword to stab.

"No!" I shouted. "This is a deed that shall stain us all." Ruthzen heeded me not, but I am not one of words only, and I ran between him and the girl, whom all save me still saw as demon. "Stop your sorcery, I will not harm you," I said to her. "Nor let others harm you." But she was afraid and trusted me not.

"Stand aside, Cheon," said the ambitious Ruthzen. "For I would do this deed, whether you wish it or not."

"You will not. She is but a child who shakes with fear."

"It is a demon which tricks you, but not me. Stand aside, for I am armed and you are not, and I would not harm you unless you force it."

"If you raise sword against me, Ruthzen, from your base ambition, I will kill you with bare hands alone, which will be no shame to me."

"Then let it be!" said Ruthzen. Yet before he could speak the demon vanished, and the little sorceress ran to me, so light and feeble that I lifted her with but a casual gesture of one hand.

"Save me, great woman, for my mother is slain, and though she told me to die before yielding, I am afraid."

"Yield not and die not, for though I am of these rovers of the sea, I shall not allow any to harm you, thin sorceress." And I looked to the others. "Begone, bloody butchers, for you have slain this child's mother who has only adopted demon guise to drive you from their tower. Now she is motherless and guilt is on all." They walked away, shamefaced, and I stayed with the sorceress. And she sat weeping while I buried her mother and marked the place with a branch cut to the shape of a palm leaf.

"How long dwelt you here with your mother?" I asked.

"All my days," she said.

"What will you do now?"

"I will live, I suppose, since none has slain me yet," she replied, anger in her voice.

"None will slay you. But will you stay here, where all will remind you of your old life, sad and lonely?"

"I have no place to go, nor any way to earn my food."

"Come then with me as my servant, and I will feed you, clothe you and protect you, for I am the greatest warrior of the north."

"But you are a woman and wear no armor."

"I wear armor all the time except this day when I have many wounds from a battle in the night against black devils."

"But I wish to be servant only to a sorceress, so that I can become one."

"I too am a sorceress, though with but little experience, and we can advance together in that knowledge."

"Then I will be your servant. For I have no mother now, and need someone who will look after me."

"So be it. And we will make love together, because that is the way of sorceresses," I said, wishing to begin with no pretense. She said nothing but looked away, her brown face becoming an orange color. "Gather then your things and let us leave this place where gloom prevails."

Soon we walked together down to the ship, I carrying her great wooden chest which she had filled. She would not look at the others of the ship, but only at me, for she held them murderers. We entered my deck house, and there she stayed nightly until we sailed. I set her to tidy it and scrub it and sent her to fetch food. Those things that passed between us ever after are not to be described, for they add nothing to my tale; but how they began is an interesting thing and worthy of recounting to arouse the sexual appetites. For I lusted after this girl as soon as I saw her.

She had a long beautiful face with hair as black as mine and brown skin. She wore a blue shift from neck to calf and her hair had a ribbon in it. For the first night she lay on the floor, but I had two of the youths make me a great bed wherein one lay in the usual place and the other across the foot, and thus she was to lie, for it is the correct way for a witchling to lie with her witch, which I was. I spoke nothing to her until the third evening when we were to put to sea the following day. She had just returned from taking my dirty plates to wash.

"Servant, stand before me, for I would now examine you to see that you are all that you should be, clean and of right mind. What be your name, thin witchling?"

She stood before me as I lay insolently on my bed.

"I am called Mtamuru, mistress."

"This name is not easy for my lips to speak, and I shall shorten it to Muru, which is anyway more fitting for a small humble creature who scrubs floors, than that word you uttered."

"So be it, madam." She spoke always so, though sometimes with a surly air as now.

"Now, Muru, take off that blue shift and let me see what kind of woman you are, who is so proud of her great name."

She looked sulky and pouted up her lips, but with a little grunt of annoyance she unfastened it and slid it to the ground. Yet beneath she was not naked as I expected, for she had on the tiny breeches that Asg and Kariasg women wear always for fear of their skirts blowing up, and showing their sex to strangers.

"Take off these ridiculous breeches also, since I wish to see you naked."

She was red in her face now.

"I will not. It is unseemly for they cover my private parts."

"I know what they cover, little fool, for I am a woman like you. But either you will take them off or I will, take your choice."

"I won't. And neither will you." She had barely finished when I picked her up like a baby and peeled the breeches off her cringing flesh. She squealed and I set her down naked as she was. She was a woman, I saw now, not a child. For though they were small flat hills, yet she had breasts with great flat brown nipples, like copper coins. And she had a tuft of long and unruly hair on her sex which grew too on her thighs, as such hair does on some women. Her buttocks were grown fat also and she had a womanly shape when naked, if very slender.

"So there you are, proud creature, you can hide nothing that I wish to see. Your breasts are but parodies of their real nature, but you have the same shrub between your thighs as any woman and your ass grows fat like a woman's." I sniffed the air and turned her in an insulting pirouette, by her ear. "You smell sweet enough, which not all girls do when naked. You are so far satisfactory. But there is more . . ." I opened her mouth and looked at her teeth. "You have dirty teeth, which I shall show you how to clean." I looked in her ears. "They are dirty in depth, you must wash them."

She said nothing, being very docile now. I said no more then, and it was not until we were at sea the next evening that I seduced her into my lustful ways. Then I called her again and made to examine her, this time as she lay on the bed. She kept her thighs tightly closed, knees together, for she felt vulnerable and wanted to protect the soft flesh between them, but this was my target, for my lust had become urgent.

"Your bosoms are not so bad as was said yesterday," I said softly, touching her great flat nipple. "For many women would love such nipples as these." I stroked it now, very gently for I knew what pleasure such a movement could bring.

"Is it so?" she asked.

"Yes. Why, they are very beautiful, I see now." I stroked and caressed, and the nipple grew suddenly pointed and swollen under my fingers and the other also grew like a little mountain.

"Such a pleasant thing it is to caress such a breast!" I said. She looked ever down, her eyes not meeting mine. Then I spoke.

"I must see now that you are well formed in your womanly

part, for if I am now your mistress I must look to your interest, must I not?''

She nodded but made no move, so I parted her thighs as wide as could be, and there nestled her sex, orange and shining with wetness on it, which she did not realize.

"It seems well formed," I said and moved my finger along her thighs, back and forward till I finally ran it along her slit from back to front, so that she squirmed with the intense sensation of it. Then I closed again her thighs, leaving her in want, before she had a chance to begin questioning the right of it.

"Yes, Muru, you are a well-formed woman, fit to serve me.''

She did not speak and her cheeks were flushed, eyes misty, for she was a woman of great sensuality.

"Now you must treat my wounds in the manner of a sorceress. For I am in need of some relief from the pain of them.''

Sorceresses cure wounds with the tongue, and so she knew that I meant her to lick my wounds. I too undressed, for I like to be naked with my servants, and I lay on the bed. At first she was nervous and only tentative, but soon like a dog she was licking my back and arms and I felt her breath on my body. And she did not stop for many minutes till all my body where there were cuts and bruises had felt her tongue and was wet with her saliva. There were no wounds on my breasts sadly, so they were still dry with great swelled nipples like volcanos before eruption. She sat up.

"I have finished now, mistress." She squatted beside my shoulder and looked at me to see what I could say.

"Why, you have not finished, for there is a great wound which you have missed." I said. She looked at me, puzzled.

"No, I have done all, I am sure.''

"What, look! Down here." I guided her a little till she knelt facing away on all fours so that her buttocks were near to my face. Her head was over my sex and I felt her breath on it.

"Do you not see?" I asked.

"No, there is no wound . . . Oh! . . ." Her voice changed for she saw now exactly what I meant, for I showed her.

"That is not a wound," she said. "For it pains you not, you did not get it by a fight and it will not be cured by my tongue.''

"It pains me greatly, for it is in a fever, and I got it in a fight, for is not one's change from child to adult a fight? And it will be cured by your tongue, as I know well, and you will see."

She giggled and still made to move. But because of our positions I could treat her wound which was always pleasure to me, so I spoke.

"You too have a wound, Muru, and is this not a good cure?"

She murmured a word of pleasure, and then we began our lovemaking in the way which must be evident to the reader. Thus did I at last make love for which I made no payment, and the return to Shawi passed in a haze of joy to me. All knew of our deeds, for we were not silent, but naught was said for fear of my wrath. But at last I needed no longer listen jealously to the sounds of pleasure coming from below.

The affair with Muru was an unequal thing, for she was but a servant, and because she had but lately lost her mother, she was pleased to turn to me for love, even though it was of a different sort. Yet all must know that real love exists only when people of equal power come together, and so though I loved Muru well, yet it was but a phase in my life which passed soon enough.

XXI

I learned much of what Muru believed to be the true gods. There were no such principles as good and evil, she said, as Cheeroneer had told me, but only the will of the three gods who were the Spider, the Crab and the Scorpion—for Cheeroneer was not a god, nor was he in the power of gods. These deeds that we did together and which I have described and which I have done with harlots and even with Meon, are the will of the Spider. And when only two principles are allowed, the will of the Spider is said to be evil. But when three are allowed, it is not evil, nor good. And so it is with all deeds. And at the moment, she told me, all the gods were at war with the Spider, and she was called evil, and the other gods called themselves good and made their will the principle of good. But Cheeroneer's will was not known, and he did not openly call the Spider evil—for it is said that he feared it. And she told me that it was foretold that the Spider's star would soon set, though it would rise again many years ahead. She said too that the Crab's days were numbered, and it would soon pass away forever, so that for many years the Scorpion would hold power on all, save Cheeroneer.

She also spoke of other beings who perhaps were gods— the Worm and the Monkey—but of these she knew little. And gods like Paten, the Ice-King, the Snow-King and others were not real, as I had always believed, just the foolish fancies of savage men who must needs imagine all things caused by tyrannical kings like their own. Whether the Spider, the Crab, the Scorpion, the Worm or the Monkey really existed, I knew not, and though I had seen the Spider in a dream and Cheeroneer too, yet I still did not know whether they were dreams alone. For I am one who must see things clear and wakeful before she can know that they are real, though I do not dismiss them otherwise as fancies, rather as things uncertain.

When we reached Shawi, it was autumn again and we wandered the rain-soaked streets, Muru and I, as I showed her the first great town she had seen. She liked not the dirt and smell of Shawi, for she and her mother had been very clean and tidy people, and it was well that I am also very clean and wash often. There was in Shawi a fortress owned by those of the Watch of Truth, where great riches could be kept, and such was the strength of arms and reputation for battle of these men of Odon, that many let them keep their money, so that they might not be troubled by it. There were scribes who could issue each one with cunningly wrought bonds which could be exchanged for their gold and jewels when needed. The bonds were made from paper imported from the Old Lands, and inscribed by the most delicate work of artists, which could not be imitated, for each bond had its secret marks. And by this means was paper of little value exchanged for true riches. And these watchbonds were sought after by people as if they were money. But they were easier to carry and easier to hide, and if kept in oilskin pouches they could be held many years. Were Shawi to fall, it would be a black day for many who hold the watchbonds, since they would at once become truly worthless. All this was in imitation of similar fortresses in the Old Lands, who issued their own bonds called by different names. And a strange thing was that those fortresses in lands which had been attacked by Hyperboreans or seemed likely to be attacked, soon found that all their riches were reclaimed by their owners, because their bonds were dubious. And so that they might persuade the owners not to remove their riches, they offered them a greater number of bonds, so that they soon had too little true riches to pay all these bondholders, if it were necessary on a sudden. And because Shawi and Odon were so strong and had no fear of barbarian invasion—for they were held as barbarians—their bonds became to be prized ever more greatly by people from the empire or Odon or other lands. And because of this, they gave fewer and fewer bonds for the same riches, and so each bond became ever more prized. Thus do honesty and strength build nations in richness, and I hold it the reason why Odon seems ever to wax in strength and never wane, even though it be but a hundred and fifty years since it was naught but a rabble of invading warriors.

For some, this explanation must be tedious and dull—women especially, since they are usually shallow and interested in little but commonplace affairs of love and family life.* Therefore I would not have spoken of it, but it had a great importance for me, for I gave most of my riches for watchbonds, keeping only such money as I needed for day to day living. And because, as you will hear, I was unable to reclaim them for a long time, I found that they had increased in value by a great amount, which was a mystery to me at the time, though I understand these kinds of matters now, for I am well able to understand anything once it is explained to me.

In Shawi, came a great sadness to me when Conderan visited me, though he was at last without his frost maiden.

---

*Cheon often makes such insulting generalizations of her own sex, especially when they have recently frustrated her love of adulation, as Conderan's wife and the priestess did. In fairness she often speaks similarly disparagingly of men. And she sometimes gives women a much better report, calling them adaptable, loyal and civilized.

"I am shortly leaving Shawi and returning to Emden, where I have lands which are held for me by my brother," he said, having found me in a favorite tavern. We had walked out into the autumn rain to sit upon the quayside.

"That is good for you," I replied, coldly I must admit.

"I shall be sorry to leave you, Cheon, for I love thee well."

"Do not concern yourself, for you have your wife whom you must love better than any, and I am but little put out for your going." I spoke with less coldness, yet pretending that the incident was of little moment to me.

"Do not speak so, Cheon, for I know that you hold me guilty for taking a wife so soon after the battle of Daycalx." He looked ever out to sea, the fine rain making dewdrops all over his beard, and the late evening sun making his scars ruddy like fresh wounds.

"You speak as if mad! What does it signify to me, whom you take, or when?"

He began some reply, but I got up and returned to the tavern, wishing him a brief good-bye. This was because I was near to weeping and did not want him to see it. For it had been said between Conderan and I, that I should go with him to Emden as companion to see the castle and lands of which he often spoke, and he was to honor me at his table; but now he had gone off as if this had never been said, because *she* would not have it. In the tavern I called for wine, and before it came Conderan appeared, seeming ill-at-ease.

"It is by your doing, Cheon. You are not true in speech and are hypocrite. For you would not lie with me, yet you are angry for my marriage. And you are greatly jealous, yet you will not own it."

"Silence, great cloddish fool!" I shouted. "Else I slay you and send your white-worm woman to hell where she will be well placed."

Conderan's face flushed and I knew that I had spoken too great an affront, but I cared not.

"You have gone too far, for my wife is a kind and virtuous woman. Take back your words."

"Take them back? I shall add more, for she may be virtuous, and is not a turnip virtuous for it sins not? But she is not kind, except to you and those she wishes to profit by. And she is not beautiful. I had rather lie with a domiden's turd."

All in the tavern ran now to the door, stairs or other hiding places, for they knew that deeds must follow these words. Conderan drew his sword violently.

"Then you will lie with the many-legged beasts that go about their affairs on this tavern floor, Cheon." He swung his sword with great strength, but I parried his blow, and another, then by a trick Bonz had shown me, I made his sword fly from his hand, by the violence with which it glanced from mine.

"There! Now your woman shall not lie with you again!" I shouted and I spat at him. But instead of raising sword I fell to foolish weeping like a child. And he gathered his sword and stood, anger gone, awkward and ashamed.

"I have wronged thee, Cheon, which I now see. Thy words are but the pain that thou feelest, which thou canst not hide. It is better that I leave." And he went.

None spoke to me until later, when Megridon said with truth: "You are a divided being, Cheon. For you love men as well as women, yet like a cripple who cannot rise, who must ever watch others walk, so you can but look on as men and women make bonds of love."

After Conderan's going I wished to leave Shawi for many reasons. First I knew that the priests of Paten were scheming to have me imprisoned or to pay a great fine. Second, I wished to leave Muru, because she had become too attached to me, and though I tried to find other friends for her, she would not leave me. But I knew that if I went she would soon get over me, who was her second mother. Third I wished to see the Old Lands, which are the wonder of the world. And fourth, if I am to speak truth, I wanted to forget Dawnwind and all those who had sailed in it. It lay now in the harbor, being stocked for a new trip to the Isles of Rain where lands were promised by king Anderman, if he could have more aid against king Morden. The wooden likeness of my head was now mounted where ships have their emblem, and a striking thing it was, with great eyes that stared, bared teeth like a leaping cat, flared nostrils and my hair battle-waxed in death-spikes.

"It is well that I do not habitually look thus," I said to the captain. "Else I would frighten away the very sun as it rose."

"Yet it is a good likeness," he said. "For the sculptor has

an artist's intuition of your fearsome aspect in battle. And
thus I have seen you, and you are terrible and dreadful, and
may the gods never place us on opposite sides of the field!''

"I would not harm you. For did I not let Conderan go free,
even though he spoke foul words against me, all unprovoked,
and drew sword while I soothed with calm words?''

"So you have said, Cheon," he replied.

I went among the captains on the shore, asking for the
price of a passage to Babax, Cshuni, or any port in the Old
Lands, and would have soon settled on one, but things came
out differently. For one night in the tavern, a Kariasg approached me, a man of dark skin and black beard with the
green uniform of a sailor.

"Do I have the great honor to address the most famous
warrior of our age, Cheon of Weltanland, bringer of dawn?"
he said very politely with a kindly air and earnest eyes.

"Yes, Sir Kariasg, I am she."

"I have heard from some colleagues of mine that you
contemplate sailing for the Old Lands. May I ask if this is so,
though it is your affair, of course, and you need not answer to
me nor any man."

I felt a great pleasure in this man's address, because he
seemed to see my value more than Conderan or Fidzer had.

"Yes, I do contemplate it," I said.

"That is a good thing for the Old Lands, since you are as
beautiful as I have been led to believe, if not even more so.
But I must not say more, for it may be impolite to express
such admiration as I feel in its full measure."

"Why, thank you, Sir Kariasg," I answered, and I felt my
face hot.

"Let me then offer you at small cost a berth on my ship,
Sombalaman, which sails tomorrow. I hardly dare hope for
your acceptance, but if you give it, I shall scarce sleep tonight
at the prospect of such honor for Sombalaman."

I thought a little, not too long, for I had not heard such
pleasant words for many a day.

"What would the cost be, Sir Kariasg?"

"Why but two parts of one watchbond, which you may
obtain at the watchfortress."

"Two parts only? It is very cheap, is it not?"

"Let me confess, for honesty is a good thing between
shipmates, I intended to ask ten, yet now that I have seen

you, I am in a fire to see you clothed in the thin near nonexistent garments of the Old Lands. Of course, I know by your reputation that you lie with no man, but that can be borne since I am of an artistic nature, and much elevated by the perception, only, of beauty."

The idea of parading in light clothing before this man and others like him was by no means abhorrent to me, since, as I have said, I like eyes on my flesh. So I replied to him:

"I accept your offer, Kariasg, because I have taken a fancy to sailing with a man so well mannered and frank." Thus like a simple creature, all elated by a few praising words, I eagerly engaged myself to the chance of hearing more.

"Ah, what a delightful prospect!" he said. "Come then at noon tomorrow, and I will show you a well-appointed cabin where you will spend a month at leisure. And now, if you will permit me, I must return to my ship, fair daughter of Thanda." As he left, he turned again and gave me a yearning look of admiration.

"I look forward impatiently to the warmer climate of the tropics," he said, his eyes roving over me.

That night, I prepared a box of necessities for the trip and spent much time selecting dresses, of which I had many, mostly from Wtodan. I took some of fine though moderate cut, but two which I had not dared to wear, except in my room with Muru. One was completely transparent except where folds of material hid the hair of my sex, so that nipples, thighs and buttocks could be seen by any who wished it. The other was not transparent, yet from under the arm on each side was a slit which went to the calf, so that my whole nude body was visible from the side, nothing hidden if I stood in a certain manner, at front or rear. These I packed, thinking: "Though they seem impossible here in Shawi, in the Old Lands things may be different. And I may stand only momentarily in this or that manner, if I wish to try the effect with the appearance of an accident." In the light of what happened, this all appears now as a great foolishness, and the reader may laugh as much as she chooses at such a stupidity, especially if she has never thought such things herself.

When I told Muru of my intention, she was not so hysterical as I had expected, for she had made a great friend who was, like me, a lover of women, and though being painfully loyal to my caresses, she was in a fire for this other woman, who knew how to arouse her to a pitch of anticipation, as she was a sorceress like me. Yet she abused me and called me a fool.

"There are many pirates and other dishonest merchants here, I have heard. And this one is like to steal your money, rape you and throw you overboard."

"No man can rape me. And this one is no pirate but an Asg lord, whose simple word is worth the sworn oath of a hundred barbarian dukes," I replied, for my head was full of this fair spoken Kariasg, and I could think of nothing else.

"You are easily taken in, Cheon, for all your portentous speech and pompous ways. A great fool, I say."

For this I took off her gown and breeches by force and reddened her buttocks with my hand, till she cried, for I would not brook such insolence. When she had ceased, I made to begin a lovemaking, but she would not and left that evening, for her new mistress, who no doubt played her mandolin all night, till it was as red as her ass. This was perhaps a good leavetaking, since both felt righteous, and there was no guilt nor tears.

XXII

For a week I was uplifted as we sailed due south on ever bluer seas, the summer waxing again, instead of waning. And the lands I was to visit always haunted my imagination, all brilliantly colored and populated by Wanins and Shrufiks— for thus was the captain called. He attended me each day, and spoke civilly and politely, explaining the principles of navigation and seamanship, which he thought were new to me. And I pretended that I knew nothing of these matters, because it was a pleasant thing to have him often at my side, especially when I began to wear my southern garments. I played the cloth around my body, as I had often seen done by women, from tavern wenches to Asg ladies in Wtodan. Always he might see this or that, but never with certainty, and never for too long a time. And his eager eyes rewarded me, naive and foolish as I was.

I was surprised to be the only passenger of the ship, and I wondered at the roughness of the crew who were a mixture of Hyperboreans, Pharns and lowly kinds of Kariasg, perhaps with a mixture of the cruder northern blood. They seemed either too sullen or too knowing and free with smiles which seemed not given from kindness. But the captain and two officers made up for this, and I played the role of civilized lady for the first time with great pleasure, though I know now how many things I did, which betrayed my barbarian origins, and which must have caused them mirth.

Sombalaman was more beautiful by a hundred times than had been Dawnwind, covered as it was with skillful carvings and equipped with pink billowing sails shaped like birds' wings stretched on each side. Yet it seemed to me that it was not treated as well as it deserved by the crew, and even as I sailed on it, damage was often done and went unrepaired. I thought that if such treatment had been meted out to it during its lifetime, it would have presented a sorry sight by now. As I mentioned this to Shrufik, he answered that it was a new crew, but lately hired, and that he would discharge them in Dadym for he liked them not. When I asked what cargo he had on board, he smiled.

"It is a very valuable one, beautiful warrior. You will see it when it is displayed for sale in Cshuni."

Even then I knew not what he meant. But it was thus: I was to be sold in Cshuni for an enormous sum of money. For though I did not know it, my fame had spread to the farthest parts of the world. My deeds when I slew Enrigras, when I stormed the ridge at the battle of Daycalx in Aday, when I defeated the Black Death with such slaughter, and when I slew the wrestler, all were known by word of mouth and by written record, for the eyes of the Asg are legion. And because of them, and because I am a woman, so I am a great wonder of the world. And if any who lives and has fair skin and was born in the northern lands, is a wonder of the world, soon she will be coveted by the lords of Dadym or another Old Land. But the way to subdue me, yet not harm me and bring me so far was a great puzzle. Shrufik however being a

man who knew how to please many women, saw that though
I am perhaps the greatest warrior of the age, yet I could be
easily vanquished because of my stupid girlish vanity and
pride in my beauty. And he saw that while I went willingly,
no shackles were needed nor ropes nor locks. And he guessed
that with my strength, once I wished to be free, great harm
would come to the crew, or me, or him. So like a proud pig
with a ribbon of commendation about its fat neck, I strutted
eagerly to my doom.

While I knew nothing of this, all was well. The sea around
changed its character, so that soon we seemed to move on a
field of liquid turquoise, and strange fish flew from the
surface and lay on the deck or slithered down the sails to
regain their home. Some fish I touched and received a sudden
shock, which I could not understand since the fish neither bit
me nor stung me. At other times great creatures rose from the
waters, ichthyosaurs and mosasaurs which I had never seen.
The mosasaurs were always green with yellow bellies, but the
ichthyosaurs were of many colors and sizes, some blue with
pink mottled back, often pale jade with white or blue veins
and stripes, others yet a brilliant orange, so that they seemed
to glow with their own fire. Though they were of the same ilk
as the northern snappers, yet they were more beautiful by far.
And I watched these often from the stern. And the sun grew
ever hotter, till Shrufik bade me wear a hat which he gave
me—a great white broad-brimmed one.

"For you can become fevered and sunstroked, and I do
not wish you to arrive thus in Cshuni," he said. This was
because he did not want my price to be lessened by illness;
but I took it for his considerateness, for my brain was already
addled, yet not by the sun, only by the Kariasg's gleaming
teeth. Seeing his civilized air, I felt shame now for the
admiration I had borne for Conderan. But it was a false
shame, for Conderan, civilized or not, was a true man and
worthy of the love I bore him. And if he took a wife and
loved her, not me, it was his choice, and it was not a thing to
be resented. I truly think that, had Shrufik wished, I would
have parted my thighs for him easily enough and without a
thought for my lost kingdom, but only if he kept up his
praising words even as he thrust. Yet it was not thus that
things were to be, and since the evenings of romance I spent
on the deck with him are now a memory which vexes me

greatly I shall not write of them. Imagine what you will of a handsome dark-skinned black-bearded buccaneer who spoke mocking words of love to a great amazon who wore soft silk and blushed under the arrow scar that pitted her face.

We traveled many weeks under the high palm-laden cliffs of the great continent of Mnoy, where all life took form and wherein all things are shaped, where the Crab and the Spider hide from the terrible Scorpion. The seas were like a playground of bright-sailed boats, fishers, men-of-war, merchant-men, but mostly pleasure craft filled with laughing merry folk, their skins browned by the equatorial sun. In their faces I saw not the lurking fear which flickers beneath the surface in the faces of the north. Easy was their life, and no shadow was upon it. And among them were Hyperboreans, men who had given service to the empire and who had forgotten the uneasy tension of life in the barbarian lands.

"Shall I meet such folk?" I spoke out loud to Shrufik. "For I would wish it, since all look so happy."

"You will meet them, I can vouch for it," he replied. "And they shall value you greatly, as I do." He ever spoke thus with his true meaning evident to any who would hear it, for his cleverness amused him, as did my besottedness.

We sailed up the great estuary of the Pin river, which was like a sea itself of milky blue, where the chalk brought from the whole interior of the continent made it opaque. And the bright green of the forests was like a line of ink on pale blue paper, and the multicolored ichthyosaurs seemed more numerous than ever. But even as I walked dream-haunted amid this alien paradise, my foolish anticipation of a new life of never-ending joy in the brown and white towns I could see, was being cruelly undermined.

"Tonight, great beauty, it will be the climax of our trip," Shrufik whispered to me on the deck. "For I feel a deep yearning in me, and we are soon to be parted, sadly. Will you therefore eat with me in my cabin before the open doors, where the warm scented southern airs will blow?"

"I will," I said with serious meaning in my eyes.

"It is enough to dazzle my senses, such a prospect," he said.

And later we ate, while he spoke ever in flattering terms, and plied me with wine.

"What a sadness it will be to me, that I was brought so

close to such beauty, yet by the perversity of the gods never drank of your wine,'' he said when he sat on his couch.

"Such a sadness. . . . But may it be not enough what you have seen?" I said coyly.

"Enough to fill a lifetime of memory, and to blind me to the beauty of all others."

I felt strangely relaxed, and my arms and legs suddenly lethargic.

"I would not be the cause of such sadness . . . maybe if your need be so great . . ."

"It is indeed so great, so deep . . ."

"Unclasp then my dress . . . Shrufik . . . for I have chosen you to be the first to sail on this inland sea . . ."

"What honor! Let me first mention one or two small reservations I have." That he had time for such things surprised me, now that such a treasure was offered him. He had unclasped my dress and I was naked and burning for what I expected.

"Speak then swiftly, Shrufik, for words become superfluous."

"It is the small matter of your face which is much pockmarked with little scars and a great arrow wound of old. Could you not put a silken bag over your head while we do this deed?"

I could scarce credit his words, and a flood of confused feelings came to me.

"What say you?" I asked, my voice slurred.

"What say I? Why, did you not hear? I say that your face be an ugly thing best hidden. And another trifle, now that you have taken off your garment, unwisely I think, your unpleasant barbarian scent, reminiscent of a menagerie begins to assail our nostrils and must soon overwhelm us, unless you are immune from it, by habit."

"You insolent man, why say you these words after so much praise? Speak fast, since you have but a few seconds before you are swimming for the shore."

"Brave words, fat she-olligan, yet your only strength now is your smell."

I tried to move but could not, and sensed now others in the room.

"Take the creature and shackle her as you have been shown. Do not attempt to slake your lust on her, for her heart may stop in her present condition, and if it does there is an end to our riches. Tomorrow when she is conscious, we shall think again. See how her lust overrunneth! It is well that she faded when she did, else I have been drawn in like a shrimp into a clam, never to see the light of day again.''

Their laughter ushered in the darkness.

Many who read this, especially women, will know what a fire of hatred Shrufik's words and actions kindled in my heart. For he had aroused the tenderest feelings in me, and I had foolishly abandoned all my dreams of being the Dawn of Truth and queen of the north, all because of his flattering words. But I was very young then, and I may be forgiven for such simple passion. Now I lay in the fetid atmosphere of a wooden cage where he had had me chained. My legs were shackled together with irons, which he had had made especially for me, and attached to a great metal ball which I could only lift with difficulty, for he had heard of my monstrous strength. And my wrists too were shackled with equally large rings. After many futile attempts to break them, I wept and shouted oaths and threats to Shrufik who came to watch me. But I did not beg, for I knew he would not release me even if I promised much, for he had the chance of much greater and more certain riches by my sale. His men all clamored for me to be brought from the cage, that they might ravish me—some from true desire, but many who wished to tell their fellows and perhaps their women how they had penetrated Cheon of Weltanland and how great was my howling as they did it.

''She may be raped or otherwise treated as you please,'' said Shrufik. ''But no cut nor any bruise nor any mark must be left on her body, and her hair must not be torn. Any man who injures her shall be thrown to the ichthyosaurs.''

Then I was let free, and the garment of rough sacking torn from me. Rude hands grasped my nipples and buttocks, and pulled at my pubic hair. But I was too strong for them, and they could not prise apart my legs, which they must do if they wished to rape me. And as I had heard what Shrufik said, I knew that I might strike about me, doing what damage I could, since they dared not retaliate. Therefore I struck terrible blows at any head that came too near my arms and must have fractured a skull or two, so violently did I resist. And

once, when they were near to parting my thighs, I suddenly
slackened my hold and gave a great kick aimed at one filthy
Hyperborean who was stronger than the others. I showed all
my lewd flesh by this movement, but I cared not, for I sent
the fellow crashing against a metal winch, so that his
head made a pleasing sound and he could not continue. Yet
because of this, one Kariasg more intelligent than the
northerners took the chance to thrust a small cask between
my knees, so that I was now exposed and vulnerable. But
even as I felt a rough hand exploring in that curious region,
so I scratched my own thigh with my long nails and set up a
great screaming.

"Shrufik! The fools are tearing my flesh! See my blood!"

He came and seeing what they had done ordered them to
cease. "You ignorant scum!" he said. "See you not that she
loses value? Do you wish to slay her so that we return empty
handed and guilty of murder, which the Odon will not tolerate,
nor the Kariasg of Dadym?"

"She has struck men and hard enough to break their heads,"
said the Kariasg. "See, Vondeg lies unconscious—a cruel
deed, was it not?"

"What of that? If he places his head under the olligan's
foot, does he expect a caress? Save your energies, for you
shall have money enough to lay every woman in Dadym in a
few hours."

The men desisted, seeing the sense of his words and the
strength of my limbs. And as they went back to their idle
pursuits, Shrufik looked at me.

"Fat barbarian, you will not profit by behaving thus when
you are with your master. For you are in any case an affront
to womanhood, and once the curiosity of your fame has
waned, you will be of little use."

"Hear this, Shrufik. Though I am slave for thirty years, yet
I will escape and hunt you down through every land of the
earth and every city of every land and every street of every
city. And one day I shall find you, and then you will remember this day. Sleep lightly wherever you be, lest you wake to
find my hands at your throat, or my knife at your testicles. If
you be a wise man, you will kill me now, for what I say is as
certain as the return of the sun. And see you not that I am
likely to be hard to restrain? Has ever slave so strong as I
been held for long?"

He looked uneasy though my words were but bluster. Yet he sneered on.

"It is not great strength that aids escape. Are not leaping cats and olligans caged all their lives? A cunning mind is needed, and yours is simple, for did you not fall in with my plan like a child?"

"It is so. Yet it was not from stupidity but vanity, for I believed your words, though they were not true as I know. My face is not smooth as a woman's should be, for I fight too often and have scars on it. My smell is not evil, for I am as clean as any other woman, be she Asg or Odon. But my size is too great and men mock it, for they fear me and think to shame me thus. Now that I know how false were your words, I shall never again be seduced by men's speech. And you will see my cunning, for it will be your death at the last. Play you at the game of armies, which is a game of cunning, shit-beetle?"

"I play, as do all Kariasg, and can beat any Hyperborean or any woman."

"You will not beat me, as I would like to show you, that you will be uneasy all your days."

"I will play with you to show your impotence."

"To put your mind at ease, as you hope," I said, for it was his real reason, as I was sure.

He fetched the game, and naked, shackled and humbled though I was, we played many games, and he could not triumph, but ever I triumphed which gave him cause for unease.

"What help can your skill at this game be against shackles and bars?" he said at last, throwing over the board.

"Not my skill at the game but the cunning whereby I obtained it, young as I am and only little interested, as women are in such things."

He spoke not but left me, sitting in the sun, as we headed in toward a tiny port, not Cshuni but a small neighbor.

XXIII

Though I was led ashore in humiliating manner, yet setting foot on the wooden jetty in that warm harbor was an experience to move the spirit. There is some strangeness in the air of the Old Lands, like the sparkle of wine or a whiff of mblobe, that makes her who breathes it glad of heart. All around the shore were palm trees and beautiful houses even in so small a place. Had it been Odon or Weltan, such a harbor would have been a dreary huddle of huts with chickens and dirty half-naked children running about. But here all was clean, bright and neat, with roads of stone, flowers twining round every verandah and shaded terraces where Kariasg sat watching as I was goaded on.

I wore an old sack to cover my body to my knees, and I had to carry the great iron ball that weighed me down. Only Shrufik and his lieutenant were with me as we entered a square where a fountain played. And once here came a man with subordinate seeming companions, a tall Kariasg he was, gray-headed. He greeted Shrufik.

"I saw your ship enter the harbor, Shrufik, and came straightaway." He looked at me in wonder. "By her size she is all you say. But you have proofs that she is this Cheon of Weltanland?"

"Of course, Wrunduin, I am a trader and know what is required. See, there is the arrow mark from the ridge. And I have her armor, exactly as described, and her jewel and all other evidence."

"The wound may have been inflicted in order to convince. Her armor could be manufactured in imitation, and there is more than one skystone."

"Take her or not, it is your choice. There are others in Dadym who will buy direct."

"What say you, woman? Who be you?"

"I am as he says, Cheon of Weltanland, believe it if you

will, for I am eager to pass from his hands, since he has cheated me and enslaved me and I cannot abide his sight or scent longer. Give me but a small stone and free but one hand, and I shall show who I be by dashing out this evil man's brain and grinding all his bones to powder, after which I am yours with no payment.''

"A voice like a great whirlpool of Shuruba, as it is said," said Wrunduin. Shrufik looked uneasily at him, as if he feared my suggestion might be heeded. But doubtless good faith must exist between these traders, else the business must quickly die.

"Bring me then her armor, clothes and the jewel, and let us speak of a price."

Thus while I sat in the dust, lapping water from a dog's bowl, so these Kariasg sat at ease at a shaded table and drank pleasant liquor, as they bargained over me and my own property. People came to see me, for my size made me an object of much interest, children pointing and speaking: "See this great white woman, mummy, why does she drink thus like a dog?" or "See, mummy, here is a man with long hair and the face of a woman." I did not feel anger, for children do not know how cruel are their words and they are ever curious. And one little girl begged her mother.

"Let us bring a parasol to her, for she is so hot and tired and cannot move for her chains."

I smiled at her. "Thou speakest kindly, child, and though I be a prisoner of thy people, yet I pray that thou never beist as I am, chained like a dog. For no woman should be chained, not Hyperborean, nor Asg."

Her mother looked at me, but her eyes were not curious nor sympathetic. "Come, Mna-Mna, she is but a filthy Hyperborean slave and carries disease."

"Such words are seldom heard now in Wnai," I said, and a shadow passed over her. She approached and slapped me a stinging blow in the face. I would have broken her skull but for her brown daughter whose eyes widened.

"Insolent sow!" she hissed, and I saw by the child's face that her sympathy had turned to fear and repulsion. For if her mother whom she loved and trusted struck me, must I not be evil and cruel?

"You are foolhardy, madam," said Shrufik. "For she is not tame yet, nor branded, and has broken the heads of many men.'' The woman walked away, beautiful and arrogant, her cheeks made pink by powder on her coppery face. I spoke not, for what use are impotent words at such a time, save to provoke acts of callousness?

Yet my barbarian nature was soon exposed again, though wrongly. For I wished to urinate but I knew not if a slave should do so at a special drain or in the gutter where I sat. And as it was urgent and words came not, I did it, discreetly as I hoped, without lifting the sack. But it was such a squirting jet that all heard and saw the foaming liquid which ran in the gutter.

''Thunderhead, does she not know to ask relief?'' said Wrunduin.

''No, it is their coarse habit in Mbora, they know no better,'' said Shrufik. ''You must explain to her, else she will shame you at the market perhaps with even worse.'' Thus is one further condemned for lack of knowledge in unaccustomed situation. For how was I to know that though I must drink like a dog, I must not piss like one?

''It is not so, we have garde-robes in Odon,'' I said.

''And thus you behave here?'' said Wrunduin.

''I knew not,'' I said, my face hot with shame.

''She lies,'' said Shrufik. ''Why, their excrement is piled high in the streets of Shawi.'' I answered not and looked away, the tears in my eyes.

The traders haggled on, and the sun lowered and cooler air blew into the square. Finally I was sold, and for a sum of money which I could not have imagined to exist. In the empire, money runs like water, and what it had taken me all of a year's fighting in the north to accumulate was but a hundredth part of the price I commanded here as a slave. I know now that this sum was much greater than an ordinary slave would have fetched—perhaps a twentyfold. Thus all the cruel deceit Shrufik had practiced, and all the trouble he had gone to, were well rewarded.*

---

* What Cheon does not record, but which is certainly true, is that Shrufik persuaded her to sign away her own freedom. By 500 DB it was not possible to sell slaves unless they had either been taken prisoner of war or had signed a pledge of slavery. All the slaves of the empire had either been born slaves or had been made slaves by one of these methods—fair or foul. It is known that Shrufik engaged Cheon to marry him and passed the document off as a traditional and only formal pledge which Kariasg brides signed to honor their husbands. To our modern eyes, it seems strange that she should admit to some of the foolish and largely self-inflicted indignities of her devotion to Shrufik, and yet keep silent about this pledge. But Cheon's mind was mysterious, even to her contemporaries, civilized and barbarian alike.

Later that evening they parted with a handshake, and Wrunduin led us away from the square with his two subordinates—who were slaves—uneasily at my side. I spoke to them, but he bade us be silent and they did not defy him.

"You must learn, Cheon, that a slave's voice has no purpose save to answer her master's command. If you do not, you will be flogged often. Let us not start by that." I fell silent, for it would have been futile, chained and bonded as I was, to begin a great rebellion, rather one must watch, wait and become accustomed to one's new situation.

XXIV

We went to a great covered cart pulled by two domidens, and into it I was made to climb through doors into a wooden compartment with one of the slaves, a half-breed of a Kariasg and some northern race.

"If you wish to ease your bowels or bladder, speak now, for we must be in here three hours," he said in a toneless voice.

"I do not," I replied. The door slammed and the cart rumbled along with the warm setting sun entering by a small barred window.

"May we speak since none hears, man whose name I know not?" I asked.

"Speak if you will. I have but little to say and am a little melancholic these last few decades."

I laughed loudly at his jest, for I love merry speech, even if it come from a corpse. He looked at me with weary forbearance.

"You find humor in strange things, Cheon, as I heard you called."

"To be melancholic for decades, it is a droll thing," I said.

"It is not droll," he replied and I laughed more.

"What be your name, if it be the custom to ask in this land?"

"My name? What need have I of name, since I am naught but a slave?"

"If I wish to call you, what must I say?"

"Call me Elix if you wish, though I'll not own it my name."

"Tell me, Elix, why do you ride in here with me, when your comrade and master are outside?"

"I am to ensure that you neither escape nor harm yourself." I laughed at this.

"If I wanted to, I could slay you now with my hands shackled as they are."

"It would be no loss to me nor gain to you."

"I know it. And I am more likely to study this land and plan an escape when I know the way of things." Elix seemed animated by my glib words.

"Escape? Do you speak of escape? You will soon abandon such foolish hopes. You will meet thousands of others who have spent their lives in slavery, think you that they are happy and love their lot?"

"It will not surprise me if I meet none who have escaped," I replied. "For they will be in other lands."

He laughed suddenly. "You are no fool, Cheon. But runaway slaves find no easy sanctuary in Dadym."

We spoke through the long journey, and I learned that slavery was the norm in the many lands of Mnoy around the great Pin river. He told me names with a strange Kariasg ring, Wnaisha-Wnaisha, Dadym, Wdozi-Wdozi, Wzojopi, all countries west of the Pin. To the east, slavery was even more usual, in Shmoboboda, Sbodi, Shodoshi, Wbofojofi and Dejai. My ear was unused to these sounds, and I caught but little of the names. I was more interested to know if there were lands where slavery was outlawed.

"There are such lands—Asg lands in the west, beyond Papeepe, two or three thousand miles . . . a long walk, even for those whose legs are as long as yours, Hyperborean. Or to the south, four or five thousand miles to Ypepeckli, or to the east, to Shtush where few would go even to escape slavery though it be but two thousand miles through desert and over water." These names I made him repeat, Papeepe, Ypepeckli and Shtush, since they were names I must know if I was to hope for freedom.

The port of Cshuni was on the east bank of the Pin's estuary, although it was a part of Dadym which was otherwise completely on the west bank. We reached it when night had already fallen and I saw nothing of it, but was led directly to the quarters of the women. Since Wrunduin was a dealer in slaves, he had many who had but lately arrived. I was put in the charge of an overseer who had no doubt been apprised of my great value, for though she had a sullen face, she spoke civilly enough and told me what I needed to know. I was given a great cot with rough blankets to sleep on, in a large room where there were ten or so other women. Some wept and others—not new to slavery—had dead eyes showing little interest in their surroundings. One only, fair-haired and fair-skinned, came to me and sat near, looking with her blue eyes.

"Who be you?" I asked. But she knew not the Old Tongue and only stared. Yet as I have a gift for languages and speak several northern tongues, so I asked her the same question first in Weltan, then Bunnish, and finally north Rainish, and she answered me with smiling lips.

"I am Lintzay, who has been sold by my parents in far Glarz, for they had too many daughters and little food."

"You be Namzen then, of a fine people, the fairest of the north."

"Is it so? From what land come you with so dark hair, yet fair skin?"

"From Weltan in Hyperborea, a warmer land than the Rainish Isles."

"Let us then be friends, for I like not these other women who are sad and miserable." At this one looked up.

"And so will you be when you have been a slave ten years, and you will not easily offer friendship if you are like to be sold next day to be forever parted from your new friend." She turned again.

"A friend for a day is better than none," I replied. "I will accept your offer, small fair thing, I be Cheon of Weltanland." As I said this name, which I ever speak in my native tongue, many looked at me, for they had overheard their master speak of me, but Lintzay could not understand him and knew not of my fame.

I spoke with her until I was sleepy, finding that she was but fifteen years and had been too small and sickly, so that her parents deemed it better to sell her than one of her healthier sisters.

*   *   *

In the morning I was washed by the overseer and dressed in the traditional garments of a queen of Hyperborea, for thus were important captives and slaves ever presented in regal garments of their native lands. This was an ironic thing, as anyone must agree who has read my story from the beginning. And thus with crown of base metal set with glow stones I was chained on a great place in the sun-drenched center of Cshumi for the slave market of Dadym, the greatest of all the slavelands. Before me was placed a shield, not my own but one of wood on which all my supposed deeds were listed under my name falsely written Cheon Warrior-Queen of Weltanland. Because of this a great fear was upon me, for was this not the fulfillment of the prophecy, and was this the reason for the mockery I saw in Meon's eyes the day when she granted my childish wish?

Five other girls stood beside me, their chains small and delicate to my eyes, I could have snapped them with my hands. None were naked, for slaves were not displayed naked in those times, until a buyer wished to make his final negotiations, having paid his deposit. And on other stands were hundreds of women of all races and nations. I saw Pasquerians whom I had never before seen, and two whites with skin shining and delicate like white shells from the sea and with hair coalesced into a white membrane which protected them in the blazing sun of Shusht where they lived. Yet these were apparently a common sight, for my stand was soon surrounded by onlookers—men and women alike, mostly Kariasg, but some rich-seeming Hyperborean or Oldonians as they were known, who lived in Mnoy. And I overheard many discussions about me, no effort of politeness made to spare my embarrassment.

"Queen of Weltan, is she? And are all Weltan like her, walking mountains of flesh?" said one.

"Is she not a man, carefully made-up—prettily enough, I own—but with unwanted appendages beneath her queenly gown?" said another.

"What use can this be? It is too big to enter my bedchamber, let alone my bed, yet not big enough to please my domidens." Even the women were lewd, and one spoke:

"Were you a man and with member to match your size, I should buy you now with any sum asked, but sadly you lack what I needed most greatly." Yet some were kind enough, and since flattery would have been out of place, I took their comments as sincere.

"She has the air of a warrior, it is true," began one man, a Kariasg soldier himself. "For she has a face slightly scarred and a keenness of eye and tenseness of stance that we can always see in a warrior. But still she is most comely, for her black hair is flawless and shines like the coat of a leaping cat. And she has the true shape of a woman, and her features are soft; and above all, her eyes though fierce are most beautiful, green as they are and with great lashes. She is a queen indeed."

"Come, Mdowruku," said his companion, a dwarfish creature, "let us go to play at cards."

"No, stay, for I am quite struck with her. If her price were not ridiculous, as it is, I would buy her and if she pleased by her manners, free her and make her wife."

"Would that I could lend you the money," I said, and there was much laughter.

"Would that you could," he said.

"Can you not borrow it?" I asked, hoping that I might yet avoid the ills of slavery. "For my manners can be most pleasing."

"Borrow 50,000? It is a sum that very few will see in a lifetime. And at all events, my furlough ends tonight and I must return to the camp." He left and I was sad to see him go.

Then Wrunduin called for bids. This was a formal procedure whereby those who wished to make offers were obliged to enter large deposits to prove their seriousness. Naturally enough, they wished to see greater evidence of my powers, for my price would have been much too high for any ordinary slave.

"Fear not, ladies and gentlemen!" said Wrunduin. "For I have arranged a demonstration for all bidders, so that if she is not all I say, the bids may be withdrawn and deposits returned." And so we were taken, I and the nine bidders—seven men and two women—to a small theater where public exhibitions were often held.

In this arena which was in the shape of a soup-bowl, Wrunduin had prepared a shameful affair, as you will see. I was taken into a tunnel where I could not be seen by those who watched—and there were hundreds, since he had advertised outside, always with an eye to money: "A contest without arms between a forest-demon and the Queen of Weltanland in Hyperborea. This contest is the first of its kind and has only been allowed because of the great strength of this freakish woman. There will be a number of other entertainments before this."

These earlier entertainments were very bloody, and I believed them to be fatal to some, whereas in reality all was false, save a few light wounds. But when I watched this I was already loath to enter the arena, for I cannot enjoy killing for the sake of amusement. Then I saw the animal I was to fight, and I became afraid, for it was of hideous appearance. An enormous ape, it stood with a bent and stooped gait, and had it had legs which matched its great body and had it stood straight, it must have been greater than I. But its legs were short though powerful, and it was made disproportionately broad with enormous arms. These forest-demons eat meat and overpower other great beasts—all fear them, save the striped leaping cat. Their mouths are filled with stained and uneven teeth, which are yet sharp like daggers. I am not less brave than any man, but to face such a being without weapons and wearing but a thin silk shift is a foolishness beyond bravery.

"I will not fight." I said, and held the iron rail that ran along the entry channel. "And if you force me, I shall run back, screaming too, so that none will believe your tale of my strength, and you will appear ridiculous and lose your money."

"Will you not?" he asked, smiling. "But what a shame for young Lintzay who must be soon eaten!" I looked out into the arena and saw that poor Lintzay was there, with great ball and chain fastened to her childish ankle and blood smeared on her belly and arms to attract the abomination's interest.

It was not yet released but already it was leaping up and down fiercely in its cage, and talking some bestial language or perhaps merely screeching in its deep voice. And they were loosing the front of its cage, preparing to run back. Lintzay did not cry out—she knew that her death was close and in the Namzen religion, those who die bravely are taken to a pleasant and peaceful land. But I ran forth now, unchained, and faced the beast, for I could not see Lintzay die for my fear. I grasped her chain, which was the lesser kind for women, and with a great jerk I snapped it and all who watched cried out in amazement and in admiration. Then I whirled the great ball around my head, though it had taken two strong men to heave it into the arena. And I gave the war cry of the ramshuners and approached the monster.

At such a point in a tale, all hope for a long and risky fight with advantage going first to one, then the other. But this fight was not so, for the ape, stupid as it was, sought not to duck any weapon of so puny a creature, and the ball smashed its head like a huge egg, so that I was covered with what little brain it had possessed. This sudden and abrupt end to what the watchers had been eagerly awaiting caused a great silence to fall. I grasped the ball and held it aloft, bloody and foul as it was.

"So will die all men who set fierce beasts on children! So will die Dadym and all the Kariasg provinces, since they are cruel and do not follow the Way. And though we have but little wisdom in the north, yet we do not enslave others. One day this land will bow before the Truth, when it returns from the north whence it has gone."

This speech, though just, was actually very foolish, as I found out from Wrunduin after the fight.

"Your strength is greater even than I expected," he said. "But surely it is matched by your stupidity, for there are many skilled archers who waited to see that the beast slew neither you nor Lintzay—even slaves may not be slain for nothing in these times. And now your deed has involved me in expense. That beast was well trained for realistic performances in the arena, used as it was to subdue with great sound and fury, yet not to harm. Now I must pay its full value to its owner, who had but two, which he hired for these fights. What a child you are, Cheon, to naively believe all that you see!"

I ceased my boasting when I heard these words, and flushed with anger.

"I am stupid, perhaps, but not so stupid as to look to your advantage. What care I if you suffer ten such debts? As for the beast, I am glad I slew it, for its life was a useless one, spent in these bloody shows. And you are a great shit-beetle, who leaves a foul trail in a fair land!"

Wrunduin only smiled at me and spoke.

"What do you complain of? You have done a deed which will ever be spoken of in Dadym, since no man has ever resisted a forest-demon, let alone slain one, without sword or armor. All speak of you, and great prices are mentioned."

It was in the afternoon that Wrunduin took me to his private garden, and there in luxurious surroundings, with his bidders' every whim attended to, the deal was to be struck. I was stripped and my arms and feet chained to concrete pillars. Each bidder could examine me in as much detail as he or she wished. They showed the kindness and ease of manner rich folk often have. And I saw now two more of them, one a woman whose face was strangely shaped, as if flattened by a blow from a hammer, with a scowling expression.

All made sure of my womanhood, since it was a part of my great value, and felt with care to ensure that I had not a man's organ artfully concealed, as can be done. It is one thing to feel pleasure in the revelations of one's body if it be self-willed, and in an atmosphere conducive to erotic thoughts, but here like a cow being assessed, it was a humbling thing, and I could not look at the bidders in their eyes, hanging my head in shame. The woman of the distorted face felt me with coarse hands and even ran her sharp nails on my flesh—not to hurt but to show me how she might hurt me. She held the part of me that is most secret and she grunted.

Then they all left for the bidding, and I stood in the orange light of the setting sun, lamenting with tears my cruel fate. None cared for me now, and I bemoaned Fidzer and Conderan and Wanin, Muru and even Ocea. But at the end I called to Meon, and loudly and without shame. For I wished to be free to return to the cold north to be queen as she promised. And suddenly I saw her come from the direction of the red sun which floated on the horizon.

"Meon! Meon!" I said. "Set me free, for I fear I cannot escape in this cruel land."

But it was not she, for suddenly her cruel face turned to me, and it was none but the woman of the flat face.

"Come with me," she said. "For you are mine, and you know little yet of the cruelty of this land."

Thus do I leave you, my readers, and you shall only learn

of my fate and if I was again free, and if I was made queen, if you read the next part of my tale. And it is stranger by far than the first part, and there is much sorcery, bloodshed and the joy of lust contained in it.

GLOSSARY

Aday: One of the northernmost of the Rainish Islands.

Belda: The region of Bhoumer visited by Cheon, with large port of Wtodan.

Bhoumer: The largest of the Rainish Islands, known also as the Sacred Land.

Domiden: A large beast of burden, an enormous kind of tapir, which never existed on earth.

Izden: A spirit made from an aromatic root.

Leaping Cat: A large fierce feline beast with excessively developed hind legs. In the largest striped form, it is not inferior in size to a cart-horse, though infinitely more agile and dangerous.

Mblobe: A pleasure-giving drug especially attractive to Asg and Kariasg.

Mbora: All that part of the Hyperborean continent that was a former province of the empire. Mainly the southern part.

Mnoy: The largest continent, a tropical region where the empire grew up. Sometimes called the Old Lands.

Mzum: A game with similar object to chess and draughts, played on a board more complex than a checkerboard.

Nightstalker: A genus of animals which hunt by night, like large foxes. The largest kind, the giant nightstalker, was as big as, and similar in shape to a crocodile, though warm-blooded and furry.

Olligan: A Baluchitherium—a beast that once walked the earth—a giant hornless rhinoceros which was earth's largest land mammal.

Skallopen: A smaller species of domiden, fast and agile, ridden by warriors.

Voshr: Ice sheet. There were two in Hyperborea, the larger Minden Voshr, and the smaller Zee Voshr.

The Way, Way of Truth: A moral code which emphasized the underlying importance of honesty both with oneself, and with others. It originated in the empire in earlier, more vigorous times.

Wdeni: Imperial province conquered by Hyperboreans who distorted its name to Odon.

Wnai: The last of the imperial domains on the Hyperborean continent. Its last years were spent as a "republic" loosely linked to the empire. It included both Weltanland in the north and Mortonland to the south, and fell to the Bunnish invaders in the middle of the sixth century.

Presenting JOHN NORMAN in DAW editions . . .

Don't miss the great novels of Dray Prescot on Kregen, world of Antares!

Have you discovered . . .

JO CLAYTON

"Aleytys is a heroine as tough as, and more believable and engaging than the general run of swords-and-sorcery barbarians."
—*Publishers Weekly*

The saga of Aleytys is recounted in these DAW books: